"You tempt me, my lady. Too much."

Elysia did not want him to go. She knew they would not speak again before his departure. Now she couldn't bear to see Conon leave. Forever.

"But—"

He sealed her protests with one calloused finger laid over her lips. "I will not fail you, Elysia. I promise." He cupped her cheek in his palm.

It required all her strength not to close her eyes and lean into that strong palm. "God speed, my lord." She straightened, needing to escape the temptation of his touch. "And thank you."

Elysia burrowed more deeply into the folds of his surcoat as she watched him walk away, praying he possessed the deep sense of honor she'd glimpsed in him.

By granting Conon her favor, Elysia had also given him a dangerous weapon—all the power he needed to break her heart...!

* * *

My Lady's Favor
Harlequin Historical #758—June 2005

Praise for Harlequin Historical author Joanne Rock

"Charming characters, a passionate sexual relationship and an engaging story—it's all here."
—*Romantic Times* on *Girl's Guide to Hunting & Kissing*

"Joanne Rock's talent for writing passionate scenes and vivid characters really sizzles in this story. Even the hot secondary romance has chemistry!"
—*Romantic Times* on *Wild and Wicked*

The Wedding Knight
"*The Wedding Knight* is guaranteed to please! Joanne Rock brings a fresh, vibrant voice to this charming tale."
—*New York Times* bestselling author Teresa Medeiros

The Knight's Redemption
"A highly readable medieval romance with an entertaining touch of the paranormal.... The plot is pleasantly complex, the setting well developed, the heroine and hero traditional and romantic and the ending happily interesting."
—*Romantic Times*

Joanne Rock

My Lady's Favor

HARLEQUIN®

TORONTO • NEW YORK • LONDON
AMSTERDAM • PARIS • SYDNEY • HAMBURG
STOCKHOLM • ATHENS • TOKYO • MILAN • MADRID
PRAGUE • WARSAW • BUDAPEST • AUCKLAND

ISBN 0-373-29358-5

MY LADY'S FAVOR

Copyright © 2005 by Joanne Rock

For Catherine Cavanaugh, Anne Sheehan and Hollis Seamon, fantastic professors at the College of St. Rose who helped me recognize my love of writing and literature through their support and encouragement. Thank you so much for making English classes such a rich and exciting experience.

And for RoseMarie Manory, who helped history come alive for a non-major. I can't thank you enough for infusing those lectures about European history with plenty of drama and intrigue!

Also, with loving appreciation to Dean, who appears in some small facet in every hero I've ever created, but most especially in Conon St. Simeon.

Chapter One

Brittany, France
Spring 1345

The garden looks more promising than the groom. Elysia Rougemont stood outside Vannes Keep, admiring the profusion of plants in well-tended rows, hoping to distract herself from thoughts of her upcoming marriage. Thyme and rosemary stood shoulder to shoulder with more frivolous herbs like lavender and sweet marjoram.

Elysia had little use for lavender or marjoram.

The fragrant patch of earth signified the only redeeming feature Elysia could discern about Vannes, the monstrous château that would officially be her home by nightfall—when she would marry the ancient Count of Vannes, Jacques St. Simeon.

She peered back at the keep, a massive structure of stone that went far beyond a simple fortified manor house. Nay, her new home could only be called a fortress, built for war and defense with its abundance of gates and projected fighting galleries that dominated the walls. Her future husband had told her he was a man of peace, but his home did not seem to uphold his words.

Swiping a slipper-clad foot through the warm earth, Elysia tried to concentrate on the pleasing quality of the fertile soil and not her aging sot of a future husband.

She could almost pretend she was back at her own keep in England. No matter that she and her mother had been subject to the will of their overlord since her father's death six years ago, Elysia had enjoyed their way of life. She'd built a small but thriving linen trade with the help of her mother, a venture she took both pleasure and pride in, a way to distinguish herself in a world that held little appreciation for the feminine arts.

And although now Elysia's wealth rivaled the most sought-after heiresses on the continent, she could not touch a farthing of it. That right belonged to her overlord, the Earl of Arundel, and would soon pass to her husband.

If her brother hadn't died last fall before arranging a marriage for her, Elysia might have been home reviewing the progress of her flax fields instead of contemplating the uses of Vannes's fanciful herbs.

Her wishful vision vanished at the sound of a deep masculine voice.

"Be of good cheer, my somber lady. You are quite fortunate the count is but two steps from the grave."

Whirling around with a start, Elysia sought the speaker of the callous words. A fragrant gasp of air caught in her throat. Surely the speaker was not the golden vision of a man across the boxwood hedge.

"Excuse me?" Elysia managed, certain she must have misunderstood.

"With any luck, chère," he continued, "you will be rid of the count before the year is out."

Of all the foul, crude things to say. She might not desire the marriage, but that did not mean she would wish any man dead. She searched her mind for the most cutting setdown she could give the intruder until he stepped over the boxwoods to stand before her, looking infinitely more intimidating at close range.

Tall and imposingly built, the newcomer was a warrior in his prime. He dressed in deference to the wedding day except for a sword at his waist. The sun shone on his tawny hair and crisp white shirt, lending him the luminous glow. Limned in bright light he appeared a favored son, smiled on by God and nature.

Elysia took a step back, wondering at the wisdom of loitering in the garden alone with a strange knight, no matter how intriguing his intense blue eyes. A niggle of fear forced her to clamp down the retort that rose to her lips. "Please excuse me, sir, I really do not think—"

He drew his knife and Elysia's heart stopped. There was nowhere to run from a man twice her size and no doubt twice as fast.

Bending, he applied the blade to the stem of a pink rose blooming on a low trellis. Exuding perfect courtly manners, he extended the blossom to her.

"I mean only to compliment your auspicious marriage." His scornful blue eyes contradicted the deferential air of a brief bow. "It seems a fair bet your husband will leave you a very wealthy widow by Yuletide."

Appalled at his audacity, Elysia could only stare at the insincere token he'd given her. "What wealth can any woman truly claim, sir? Widow or not, I will forever be ruled by one man or another."

The knight reached toward her. An inner voice screamed

at Elysia to move away from him, but he possessed some compelling quality that left her rooted to the spot.

His fingertip grazed the egg-size emerald dangling from a necklace her betrothed had presented to her as a wedding gift. She could almost fancy that she felt the heat of his hand through the impassive stone.

His eyes were alight with an emotion Elysia could only guess at. Perhaps it was wistfulness she spied as he stared first at the jewel, and then at her. "You stand to inherit a centuries-old dower property, my lady. I shouldn't think you are too disappointed in this match."

The news of it had almost killed her, in fact, but what would this coarse man understand of her dreams?

"And the rewards would be even better," the stranger continued, fingering a fragrant blossom, "if you can only manage to bear an heir—"

"Enough." She barely whispered the sentiment, anger robbing her of her voice. It did not matter that his words mirrored those of her overlord, the Earl of Arundel, when he had announced she must wed the lord of Vannes Keep a scant two moons prior. Elysia threw the rose at his feet, but not before one of its sharp thorns tore her thumb.

"You think I purposely sought the lord of Vannes for a husband?" Ever since her father died, she had told herself she would only wed a man who recognized a woman's true worth and not just the size of her bridal portion. Her parents had found the fulfillment of true love, and while it hurt to lose her father while she was naught but a girl, she'd consoled herself that at least he had been happy. "As if I were so eager to trade every shred of pleasure I've ever known. How dare you?"

"No, lady, there will be some gossips who whisper how dare *you,* when you walk away with a lucrative property after a scant year at the count's side." His grin remained as disarming as the first moment she saw it, at odds with his scathing remarks. "But not I."

She considered fleeing, but some part of her feared offending her husband's wedding guest, no matter how discourteous. She was no longer mistress of her own actions—she had a husband to answer to now. A husband who had seen naught but her bridal portion when he looked at her.

So much for the idle dreams of her girlhood.

The stranger lifted her hand to examine the small cut on her thumb. Blood trickled down to her knuckle in a crimson stream against her pale skin. Wiping the red trail away with his finger, he stepped closer still.

Never had anyone dared to touch her in so brazen a manner. She became aware of the heat of his body, her own racing pulse.

He retained his hold, lifting his gaze to hers. "The bride has my complete and heartfelt best wishes."

The slight lift at the corner of his lips mesmerized her. He loomed nearer as he bent over her hand and kissed the soft pad of her injured thumb.

Her flesh tingled under his lips for one frozen moment, and then indignation reared through her at his impudence. She wrenched her fingers from his grasp.

He bowed with mocking reverence. "Good luck, chère."

Infuriated by his disrespect, more upset by her own inaction, Elysia could no longer hold her tongue. Who was this man? And why did he seem so intent on piercing her with his disdain, his words finding their mark as effectively as the rose's thorny stem?

"You can be certain the count will hear of your taunts, sir." Thankfully, her voice did not quaver the way her insides did. Although his words stung and his kiss was meant to be insulting, Elysia could not help wondering why her future husband could not look more like this man, whom she guessed to be some ten years older than her eighteen summers. "May I tell him whom among his guests thinks so little of him that they would accost his bride and insult the sacred nature of his wedding vows?"

His smile came as easily as it had before, as if the man was long accustomed to charming his way out of trouble.

"Tell him his nephew, Conon St. Simeon, has been kind enough to welcome our English guest on this momentous day." He made a curt bow. "I am certain he will approve."

"Are you, my lord?" Recklessness crashed through her in time with her anger. She ignored the discomfiting thought of this imposing creature as her nephew by marriage. "I am not so certain he will appreciate your speculation on his demise. Perhaps you would be wise to keep your distance."

The golden-haired stranger quirked a brow. "Perhaps you would be wise to hold your tongue with my uncle. I assure you he will not find your wayward mouth half as…entertaining as I do."

Bowing again, the knight turned on his heel and left, disappearing into a grove of yew trees on the garden's south end.

The cad. Oddly, they had agreed on one thing. The younger St. Simeon opposed this marriage as adamantly as she did. Elysia bent to retrieve the flower he'd given her. She caressed its soft petals, telling herself the bloom should not be wasted merely because it had been presented by a churlish knave.

Did he stand to lose his position in the family now that she would wed his uncle? Perhaps that's why he'd been rude. Didn't he realize *he* could follow his dreams? He was not dependent upon a man as she was. No matter how successful her linen trade had grown, she'd known the day would arrive when her overlord would steal it out of her hands and make her wed. Now that the day had arrived, she had little patience for Conon's taunts when he had the world at his feet.

She grazed the rose across her cheek, reminding herself that resentment would not alter the outcome of this day. She was fated to become the next Countess of Vannes, to wed a man older than her father would be now.

God have mercy on him. She thought of her father and smiled, knowing that if he were alive, she would not be forced to wed the count. Or if she had wed someone last fall, before her brother, Robin, died, she might have had some choice in the matter. But she had put the matter off, happy to immerse herself in pleasant labor, consumed with running the linen trade. Now she would pay the price for failing to choose a husband.

Only one thing could halt the wedding to Jacques St. Simeon today, and she planned to try it right away.

Father in Heaven, she prayed, *please, please, let it all be a dream. May I wake up any moment in my bed at Nevering, ready to face a day of linen weaving and flax growing….*

But as more wedding guests arrived and the day passed in a blur of preparations, Elysia lost all hope for divine intervention.

The fresh wound on her thumb continually reminded her of her new role as Countess Vannes. Oddly, the kiss that young, virile Conon St. Simeon had placed there seemed to linger as much as the thorn's sting.

What the hell had he been thinking to kiss her?

Conon cursed his actions as he stomped through the

winding stone passage to his Uncle Jacques' chambers. The convoluted corridors and mazelike interior of Vannes Keep did nothing to clear Conon's mind as he trudged upward. His uncle had spared no expense to build this elaborate fortress with its passages that led to nowhere and its wealth of private rooms—a luxury unheard of in all but the newest defense structures. He had only intended to introduce himself to the future countess, to look her over as his uncle had commanded.

She was beautiful, despite her rigid posture and the cool reserve she wrapped about herself like a cloak. Her long dark curls and heart-shaped face struck him as romantic features out of place on such a serious woman.

Still, something about Lady Elysia's proud defiance had made him want to touch her, taste her. He had seen the flash of fear in her eyes when he'd neared her, yet she'd stood her ground and defended herself. The warrior in him admired her backbone.

Besides, what self-respecting Frenchman wouldn't kiss the hand of a woman new to his acquaintance? Conon's time at court had taught him the excessive gallantry expected of a nobleman, even though Conon lacked the title and wealth that normally accompanied such chivalry. He'd earned respect with the accurate slash of his sword in battle.

He reached the door to the count's private chambers and paused. Conon dreaded meetings with his uncle, but it seemed even more awkward to face Jacques after the encounter with his future bride. Ruthlessly, Conon thrust thoughts of Elysia from his mind.

Best to dispatch the visit quickly. He knocked twice before a slurred voice bade him enter.

The master quarters were richly appointed with tapestries and woven mats, yet the chamber perpetually smelled of strong drink and stale air. Jacques reclined in his bed, a cup of ale perched haphazardly on his generous belly.

"Welcome, Conon!" His kinsman's attempt at a hearty greeting lacked warmth. The vibrance that surrounded him in youth had vanished after his first wife died. "Care to join me?" Ale sloshed from the cup as he lifted it in question.

"No, thank you, my lord." He could not imagine choking down a drink of any sort in the fetid room. "I have come to inform you I visited your bride."

"A beauty, isn't she?" A feral grin crossed Jacques's flushed face. "All that money and a luscious young body to go with it. I have done well, have I not?"

Conon was unprepared for the wave of jealousy that assailed him. The thought of Elysia Rougemont beneath his uncle's corpulent form filled Conon with an unwelcome surge of protectiveness. "She is indeed attractive."

Laughing, the count reached for the pitcher at his bedside and filled his cup again. His gaze turned dreamy and unseeing. "She has hips fit for bearing children."

Conon fought the urge to slam his fist into something. In Jacques's eagerness to produce an heir, he no longer remembered his vows to gift Conon with a small keep for loyal service. Years of drink and dissolution had worn away the count's memory along with his sense of decency.

"I am sure she will provide you with the heir you seek, my lord. Although I must say she seemed about as warm and welcoming as an English winter." Conon clenched his jaw to staunch further comment. "If that is all?"

"Nay." Jacques huffed for breath as he struggled to rise. From long habit, Conon moved to help the older man. The count stood, though not without considerable wa-

vering. He grinned and clapped Conon on the shoulders as
he steadied himself.

"I have a gift for you, son, one which I'm sure you will
enjoy."

"Thank you, my lord." Conon felt the disgrace of his status as a poor relation even as the words kindled a wary hope
in him. With the Vannes wealth at his disposal, Uncle
Jacques's gift might be enough to bolster Conon's finan-
ces until he put his sword arm in service to the highest bidder.

The Count of Vannes laughed again, his hearty guffaws
jiggling his cup. Ale spilled onto Conon's surcoat, staining his best garment.

"Thank me you will, son, when I tell you that I have
brought the fair widow Lady Marguerite here for you. Such
a liaison ought to please even a man of your notorious reputation, Conon."

Jacques's laughter echoed hollowly in Conon's ears.
Conon knew liaisons were all he could allow himself, since
he couldn't provide for a family. Still, he resented the implication he was little more than a wastrel.

Disappointment choked him as he managed a stiff bow
before departing the stale chamber. His gift would be no
monetary prize or valuable token of his uncle's affection,
but a lusty young widow who had chased Conon all over
the French court. Unbidden, an image of his uncle's haughty
future wife came to mind. Conon was willing to bet Lady
Elysia wasn't the kind of woman to have a liaison.

Amid the arriving wedding guests and preparations for the
evening feast, Conon sought his chamber. What had he expected from Uncle Jacques? That after a lifetime of assuming Conon to be naught but an entertaining table companion,
the count would suddenly realize new respect for his nephew?

Inside his chamber, Conon scrubbed his stained surcoat. Despite noble birth, he was all too familiar with menial labor. He counted himself fortunate to have come this far. At least he had a reputation for his sword arm in France and beyond. With any luck, he'd find lucrative work as a mercenary, preferably somewhere far from Brittany.

After wringing out his garb, he brought the material toward the only source of light in the room, a narrow arrow slit that looked down upon the keep's gardens.

The matter of the surcoat went forgotten as Conon spied Lady Elysia idly picking her way through the rows of herbs and flowers. Her white linen gown gave her an ethereal air among the colorful blooms. An odd sensation clutched at his chest as he realized she carried a wilting pink rose in one hand. Surely, it was not the same one he had picked for her.

He couldn't help wondering if she was truly the money-grubbing wench he'd accused her of being, or if she, too, had unfulfilled dreams.

The lovely vision she presented only further convinced Conon of the need to leave Vannes. Let Jacques enjoy his English heiress with the childbearing hips. Conon could finally leave France now that his ailing uncle would be cared for by Lady Elysia. As he rifled through his sparse belongings for a fresh garment, Conon determined he couldn't possibly get away from Vannes Keep fast enough.

Chapter Two

Even though the sun had not fully set, Jacques St. Simeon's wedding guests carried candles to welcome Lady Elysia to the Vannes family chapel. Conon admired the whitewashed stone tower standing apart from the rigid symmetry that marked the rest of the keep. A small building designed as an afterthought, the little chapel revealed the scant interest Uncle Jacques paid the church.

Studying the boisterous, ornamented crowd that gathered there, Conon wondered how the bride would react to his uncle's idea of a wedding. There would be little entertainment this eve, but much drink. Nobility from far and wide attended the event, not so much to see the bride, but to pay their respects to one of the region's most powerful lords.

Conon swatted a bug that flew about his neck while he waited for the bride to appear. Hot wax dripped on his finger.

"Damn," he muttered, peeling the soft wax off his skin.

Marguerite's sultry voice purred over his shoulder. "Shall I kiss it, my lord?"

He had almost forgotten she posed, pouted and flaunted beside him. No matter that Marguerite had a body made for sin and an appetite to use it, Conon had been plagued with thoughts of proud Elysia Rougemont all day. The rose-washed taste of her skin, the slightly metallic tang of her life's blood, haunted his lips.

"Aye, chèrie," Conon responded, forcing himself to notice Marguerite's lush curves and daringly low-cut gown. With silky dark hair and a flirtatious manner, the young widow remained most sought after since her first husband left her a profitable estate. But she seemed content to indulge her independence, purchasing extravagant gowns of velvet, silk and beads as if she'd poured her entire fortune into an elaborate effort to showcase her natural beauty.

She leaned close, swirling her tongue around his finger in an effort to soothe his burned skin. Conon scarcely noticed her moist ministrations, but he heard the bridal party approach long before anyone else on the chapel steps.

His focus narrowed to Elysia as she rode by. She sat atop Uncle Jacques's best white palfrey, her green gown a vivid contrast to the mare's pristine coat. The brown hair that scarcely peeked out from her veil earlier in the day now cloaked her in sable silk. A chaplet of violets crowned her like Persephone in her glory.

Conon watched her descend from her mount with the help of two squires. She would be married on the chapel steps in a few more moments. Did she appreciate the fact that she achieved lifelong security with the simple exchange of vows? Did she long for children, as Conon did, or did she look at Jacques and see only his gold?

The emerald necklace glittering about her neck answered that question clearly enough. His uncle's betrothed might have intrigued him, but she was no doubt as greedy as every other minor heiress that had traversed Vannes's threshold the last five years. Women of all ages were willing to wed a drunken old man for the security of his money. Why would Elysia be any different? Tonight she would assure her future while Conon questioned his own, but for love of his uncle, Conon vowed he would harbor no malice. Tomorrow he would obtain freedom from Vannes forever. The niggling of temptation Elysia presented would be easily ignored once Conon was on the other side of the continent.

As he watched the dignified woman in green wend her way through the crowd to join Uncle Jacques, Conon knew he had to thank her even as he resented her. She might be effectively ending any hopes for inheritance, but she would also provide him with the only extended independence he'd ever known.

If he used that freedom wisely, perhaps he would be the one greeting a breathless bride on the chapel steps in a few years' time.

Heaven help him, he hoped *his* bride welcomed him more warmly than the aloof Lady Elysia.

Heaven help her, Elysia hated being a bride.

The wedding had passed in a blur of Latin and rice, until at last she and the lord of Vannes were seated at their banquet table.

She perched beside her new husband in the glow of the evening's torchlight and watched him down the contents of his cup for at least the tenth time. After he called for a refill, Elysia pretended not to notice as he pinched the wine bearer's backside. Although she resented having to marry such an odious creature, Elysia would not allow her dignity to crumple because of him.

The count was a huge man. He was reputed to have been a formidable warrior in his day, but it had been many years since he gave a care to his health. His jeweled sword belt did nothing to hide his girth, one of many indications that he indulged himself too freely. His ruddy nose and the high color in his cheeks suggested that he consumed great amounts of wine along with his ravenous appetite for food.

For this, Elysia did not condemn him. His penchant for ogling every woman under fifty, however, gave her a sense of impending doom.

Shuddering, she turned away from him to sweep the great hall with her gaze. She tried to ignore her husband's arrogant nephew. Conon St. Simeon sat at the table closest to the dais, a giggling beauty wrapped about him. The younger St. Simeon displayed none of the defects of the elder. Strong, handsome, articulate, he held the crowd at his table in thrall with some tale or another, his animated face and wild gestures bespeaking only good humor, not drunkenness.

Elysia knew from his behavior in the garden this morning that he was not the angel among men he appeared. His lingering kiss and forward manner proved his lack of chivalry.

She did not mention Conon's behavior to the count. Nor did she have any intention of doing so. She spoke little to her husband, who seemed just as happy to immerse himself in good food and abundant wine.

Elysia's overlord, the earl of Arundel, leaned close on her other side. "You must admit, Vannes Keep is far more sophisticated than your little stone tower at Nevering." The earl smiled benevolently, as if ready to forgive her for not wanting to come to France.

"Nevering is far more than a little stone tower, my lord, and we are both well aware of it." Elysia could not help the edge to her voice since she had striven for years to make Nevering a strong keep as well as a gracious home. Besides, fear about the night ahead knotted her belly.

"Ah, but here you will be a lady of leisure," her former overlord countered. "The count will provide well for you, and you will not have the worries associated with the linen trade. You can rest easy knowing Sir Oliver Westmoor will take good care of Nevering and watch over your mother."

He will soak up all the profits until he runs the holding into the ground. She mustered a tight smile that hurt her face to bestow. Did he expect her to thank him for reminding her of the greedy neighboring lord back home who coveted Nevering and its modest wealth?

A tall knight approached them, bowing deeply before the dais table. "My lord," the newcomer addressed the count, though he wore Arundel's colors on his sleeve. "Might I hope for an introduction to the bride?"

The count leaned close to Elysia. "My dear, this is Sir John Huntley, Arundel's right arm in battle."

Elysia took in the looming height of the tall knight, his angular features and sandy brown hair pleasant enough, though his eyes held a lingering familiarity that uneased her. Her new husband draped a heavy arm about Elysia's shoulders to draw her near to him, his bejeweled surcoat scratching her skin through her fine silken garment. The informality of his manner announced his drunkenness to the entire hall while the attending knight bowed again.

Arundel leaned over to whisper, "He is as important to me on the field as Sir Oliver is to me back home."

Even if John Huntley had not been looking at her as a cat eyes a caged bird, the comparison to Sir Oliver would have put her on guard.

"Huntley," Jacques continued. "The new Countess of Vannes, Elysia St. Simeon."

She had no choice but to offer her hand, which the well-favored warrior quickly kissed.

"I am pleased to meet you, sir." She smiled so as not to offend her husband, but her fear and apprehension of the coming night grew to painful proportions as the count squeezed her to him in a proprietary gesture.

"It is the greatest of honors, my lady." Huntley straightened. "I beg you to consider me your champion and protector should you ever be in need of one."

"Gallant words, son." The count laughed, allowing his touch to stray down Elysia's hip. "But I daresay she has all the man she needs."

The lavish jewels on the count's fingers snagged in her gown. His rotund body radiated warmth as if she were seated near a brazier. Elysia tilted her head to one side to escape his pungent breath on her cheek.

Bowing, Huntley departed, though Elysia felt his eyes upon her at all times.

Through the count's uproarious mirth, Elysia heard a persistent ringing in the hall. As others became aware of it and quieted to listen, all eyes turned to Conon St. Simeon, banging his knife against his silver cup for the guests' attention. Elysia edged away from the count, eager to put as much distance between them as possible.

"Ladies and gentleman," Conon called, rising to his feet as the hall paused in its merrymaking. "A toast to the count and his bride."

"Conon is my nephew," the count whispered, wrapping one heavy arm about her waist and pulling her close to him once again. Elysia tried to mask the shudder that went through her at his touch. His breath nauseated her while his sweaty hands left damp imprints on the silk layers of her gown's overskirt. Apparently his drunken state had robbed him of all sense of propriety.

Conon approached the table and raised his glass to the

new couple. Elysia found it impossible to meet his gaze, as if he might be able to guess she had been thinking about him all day.

Intellectually, Elysia knew it did not matter whether she wed a handsome young man or an elderly lord. Marriage signified the end of a woman's limited freedom, and a lifetime of domination by a man. Yet she couldn't help but look at the count and wish fate had presented her with a more desirable groom.

"I wish you health and happiness and many babes to share your joy." Conon's voice rumbled through the hall as he made his pledge.

Elysia's face flamed.

"May you make our name one to be feared and respected," he continued. "And may your children be stalwart guardians of Vannes for another generation. To that end, I will faithfully serve you and your family."

For the first time since she and the count had exchanged vows, Jacques St. Simeon's expression grew serious as he looked upon his nephew. "Thank you, son."

Cheers went up all around and in that moment, she braved a glance at Conon to find his gaze upon her, serious and contemplative. Perhaps her attention called him from his thoughts, because a grin suddenly stole over his face.

"Lady." He raised his cup to her alone, then downed the rest of his wine in her honor. After slamming the vessel on the table, he crossed the room as if he could not wait to put distance between them. He pulled his dining companion into his embrace and headed toward the gathering dancers.

Elysia found her gaze would not stray from him. He wrapped the other woman in strong arms outlined by his narrowly cut tunic. Although Conon possessed the broad shoulders of a warrior, his step was light as he whirled his partner around the floor. The woman tossed her head back and laughed.

What would it feel like to be so carefree?

Elysia's fanciful thoughts scattered as the count attempted to lean close to her and lost his balance, pitching forward. She buoyed him up with her arms, but he remained oblivious to her effort. He gestured to the dancing couple. "They make a beautiful pair, do they not?"

Elysia affected a smile in response. She had never found much to recommend beauty.

"She is a widow, you know." The count nodded in the direction of Conon's companion. "In our country a widow is allowed a bit of freedom to seek what company she wishes."

In my country, too, Elysia reflected, wondering if she would ever know a time in her life when she was not bound to answer to a man. For a moment, she envied the woman. But it was certainly because of the widow's autonomy and not her proximity to the dynamic presence of Conon St. Simeon.

Her husband flashed her a knowing grin. "'Tis why my nephew seeks out the grieving widows. They are mistresses of their own hearts—and their own bedchambers."

He gave a loud guffaw at his joke, his fit of laughter soon turning into a fit of coughing. When his face turned red, Elysia feared for him.

"My lord, perhaps you should rest."

"Rest?" He spluttered, apparently incensed at her choice of words. After another round of coughing, he rose to his feet with slow deliberation. His eyes issued a distinct challenge.

"Perhaps we should retire for the night and you will learn what your lord is made of." His voice boomed with the complete lack of awareness of a drunkard. The entire hall stopped to turn wide eyes on the bridal couple.

"We retire!" the count shouted, yanking Elysia roughly to her feet beside him.

The crowd fell silent, until one lone clap broke the quiet. Elysia did not need to turn around to know which bold wedding guest instigated that noise. No matter how opposed Conon might be to his uncle's wife, he supported the marriage in public. Elysia couldn't deny a flicker of admiration for his family loyalty. Thunderous applause and whistles broke out amongst the well-wishers, who quickly followed Conon's suit.

Fear, cold and still, choked her. She tripped behind the count as he pulled her through the hall, stumbling up the stairs leading to the sleeping quarters. She hadn't prepared herself for this yet. Not that she would *ever* be fully prepared, but the count dragged her to bed hours before she'd thought they would retire.

Tomorrow she would wake up defiled by a lecherous old man, with nothing to look forward to in her life but more of the same, night after night. Arundel told her the count wanted to have another child, as his two children from his first marriage had died in infancy.

The fact that Elysia's mother had told her exactly how babes were conceived only added to her anxiety. Knowing what her husband expected of her filled her with panic since Jacques St. Simeon did not seem to be a gentle man.

By the time they reached the lord's chambers, Count Vannes appeared winded, his ire from the hall vanished in an effort to gasp for air. He looked much older than his fifty years. Elysia had a sixty-year-old tenant at Nevering who displayed twice the energy and health of her new husband.

Elysia watched his breathing slow, and he seemed to collect himself. Opening the chamber door, he smiled with some of the mocking self-deprecation she had seen in his nephew. "After you, beautiful one."

Stepping hesitantly into the opulent chamber, she gasped when he wasted no time pulling her backward against him.

"After tonight, you will never again suggest your husband is some kind of invalid who needs to rest." When he ran his hands possessively over her hips and down the fronts of her thighs, Elysia fought the urge to shove them away.

How would she get through the night? She was accustomed to being her own mistress, to managing her own life. How would she lie submissively beneath this drunken cad when she longed to run from him?

"There will be so much delight for you tonight, innocent one. I will be very gentle with you, I promise." His words slurred together as he swayed on his feet and leaned against his wife, mashing her with his bulk.

Unable to support him for long, she stepped toward the room's one chair, hoping to convince the count to sit down.

"Please, my lord." She strained under his weight as she maneuvered him around the huge bed to the high-backed seat next to it.

Not in all her years as a starry-eyed girl did she envision this debacle for a wedding night. When she dared to dream of it, she imagined a man gazing upon her with adoring eyes as he initiated her into womanhood. An incredibly handsome man.

Like Conon.

Tripping over a protruding claw foot of the monstrous bed, Elysia lost her balance. The count fell into the linens, his arms still wrapped about her midsection, dragging her down with him.

The oaf.

"Please my lord, I—" Wriggling away from him, she stiffened when he seemed to regain control of himself.

"This is very nice, Lady Elysia."

Pinning her body against his own, he rolled with her until he lay atop her. Her back bent at an awkward angle as her feet remained on the floor.

The count kissed her and ran groping fingers over her breasts. Elysia squeezed her eyes shut, wishing she could close down all her other senses.

Muttering incoherent words in her ear, he pulled at her clothing in all directions—yanking her gown from one shoulder, tearing the fabric at her neck, hoisting up her skirt.

Elysia froze. The count grinned down at her, eyes glazed and unseeing. His hands fumbled with his clothing, pawing between their bodies to loosen his braies.

And then the pain came.

Sharp and heart-stopping it felt like a dagger, jabbing into her with considerable force. Her mother had said it would hurt but a moment....

"Damn!" The count looked down between their bodies in dismay. "I forgot to sheathe my eating knife, love." With a tipsy lack of grace, he slid the blade clumsily from her thigh. "Does it hurt overmuch?"

Blood poured from the wound, staining her dress and the bedclothes.

"I will be fine." Grateful for the reprieve despite the pain, Elysia pressed her kirtle to the wound. "I need some wine to bathe it, however, my lord."

"I am so sorry." Like a chastened young squire, Count Vannes hurried across the room to retrieve the flagon. "Damn clumsy of me."

After cleaning and bandaging the small gash, Elysia

helped Vannes remove his eating knife from its place at his waist.

"Perhaps I have gone about this all wrong, my dear." Grinning sheepishly, he tugged her torn tunic sleeve back over her shoulder. "I think instead, you should disrobe for me."

He cannot be serious.

"A sweet young girl like you is unused to the careless hands of a man. It will go easier for you if *you* do it."

I pray he is not this careless all the time. His conquests must be fortunate to survive the night in one piece.

He settled himself upon the bed, glassy eyes looking close to sleep. Perhaps if she took her time about it, he would pass out before she finished.

Heartened by her new plan, Elysia pulled her slippers from her feet, then slowly ungartered her hose and slid them from her legs.

Still awake.

Unwinding the ties from each sleeve was a painstaking job, but it did not take long enough to lull the count into unconsciousness. In fact, his eyes widened in anticipation.

Elysia slipped the gown from her shoulders and it pooled at her feet, leaving her clad in only her sheer linen tunic.

The count's eyes grew huge. Elysia thought it peculiar she would engender such a response. The man surely had vast experience with women. Did he find her so terribly different? Fear and embarrassment gripped her, but it was now or never.

Lifting the hem, she pulled the slim-fitting tunic over her head, baring her body to a man for the first time.

Shyly, she glanced up to see his face…convulsed in agony.

Chapter Three

"My lord?" Panicked, Elysia rushed to the count's side where he sat, his body twisted to one side and frozen in place. "Are you all right?"

His glazed eyes were unseeing. He did not breathe.

Her heart dropped in her chest.

"Please, my lord, you must lie down. Catch your breath." She eased him back to recline on the bed. "I will get help." Yanking the linen duvet from the bed, she clutched it to her breast and ran to the door.

"Help!" she shouted the plea, but she need not have yelled. Conon St. Simeon strolled down the corridor, the voluptuous widow from dinner still clinging to his arm.

Elysia reached for him, needing him far more than the widow did. "Your uncle is unwell, sir. Please—"

Conon shoved past her into the bedroom without hesitation. "Wait for me down the hall, Marguerite," he called over his shoulder.

For good measure, Elysia shut the door to the young woman, not wanting anyone else to witness the shambles of her wedding night.

"Unwell?" Conon turned accusing eyes to her from the count's bedside, where he clutched his uncle's wrist. "He is dead."

"My God." The room swirled, and for a moment she thought she would faint. She gripped the blanket to her like a lifeline.

"What happened?" His harsh tone forced her to think clearly.

"I do not know." Still reeling, she sank into the chair beside the bed, recalling how she had struggled an hour ago to help the count into that very seat. "He seemed out of breath all evening, but I assumed it was because of the wine. He drank so much at dinner—"

"What happened after he brought you up here?"

Elysia felt the heat rise in her cheeks, but she knew it was sinful to think of her modesty at a time like this.

"I helped him to the bed and then…" She could not tell him about the incident with the knife. It was too embarrassing and had no bearing on the count's death anyway. "And we…lay together until he bade me to rise and disrobe."

"And?" His face betrayed no hint of the charm she'd spied at the wedding feast. Blue eyes bored into hers in their search for the truth.

Her face flamed. She prayed she did not have to relate the details of this night to anyone else.

"And he grew…amorous. His eyes widened and—" This was awful. "I thought…well never mind what I thought. I did not realize he was unwell at first. Feeling a bit shy, I could not meet his gaze again until it was too late. When I glanced back up at him he seemed frozen, like that." She nodded to the still form of the count.

Conon wiped a gentle hand over his uncle's face, shuttering the dead man's vacant stare. Closing his own eyes at the same time, Conon kneeled beside the bed for a long moment, whispering words of prayer.

The scene, so gentle, flooded Elysia with guilt. It had not occurred to her to pray, and she was the count's *widow*. She should be on her knees begging God for forgiveness that she had not saved her husband, that she had come to the marriage bed full of dread and selfishly pining for a husband who wanted more in a marriage than a house full of heirs.

"I am so sorry."

As she intoned her own supplication for the count's soul, Conon found his feet once again, detached and matter-of-fact.

"The union was consummated then?" He did not look at her as he asked, thank goodness, but appeared to focus on the bloodstains on the bed.

The creak of the chamber door startled them before she could speak.

"You did not lock it?" Conon rushed toward the entry, but not before his widow friend stepped through the portal.

And screamed Vannes Keep to the ground. "He's dead!" she shrieked.

Answering footsteps resounded in the hall.

The woman stared at Elysia in openmouthed horror. "You killed him, you greedy witch."

Conon wrapped restraining arms about his paramour and covered her mouth with his hand, speaking softly into her ear. "No one has killed anyone, Marguerite."

Elysia's maid appeared at the door amid a growing number of curious wedding guests. Every avid gaze fixed upon her deceased lord, and beside him, the bloodstained sheets.

"Belle, take your mistress to her chamber and help her dress." Conon's brusque tone rang with authority.

"Dear God!" Arundel burst through the small crowd to

gape at the dead man before Elysia could escape the scene.
"What has happened here?

He turned accusing eyes to Elysia.

With shock, she noticed everyone else in the room
shifted their attention to her in that same, peculiar way.
Awkward and self-conscious, wrapped in the bed linen,
Elysia wished she could disappear.

Conon stepped in front of her, shielding her from the
chamber full of wedding guests with his body. "My uncle
is dead, Arundel. No doubt helped to his grave by his foolish notion to take a young bride and start another family."
Conon did nothing to hide his frustration, though he directed it more toward the earl than Elysia at the moment.
"His health proved too weak to support his fancies, I fear."

"Hah!" The woman called Marguerite stepped forward.
"She probably hastened him to his death." The widow nodded in Elysia's direction. "I hear she stands to inherit her
own lands whether or not she bears an heir."

"I do not need anything from the count," Elysia murmured,
pulling the duvet more tightly around her. "I never have."

"Though you will benefit." Conon turned to glare at
her, still blocking her body from the view of the rest of the
room. "As my uncle thought he would from this marriage."

"It was your uncle's idea to wed, Conon." The earl's voice
held a note of warning. "He came to me with the notion."

Elysia grew more uncomfortable by the moment.

"After you paraded your prize morsel before his nose
when he came to England last fall," Conon muttered darkly.

"He fell in love with her," the earl countered.

Conon made no response, and it seemed to Elysia that
every observer heard the false ring of the words.

"He wanted her," the earl amended. "Who am I to say
nay to the girl for making a good marriage?"

"I'll say it was a good marriage," Marguerite huffed. "The English heiress has but to spread her legs once and—"

Elysia flinched, not so much from the woman's crude accusation, but from the fury that came to life in Conon's expression.

"Get out, Marguerite."

"But it is true—"

Seeing Conon's rigid stance, Elysia silently urged the woman out the door.

"Out." The word was not shouted, but the fierceness of it sent the young widow hurrying from the bridal chamber.

Arundel wandered over to the count as she left, peering at the man's body and the bedclothes. Elysia gauged the distance to the door and wondered if she could sneak out before the conversation turned back to her. She wanted to wash and dress and escape the nightmarish scene.

"Too bad the marriage was consummated," the earl observed.

"But—" Elysia intervened, preparing to explain the matter, no matter how embarrassing it might be. With no consummation, she could not call herself a true widow.

Either Arundel ignored his former ward, or else he did not hear her, for he continued to speak. "She would bring more wealth as a virgin."

His words shut her mouth. For him to speak of her as if she were no more than an object for sale to the highest bidder…the notion galled her.

How could he think about marrying her off to someone else already? Was he that unfeeling? She had yet to bury this husband.

Perhaps Conon had heard Elysia's attempt to speak, for he suddenly looked hard upon her. "It *was* consummated, was it not, Lady Elysia?"

If it had been consummated, she would be considered a true widow to the count, and safe from marriage for at least another year. Maybe longer.

She would be free. Her life would be her own again, and she could return to Nevering. To her linen business. She would not attempt to take a farthing from Vannes, no matter what Conon thought to the contrary.

Yet she could not force the lie past her lips. "I am sorry, my lord but—"

"*Jesu,* Conon." Arundel strode to Elysia's side and put a protective arm about her. "How can you humiliate the girl in front of the whole keep? 'Tis obvious the deed was done."

Conon stared at her bare shoulders and the linen duvet wrapped carelessly around her body.

"Belle, get her dressed, *please.*" His voice held a gruff edge. "There will be little sleep for any of us this night."

"Yes, my lord."

Elysia felt like a child, but saw the wisdom of clothing herself. It frustrated her, however, that Conon just stepped in and assumed control. The men, she knew, would decide her fate without her. By the time she returned, Arundel and Conon would probably have the rest of her life planned without so much as a glance in her direction.

She needed to tell them the truth of the situation before they began discussing her future. Elysia looked back to the chamber, weighing her options.

But she did not want to return and bring up the awkward situation in front of a crowd of gossipmongers. She would go to the earl later, when he met privately with Conon, and tell them what really had happened.

Belle hustled Elysia down the hall and to a private chamber. She scarcely noticed what garments Belle chose for her as the maid dressed and groomed her with expert thoroughness.

Elysia focused on the upcoming meeting with the earl and Conon. She would tell them she would not marry again unless forced. Tonight's experience surpassed humiliation, and for all she knew, it was because of her ineptitude as a wife that her husband died.

"Do not fret, sweeting," Belle soothed. The French maid had served at Vannes prior to Elysia's arrival, and Elysia had liked her from the moment they met.

"It had nothing to do with you, you know," the servant continued. "The lord has been drinking with no care for his health for as long as I have been here, and from what I hear, for twenty years before that. No man can abuse his poor body that way and expect to escape unscathed."

"Perhaps I hastened him to his grave." Elysia hid the knife wound on her thigh as Belle helped her into a fresh gown. Elysia would tell Arundel what happened, but she didn't want the servants to hear the news first. "The excitement of the marriage and the strain of the wedding day. It was too much."

"If so, he has no one to blame but himself. If you had not consented to wed, he would have found another young woman half his years."

But guilt racked her. Guilt because the count died. Guilt because she let his nephew and Arundel think her wedding night left her a widow.

The whole mess required unraveling. She would proceed immediately to the earl's chamber and tell them what happened—and hope with all her heart Arundel did not immediately marry her off to some other unfortunate soul.

After giving instructions to the staff for moving the count's body and cleaning the master bedchamber, Conon sent for his fellow knight, Leon de Grace, to oversee the movement of the count while Conon met with Arundel.

A trusted friend, Leon had fought beside Conon during Conon's first battle. Some odd command of the Fates had left them standing when hordes of other men had died all around them. They'd stuck together after that, neither one willing to turn his back on a partnership that seemed somehow preordained. Neither man had a family, but for ten years, they'd counted on one another as if they'd been born brothers.

De Grace arrived immediately, offering his condolences by clapping Conon on the shoulder. "He is at peace now, my friend."

Conon nodded, heartened by Leon's presence. Ten years older than Conon, de Grace would handle everything with his usual efficiency. The man was endlessly capable.

"You are to meet with the girl's overlord now?" de Grace asked, peering around the room as the maids removed the linens to clean the chamber.

"Arundel will want every facet of the bridal contract enforced, of course," Conon remarked, trying unsuccessfully to keep the bitterness from his voice.

"As is his right, of course." The voice of wisdom returned as he tore off a bit of bread from the food on the sideboard.

"And I will honor it." Conon swiped a hand over his face, weary of the day. "I am a man of honor if not wealth."

"'Tis a better recommendation for a man anyhow," de Grace reminded him between bites of bread. "If only your uncle had possessed a bit more of the former, you would now be possessed of a bit more of the latter."

"Aye." Conon knew his friend meant no insult. "He was a good man once."

De Grace gazed upon Jacques's bloated body and nodded. "You lost that man long before tonight, Con. Just remember his bride knows naught of his empty promises to
you. 'Tis not her fault he did not keep them."

Conon thought of Elysia's frightened eyes tonight, the
way she had looked when she'd realized the count was
dead. Had that been sorrow he'd read in her expression?
Or relief? "Nay, but it is her fault I cannot leave Vannes
now. I will need to stay here a bit longer while matters are
settled."

If Elysia carried his uncle's heir, Conon would need to
make arrangements for the child's care and protection. For
that matter, he would be honor-bound to protect the child's
mother.

"We will leave when you are ready. I am in no hurry,"
de Grace assured him.

Of course Leon was in no hurry to find work as a mercenary. He had a modest fortune stashed somewhere on the
continent thanks to more wars fought than Conon. This
new delay was a blow to Conon's coffers.

They parted company then. Conon traversed the dimly
lit corridors toward Arundel's chamber, preparing himself
to face the earl and discuss the fine points of his uncle's
marriage contract. No doubt, Conon's fears would be confirmed—he would learn his *grandmère's* dower property
would indeed fall into Elysia's hands. Before Conon could
knock at the earl's door, it was flung wide by Arundel's
squire.

"Very good, then, St. Simeon," Arundel muttered, waving him inside the sparsely appointed chamber. "We can
proceed now."

Conon wondered what had become of the furnishings.
The last time he had been in this room, rich tapestries

adorned the walls and woven mats covered the floors. Now there was little to recommend the cold chamber except the fire that crackled merrily in the hearth.

Ten men crowded in the earl's small solar, all Englishmen loyal to the earl. The only one Conon recognized was Huntley, Arundel's crass second in command.

"Sorry about your uncle, St. Simeon. He was a good man." The earl shook his head in sympathy as he clapped a hand on Conon's shoulder. "An honorable man, too. 'Twas one of the reasons I consented to wed my ward to him."

Shaking off Arundel's grip, Conon did not care to be wheedled. "I will honor the bridal contract. Let us go over it in detail."

Although the earl nodded politely at Conon's acquiescence, Huntley had the gall to grin, as if he were solely responsible for winning a great battle.

"But I would see *him*—" Conon addressed Arundel as he jerked his head in Huntley's direction "—and his disrespect out of the room before I do so."

Huntley would have protested, a black look marring his face, but Arundel stepped in. "Perhaps that would be best." He nodded to Huntley and the other knights. "Excuse us, please."

Chain mail clinking, the knights filed out of the room with Huntley muttering under his breath. Conon did not care. He turned to the earl, ready to discuss the specifics of Jacques's agreement with Elysia and her overlord.

"I understand Lady Elysia will inherit the Vannes dower lands, even if there is no heir?" The dower property represented a small fraction of the Vannes holdings, but its worth was immeasurable to Conon. His happiest childhood memories revolved around the nearby keep and time spent there with his grandmother. He had inherited his *grandmère's* family pride while a boy at her knee.

"Aye. But she inherits much more if she has conceived."

Pacing the length of the solar, Conon rubbed his temple in a futile attempt to relieve the pounding in his head. He didn't want to ask for clarification, but he had to know. "All of it?"

Arundel pulled the contract parchment from his surcoat and allowed the scroll to unravel onto the chamber's only table. "Everything. At least until her eldest son comes of age."

Conon should have expected this. Hell, hadn't his uncle practically told him as much? Still, he had hoped Jacques would realize how unfair that would be. Conon would be left with nothing, unable to afford a noble marriage and family. He schooled his features in spite of the knife his dead uncle had just twisted in his back.

"It is unlikely there will be an heir after such a brief marriage." Conon glared at the words upon the scroll, willing them to be different.

"Perhaps," Arundel agreed, stroking the tuft of beard at his chin. "In which case I will send her home to Nevering until I have found another suitable match for her."

Conon paused in his pacing. "She would not live on the Vannes dower lands?"

"Nay. She is a wealthy heiress in her own right, and a prize I must safeguard. Her bridal portion is worth almost as much as the Vannes fortune. Many a man would lay claim to her."

For a moment, Conon envisioned himself wed to the English woman. Although her slender form had looked enticing as hell wrapped in naught but a linen blanket, Conon guessed she was cold as a hard frost. The curves he had detected beneath her impromptu robe didn't soften her perpetually stiff spine or proud bearing.

Yet her skin had been soft enough beneath his lips, a contrary part of his brain reminded him.

"If she is so damn wealthy, why does she need the dower lands?" Conon asked, not expecting an answer. He should have found a way to ensure the inheritance Jacques had promised him long ago. Conon didn't care about the money. He cared about his family seat.

"'Tis the politics of marriage." The earl rolled the bridal contract with brusque efficiency and returned it to a pouch at his waist. "I knew you would be difficult about this."

"What if she killed my uncle?" Conon inquired. It was entirely possible. Heaven knew it had been the first thing Conon thought when he entered the bedchamber tonight and saw the count lying on the bed. How many young maids would go eagerly to the bed of a lust-ridden, aging knight?

"How?" Arundel scoffed. "By being too damn beautiful for an old man's heart to bear? Surely you jest."

"I have heard she has knowledge of herbs." Even though Elysia struck him as proud, Conon did not truly think she had killed his uncle. She had looked too genuinely horrified at the sight of Jacques's face in death.

"Flax plants for linen, but I assure you that is all. Elysia is no wisewoman."

"Mayhap she contacted one to be rid of an unwanted groom," Conon pressed, wondering why he bothered. Some part of him seemed to want reassurance she could not have committed such a crime.

"You impugn the honor of your countess, St. Simeon."

"I say nothing the whole keep has not secretly thought already. But I will give her my protection as my uncle's widow until it is known whether or not she is breeding. Once it is proven she is not, I want her out of Vannes." And then Conon would be rid of the unwanted temptation she posed.

"I cannot afford to wait that long. I will leave Huntley here to protect my interests and a few men to guard the countess until that time." The earl scooped up the parchment, making it obvious he wanted Conon to leave. "Keep in mind, St. Simeon, if Elysia carries the next Count of Vannes in her belly, 'twill be *you* who is ousted."

"Aye." Conon raised a brow in the earl's direction as he stepped into the corridor. "Unless, on top of being a fortune-hunting opportunist, your ward proves to be a murderess."

The earl made no reply, despite the furious blue pulse that leaped in a thick vein down his forehead.

Conon departed the guest tower for his own quarters in the family wing of the keep. His door was one removed from the Countess of Vannes, the only other occupant of the wing.

He lingered in front of Elysia's chamber for a moment, noting the light that still shone brightly under her door. Was she upset by the count's death and unable to sleep? Or was she privately celebrating her success in ridding herself of an unwanted bridegroom? A cynical thought, mayhap, but Conon could not dismiss the sense that the countess had been hiding something about her wedding night.

Perhaps she would think him rude to interrupt her in the middle of the night, but she was evidently not sleeping anyway. "Lady Elysia?" He rapped on the heavy barrier.

Silence answered him for a long moment until the door creaked open to reveal his uncle's widow illuminated in the glow of a blazing fire. She blinked slowly, as if surprised to see him.

Unrepentant for his late intrusion, Conon shoved the door open the rest of the way and invaded the bright chamber.

Candles wreathed the room as if it were a church. Conon shook his head at the blatant extravagance. Since leaving the comfortable household of his father almost fifteen years ago, Conon had not wasted so much as a drop of wax or a skinful of wine. His frugal existence forbade it. Lady Elysia, on the other hand, was evidently used to indulging herself.

"Do not answer your own door," Conon admonished, pushing his way into the room before someone saw into her chamber. "Where is Belle?"

The temperature soared as hot as midsummer in the chamber, and Elysia was wrapped in a jumble of blankets.

"I am afraid the heat made her sleepy, though she fought to stay awake by me."

His eyes found the maid, sprawled across Elysia's rumpled bed. This was not the chamber the countess had briefly shared with Jacques, but the smaller, private quarters she had been appointed upon her arrival a fortnight ago.

"You should be abed, as well." He worked his way around the room, pinching candles as he went. "It is almost dawn."

"I have been worried. I was denied entry into the guest tower, let alone the earl's solar. I wanted most urgently to speak in my own behalf—"

"Denied entry?" Conon hovered over a candle, focusing on Elysia for the first time since entering. Her hair hung in a shimmering black mass down her back, rumpled and out of place. She had the delicious look of a woman who had just rolled out of bed—an enticing contrast to her usual stiff posture and cool reserve.

. Her eyes, however, were sunken and dark; her skin pale. She seemed to shiver right through the pile of blankets that covered her.

"Who denied you entry?"

"Sir Huntley." Her tone conveyed her distaste for the man. They agreed on one thing, anyway.

"Huntley is an arrogant son of a—"

"I know." She put her hand up as if to ward off his forthcoming curse. "He is a vulgar man, and my words with him topped off an already horrifying day." Voice breaking, she crumpled to the bench by the fire. "Please excuse me, sir, if I am not myself."

For a long moment, she did not speak. Seeming to collect herself, she fixed him with her gaze, chin high and proud in spite of her nearness to the breaking point. Unshed tears glittered in her eyes, refusing to fall.

A wave of pity tempered by admiration washed over Conon, surprising him with its force. Perhaps there was more to this woman than he had anticipated.

"But I have to know." She took a deep breath, as if frightened of his response to her words. "What did you discuss with the earl? What is to be my fate?"

His pity dissolved when he recalled the discussion with Arundel. "You mean how much of Vannes will you walk away with?"

All signs of weakness vanished from Elysia's expression as she stood, though she kept the blanket wrapped about her. Conon tried not to remember how unsettling it had felt to view her with nothing but bedclothes to cover her earlier tonight.

"Nay, sir." Her voice cold and controlled, she sounded at odds with her vulnerable appearance. "I am not concerned with the Vannes fortune, but with my person. Because you are a man, you cannot possibly understand the frustrations of being unable to control the most basic decisions of your life."

"As a man who stands a good chance to be disinherited,

chère, I can tell you exactly how frustrating it is to have no control over your life. And to be undermined and outmaneuvered by a woman is especially insulting." Crossing the room to stand toe to toe with her, he willed her to be intimidated.

Stubbornly she stood her ground, though she was forced to look up at him. "How could my marriage possibly disinherit you? Do I look like a successful candidate for Count of Vannes?"

"Nay, lady, you do not." She looked more like a petulant child in need of sleep, but he was not cruel enough to say that.

Some surge of protectiveness moved Conon to tuck a stray strand of her midnight hair behind one ear. The dark, rumpled locks felt as soft as they looked. Softer. He recalled the impetuous kiss he had given her earlier that day. Her skin had been warm and smooth, too. Now, she stiffened at his touch, though she did not pull away.

"However, you might carry the future count within your womb. If that is the case, you have dispossessed me of much."

"No." Stepping back from him, she walked toward the fire and gazed in its heated depths. "That will not be the case. I am certain of it."

"You cannot be sure, Countess." He forced her new title past his lips. "That is why the earl and I thought it best you remain here until such time it may be proven one way or another."

Her gaze flew to his, revealing a depth of vulnerability Conon would not have thought her capable of, before returning to the safety of the fire.

"As you will," she responded with quiet assurance, indicating no hint of the anxiety he had seen in her countenance. "Yet I am certain I will carry no babe. Am I free to leave once that is…established?"

She spoke with such quiet conviction, Conon wondered about the events of her sordid wedding night. Of course the blood on the sheets told the story anyhow, but the countess spoke as confidently as if she knew no heir would result.

"*Aye.* You may leave." With the deed to *Grandmère's* dower lands as a prize for her virginal sacrifice.

Perhaps one day she would allow him to buy it back from her. Surely she would exchange a fortune for a plot full of memories.

His gaze flitted over the countess's rumpled hair and pink cheeks. Despite her more approachable disheveled state, Conon could not imagine the stiff-necked Elysia Rougemont knew anything of love or sentiment.

"And if that is the case," Conon continued, backing toward the door, "your time in France will have been more brief than either of us could have imagined."

By month's end, he could well possess the security he had longed craved, but he would never see the fair lady again.

Chapter Four

She had lied.

The knowledge ate away at Elysia long after Conon's departure, keeping her awake into the morning hours. Although she'd never actually *told* a lie, her failure to correct the popular misconception that her marriage had been consummated was as good as an outright falsehood.

Brooding as she stared into the cold ashes of her bedroom hearth, she regretted her continued silence. She had every intention of revealing the truth to the earl last night when she went to meet with him and Conon.

But she hadn't been allowed to see them.

Although unaccustomed to such treatment, Elysia knew such was most women's lot. At Nevering, she had ruled the keep. Even while her brother lived, Elysia had been the one to oversee the linen trade and issue orders. How galling to go from a position of importance—one which she enjoyed immensely—to being treated with open disrespect.

Recalling Huntley's rude treatment the previous evening riled her all over again. She had assumed the earl instructed Huntley to keep her out of their private meeting, though Conon seemed genuinely surprised when she mentioned she had been denied entry. Perhaps it was only the earl who wanted her kept in the dark.

In her anger, she decided if the earl did not want to share his plans for her, she would not bother to confide the truth to him. This morning, when she had calmed down and realized she had a moral obligation to tell him the truth no matter if she had to fight Huntley to do it, she discovered Arundel had already departed.

Since first light she had paced the floor, fearing for her soul with so grave a sin to hang upon it. She thought, too, of Conon and his fear that an heir would usurp his fortune. But how could she tell *him* the truth? The matter was most delicate.

She would have to live with his anger for another couple of weeks until it was proven she would not bear the next Count of Vannes. Surely, once she displayed no signs of being *enceinte*, she would be allowed to go home. She would simply confide the truth to her overlord when she saw him once again.

Who would it hurt if she kept the truth to herself at this point? After all, she would take nothing from Conon's inheritance except a small dower property, and that could be returned to him as soon as she spoke with her overlord. It wasn't as if she would be dragging the French estate home on horseback. Besides, Conon had an enormous estate to live in now, so he wouldn't miss the deed to a minor keep for a few weeks.

Somewhat appeased by her plan, Elysia donned her old gardening kirtle to work among the flowers she'd spied the previous day. She hated idle hands. In the garden she would escape the oppressive keep, with its reminders of the horrible night before, and soothe her frayed nerves with a healthy dose of weeding.

Scarcely aware of the departing wedding guests, Elysia lost herself in the mundane task of tending an unused section of the garden, visualizing the seeds she would have planted to best utilize the space.

The male voice startled her.

"The garden seems to be a common hiding place for you, Countess." Conon appeared out of nowhere as he had the day before.

When his kiss upon her hand had seared her flesh.

Although he was as incredibly handsome as the previous day, Elysia noted the shadows under his eyes, the sadness that lurked within. Guilt nagged at her.

As Conon helped her to her feet, she tried not to wince at the pain in her thigh from the count's knife wound.

His eyes narrowed as he assessed her, obviously seeing the hurt.

"What is it?"

Embarrassed and guilty, she could not look at him. "It is nothing, I—"

"You should not be out so soon after a wedding night, Elysia." His voice was as rough as the hand that still gripped her arm.

"I am fine, truly—"

"There will be talk all over France about the beautiful young English woman who came to Brittany to wed a rich count, poisoned him on his wedding night, then flaunted herself about the gardens the next day as if nothing were amiss." His words might be accusing, but his tone was merely tired.

Ignoring the unwelcome warmth that still tingled where he touched her, she stepped out of his grasp. "Poisoned? Is that the verdict this morning?"

"*Aye.*" He smiled halfheartedly. "Though that verdict is

subject to change several times by the end of the day and will no doubt become more embellished as the tale travels to all corners of France and England."

"Do *you* believe I had a hand in the count's death?" She brushed the soil from the worn linen kirtle she favored for gardening.

"Your refusal to stay in your chamber like a proper grieving widow today does nothing to ease my mind regarding your possible guilt."

"What does staying shut up in my chamber have to do with how much grief I feel?" Elysia was surprised at the sting of tears in her eyes.

"You cannot convince me you mourn his loss."

"Just because I was not overly eager to wed him? By all the saints, that does not mean I wished his demise. I imagine at least half the brides who have ever sought the altar have feared and regretted the choice of husband made for them. That does not make them bloodthirsty killers."

"*Aye.* But their husbands do not end up dead on their wedding nights."

"Very well then, my lord." *How dare he accuse her of something so foul?* "Your uncle *was* poisoned."

Conon's eyes widened, a flicker of shock and disappointment crossing his expression.

"Poisoned by drink and self-indulgence," she snapped. "And mayhap by uncaring relatives who closed their eyes while he had been slowly killing himself for heaven knows how many years."

"*Touché, chère.*" The wind caught his hair and gentled him with unseen fingers. "However, I assure you my lack of interference in my uncle's life was not the result of indifference. Had he been my father, perhaps I would have felt

I had the right to...." He paused in thought, far away from the garden and Elysia. "Yet it does not matter. He is gone."

"I am sorry."

"So you say. I merely came to inform you that Arundel departed, and he has left John Huntley to be your guardian while you are in residence here."

"Sir Huntley?" She could not imagine a more loathsome protector.

"Everyone else is leaving except for Leon de Grace and myself."

"De Grace is loyal to you, I gather?" Elysia wished she had an ally here. She did not relish the thought of spending any more time at Vannes, but it seemed a small price to pay for her freedom.

"He is his own man, and he seems to think I will need his help in the coming weeks." A wry smile tugged at the corner of Conon's mouth. "I could not get rid of him if I tried."

"You are fortunate to have such a friend."

"Fortunate with no fortune. But you are right, Countess." Bowing, he turned toward the stables. He was but a few steps from her when he looked back. "Elysia."

"Aye?"

"While I understand the need to lose oneself in activity during a crisis, most of our remaining guests do not." He nodded in the direction of the road, where a small party of knights rode away from Vannes, casting curious glances toward the scene in the garden. "Would it hurt to smother any more wagging tongues?"

"Certainly." Duly chastened, Elysia nodded, sorry she had not thought to stay within the keep for that very reason. "I will retire to my solar."

Dusting off her small shovel, she had to admit Conon St.

Simeon possessed a quiet wisdom she had not expected in so carefree a man. His frivolity at her wedding, his open liaison with a wealthy widow, had made her regard him as an insubstantial man, but now she doubted such was the case.

Thrusting aside disturbing thoughts of the enigmatic new count, she hurried to Vannes and found Belle tidying her large wardrobe. The maid curtsied when Elysia arrived.

"Morning, mistress. Perhaps you would like to change?" Belle's pointed look at Elysia's dusty clothes conveyed her disapproval.

"Aye." Elysia sighed. "I do not know what I was thinking to work in the garden this morning, Belle. The count's nephew is annoyed about it."

"'Tis easy for a girl to forget what is expected of her when she has been through all that you have, my lady."

Elysia shook her head sadly as she finished washing with the fresh, cold water Belle brought. "My husband has not even been properly buried. I must plan a mass for him. It was selfish for me to think of my own needs at such a time. My mother taught me better than this."

With quick efficiency, Belle had Elysia dried, dressed and seated, ready to begin the monotonous task of brushing and braiding her hair.

"You miss your mother then, my lady?"

"Aye." Elysia thought of Lady Daria Rougemont at Nevering. Was her mother immersed in sewing and stitching to keep up with the linen orders? Or was she reveling in the freedom of escaping from her taskmaster daughter who had ensured everyone at Nevering did their share of work? "She and I grew close when my father died. Closer still when my brother, Robin, died. It hurt very much to leave her."

"Does she tend your linens now that you are gone?"

Elysia smiled at her thoughtful maid. "I do not know if

she will try to run things or not. She does not like to be plagued by details. My mother's greatest contribution has always been her fine needlework." Much as Elysia adored her mother, Lady Daria made no pretense that she enjoyed the labor involved in maintaining Nevering's trade.

"If your mother does not oversee the business, who will?"

Who indeed? That very question had been the biggest deterrent to Elysia's marriage. Of course the earl had not cared. He did not understand the finer points of the linen trade, and assumed that anyone, even his dolt of a vassal, Sir Oliver, could take the reins once Elysia left.

"Our esteemed neighbor to the north, Sir Oliver Westmoor."

"You do not care for this man, Countess?" Belle pulled one braid over the crown of Elysia's head and fashioned it into a slender circlet.

"Envision a less bulky, more insipid version of Sir Huntley."

"Not a pleasing picture." Belle secured the final braid and stood back to admire her handiwork. "How will your mother handle such a man?"

"I admit the thought has frightened me." Stepping to the window, Elysia looked down into the courtyard to watch the latest wedding guests depart. "She should be fine until I return. Oliver cannot possibly have found reason to interfere in the scant moon since I left."

"What if you cannot return, Countess? If you are with child, my lord Conon will not permit you to leave."

Guilt nipped her once again, a familiar companion since the moment the whole household assumed she was no longer a maiden.

"I am not with child," she whispered, more to herself than to Belle. Elysia's hand strayed to her flat belly, and for the first time wondered what it would be like to carry a babe.

The thought held appeal if only she could wed an honorable man who was interested in a true partnership between husband and wife. Did such a man even exist?

Elysia warmed at the vision of herself cradling an infant with an impish twinkle in its bright blue eyes. Realizing with dismay that she'd given her baby Conon's eyes, she turned away from the window view and tamped down the yearning for things that could never be.

For the next several days, Elysia did little more than think and brood in the confines of her room. Although Conon encouraged her to enjoy the weather and roam about the keep after the wedding guests departed, Elysia felt cruel and uncaring to go on with daily life as if nothing had happened.

Her husband was dead.

At least he had been honored and buried now. She saw to every detail of his mass and memorial gathering.

"My lady?" Belle called to her through the fog of her gloomy reverie.

"Aye?" Elysia turned from her needlework, an elaborate tunic she planned to give Belle with an embroidered bee hovering over a delicate flower.

"Your guardian is at the door, my lady. He wishes to see you."

She had not even heard Sir Huntley knock. It was past nightfall, an unseemly hour for her to receive guests in her solar. "He must know better than to—"

"Good evening, Countess." He suddenly stood in the middle of the solar floor, not appearing to mind that no one had admitted him. He wore a surcoat trimmed with ermine and a weighty gold medallion adorning his thick neck. A lock of damp hair fell across his forehead, suggesting he had recently bathed.

He was handsome enough, Elysia supposed, but his looks did nothing to mitigate her impression of him as a cruel man.

"Sir Huntley, really, I beg your pardon, but—"

"Nay, lady." He bowed, smiling wolfishly. "It is I who should be begging yours for intruding so late, but I could find no other way to speak with you. You have been a bit of a recluse this past sennight."

"I am in mourning." What coarse manners to intrude upon a widow a scant few days after her husband's death. Anger brewed inside her, drawing her out of the gray depression that had hung over her all week. "What is it you wished to speak with me about, sir?"

Kneeling with respectful courtesy before her, he stared at her with an impudent gaze. "Marriage."

Elysia reeled. She heard Belle gasp behind her.

"Really, sir—"

"Call me John."

It upset Elysia enough that she had no say in her life anymore. But now Huntley did not even give her the courtesy of speaking without interrupting.

"Nay. I could not," she assured him. "Sir Huntley, I have only just lost my first husband. My devotion to his memory forbids me to even consider—"

Grabbing her hand in both of his, he yanked her a step closer to where he knelt. "You knew him less than a night, Elysia."

What manner of man thought he could woo a woman by not ever letting her finish a sentence? The same kind who would attempt to court a new widow, apparently. She balked at Huntley's familiarity and withdrew her hand. "Nay, I—"

"I will be a good father to your son, should you bear one."

He looked reverently toward her belly, and Elysia got the sneaking suspicion he had rehearsed this speech. No wonder he would never allow her to speak. Her commentary would probably confuse his practiced words.

"I must mourn my husband, sir, and even then it is up to the earl." Part of her longed to give him a stern set-down for his crudeness, but instinct warned her John Huntley would not take such a slight with good grace. He was a dangerous man, lacking the restraint Conon possessed.

Conon. Strange how he came to mind at the oddest times.

"The earl will give his consent if you agree, Elysia. I am his most trusted knight. He owes me much."

"But he does not owe you *me,* Sir Huntley, and I am not ready to wed again."

He looked offended, and dispensed with his courtly guise to address her in a more serious fashion. "You need a strong knight to guard your considerable wealth, Elysia. And if you bear the heir to Vannes, you'll have all the more need of me."

"I will not bear a child." Elysia's face flamed at her blatant mention of the situation, but she became more annoyed by the moment. Exasperated, she gave in to the urge to send him away. "Now I must ask that you take your leave, sir. I am overwhelmed by your proposal, and I am still in mourning. Pray speak no more of it."

With admirable discretion, Belle opened the solar door and cleared her throat.

Huntley looked back and forth between the women, obviously wondering how far he should push his luck. "Very well then, Countess. I will leave you, for now." He smiled graciously, though his eyes remained lust filled and greedy. "My offer still stands, however. I would have you think on it."

With a curt nod, he vacated the solar, leaving Elysia irritated but enlivened. If nothing else, Huntley's visit helped dissipate her sadness.

Soon she would go home. If her moon cycle proved as well timed as usual, she would have less than a fortnight to remain in Brittany, and then she would leave all remnants of her ill-fated marriage behind.

"You say Huntley departed her chamber well after nightfall?" Leon de Grace asked Conon for the second time, as if oblivious to Conon's desire to speak no more of it.

"Aye." Conon swung his sword in a wide arc, narrowly missing de Grace's head as they practiced in the vast courtyard outside Vannes Keep the following morn.

"Did he look well pleased?" De Grace darted a blow and backhanded Conon's blade, relieving him of his sword.

A string of unholy curses erupted from Conon's throat as he stood at his friend's mercy. "What do you mean by your question?"

Grinning, Leon stood back, his once vicious sword becoming a harmless staff in his hand. "You are obviously annoyed to think Huntley had some sort of tryst with your uncle's widow. Are you not?"

Conon stalked to retrieve his blade, angry with himself for allowing de Grace to best him. Conon was ten years younger. And faster. And stronger. But he would never find wealth on the battlefield with that kind of performance. He had to focus on something besides Lady Elysia, damn it. "Not annoyed. Just insulted for my uncle's memory."

"Well you need not be if the man did not look well pleased, you see? A man who leaves a beautiful young woman's room past nightfall is only having a tryst if he has a very self-satisfied look upon his face."

Dusting the dirt from his blade, Conon tested it in a series of quick swings. "He did not look pleased, but neither did he look like a man rebuffed. Perhaps he is making headway with the countess."

Conon waited for his friend to respond. When he received no answer, he turned to look upon him, and witnessed a troubled countenance. "What is it?"

De Grace stared down at the wildflowers and grass at his feet. "It is nothing, only—"

"What?" Conon felt a chill in his soul, anticipating an unwelcome answer.

"It merely occurred to me how much Lady Elysia has to gain by having a child to show for her marriage. I hope she has not taken it into her head to conceive one at all costs, even if it means taking Huntley as…"

Leon's words died as a feminine voice swirled through the air on a musical note, light and sweet. Both men turned to see Countess Elysia Rougemont St. Simeon stroll out the keep gates and onto the wide path that led to the garden. She had a flat basket slung over one arm, the cutting knife inside it bouncing carelessly in time to her step. Her dark hair was caught midway down her back with a limp green ribbon. She wore a matching linen surcoat, richly embroidered with all manner of flowers and bees.

"Morning, Countess," Leon called, halting her in her tracks along with her song.

With a polite curtsy, she waved away a raven tendril that escaped the rest of her hair and blushed a soft shade of pink. Her quiet song, her light step, softened her usual cool reserve.

Something contracted painfully inside Conon's chest

just to look at her. Could one so lovely be ruthlessly plotting against him?

"Good morning." Her voice sounded breathless and warm, as alluring as her sweet song.

Not bothering to consider his actions, he approached her, watching her eyes grow wider with each step he took. "How long have you been receiving late-night guests in the privacy of your chambers, Countess? Only since your husband died, or has this been an ongoing indulgence?"

All signs of pleasant charm evaporated at his words. Spine straightening, she transformed into a worthy adversary before his eyes.

"I'll thank you to give me a key to my room, my lord, so I can prevent fortune-hunting knights from forcing their attentions upon me at will." The voice that had sounded so melodic and sweet stung him with its sharp bite. "As long as I am under your roof, it is your duty to protect me."

As if she needed protection. Conon had never met a more capable woman. He found it difficult to believe she could not fend off one boorish knight while in the safety of her own home. "Of course, my lady. It must be difficult to stave off so many poor men."

His barb found its mark. He could see the wound flash briefly in her eyes before she recovered herself, but not before he felt a moment's regret for his temper.

"I hold you responsible if he gets in again." In a swirl of skirts and swinging basket, she marched down the path to the garden.

Leon emitted a low whistle through closed teeth. "Tougher than she looks, is she not?"

"Almost makes you wonder if she is not tough enough to poison a lecherous old man to spare herself a life beside him."

"It is a challenge to read the quiet ones," Leon observed as they stared after her.

"You are an expert all of the sudden?"

"*Aye*. I know plenty about women. Why do you think I'm not a married man?"

"No luck, perhaps?" Conon watched Elysia bend toward a crop of flowers and apply her cutting knife to the stems with forceful swipes.

Leon ignored his words and pointed in Elysia's direction instead. "You see what I mean? She is imagining that poor bloom is your head at this very moment. Women are dangerous creatures."

Conon scraped a protective hand over his throat. Perhaps the countess warranted a bit more of his attention. What did he really know about her other than that she had strolled into his uncle's life and convinced him to wed, and now she would benefit tidily for her efforts? Despite what Leon said, Conon also knew she didn't have much trouble speaking her mind. And she had a talent for making money wherever she went.

But he needed to know more. The future of Vannes might rest in her hands. In her womb.

Yes, he'd do well to keep a better eye on this woman. And damn the consequences, the idea pleased him.

Chapter Five

⚜

The moon had risen in nearly all its phases since her wedding, and still Elysia remained at Vannes. She had passed the days by working in the garden and the herb-drying room. Her most recent project had been to refresh the latter, and now Elysia allowed herself a moment to enjoy the restored order.

All forms of plants and flowers hung in neat rows from overhead beams that ran the length of the room. The mortar and pestles were spotless, carefully positioned at regular intervals along the plank table. Swept clean of leaves and debris, the floor was covered with sweet-smelling rush mats woven with dried herbs.

As the satisfaction of a job well done faded, however, she realized there were no more tasks left that required her tending. She had gone through the keep systematically over the past two weeks, lending eager assistance wherever she could.

Elysia hated idle hands.

Now her only choices for activity were reading or sewing, both of which were too passive for the nervous energy that danced through her these last few days.

Her flux had arrived.

She had possessed the proof that she would not bear the future Count of Vannes for three days, but found she could not delicately broach the matter to Conon. Though she longed to return to Nevering and her linen trade, she decided she would have to wait another fortnight or so until he brought up the topic once again. Her monthly courses were too private a subject for polite conversation.

And, oddly enough, she had mixed feelings about leaving Vannes and its new lord. As much as Conon could make her angry, Elysia had also seen hints of his quick wit and clever mind. After their disagreement about Sir Huntley, Conon had wordlessly provided her with a key to her bedchamber, allowing her to lock herself inside each night. In doing so, Conon had become more of a protector than her assigned guardian.

Opting for a quick walk around the courtyard to enjoy the warm spring day, Elysia hurried out of the drying chamber. The courtyard buzzed with other people spending the day out of doors. Too late, she spied the one person she had been avoiding.

"The gods must smile upon me today, lady," John Huntley greeted her a moment after she stepped into the bright sunshine.

Fighting the urge to hide in the cool darkness of the drying room, Elysia hugged her arms around herself and calculated the distance to her rooms at the keep.

Too far.

"There is but one God, sir," she murmured distractedly. "And He smiles not upon those who say otherwise."

Undeterred, he plucked up her hand to plant an impudent kiss upon the palm. "He sends me you to guide my erring foot onto the true path, lady, so I am grateful."

Elysia yanked her hand away, not bothering to hide her disgust. "I have not been sent to you, Sir Huntley, I assure you. Now if you will excuse me, I must—"

She made a move to sidestep him, but he blocked her path with the breadth of his body.

"Perhaps you should give a thought to your future, Lady Elysia, and anger me no further."

He backed her into the trunk of a lofty oak and narrowed his gaze, daring her to gainsay him. Yet this was no idle challenge. Elysia read the threat in his eyes.

"Have I angered you?" Rethinking her approach, Elysia struggled to adopt a more pleasant demeanor, idly plucking a nearby daisy as if his answer were of no consequence. "I only mean to return to my duties. I must say I find you a rather intimidating companion, Sir Huntley." Forcing a smile, she tried to peer around Huntley to search the courtyard for Conon. A small quake of fear tripped through her when she saw no sign of him.

Huntley grinned in appreciation. "Intimidation is what being a knight is all about, Countess. Now if only you'd grant me one last favor, I'd be on my way."

Elysia waited, her dislike for the man growing with every breath she took.

Without warning, he seized her arms and pulled her against him, planting wet lips upon hers. The scent of toil, horse and man burned her nostrils. His tongue probed her lips for entry.

Elysia fought back the wave of nausea that roiled, and pushed at him with all her might.

Oblivious, her attacker bent her backward more forcefully, increasing the pressure of his thumbs into the softness of her upper arms. Though her determination to keep her mouth shut prevented her from screaming, she pounded

on his shoulders with as much force as her paralyzed arms
would allow.

"Huntley." A sharp male voice gave her captor pause.

Leon de Grace called across the courtyard, where several other onlookers gawked, greedy for morsels of gossip. Where had they been moments ago when she needed
assistance?

Fear, grown sharp and unreasonable, propelled Elysia's
hand forward to connect with stinging clarity upon Huntley's cheek before she ran across the courtyard, stumbling
over a jutting tree root on her way to the stable.

Heart pummeling the walls of her chest in a jerky
rhythm, she threw a saddle on the small beast designated
for her use. Impervious to the heavy leather or the dirty
stain it made across her gown, she struggled to tighten the
strap around the horse's lean girth.

From the courtyard, she could hear de Grace calling her
name. She ignored him. Nothing would make her face
John Huntley or his odious advances now.

Tearing from the stable with the mare partially bridled
and as nervous as her rider, Elysia traveled west from
Vannes with all the speed the horse could muster. She rode
until the erratic drumming of her heart settled into a more
even rhythm, eventually keeping time with the horse's hoofbeats.

Huntley wanted to wed her for her money. As the late
Count of Vannes had. As other men most certainly would.
She was a rich woman with a fat dowry, and would no
doubt be a target for greedy males across England and
throughout Europe. Once again, she would have no say in
her husband, but would be pawned off like any other
valuable battle prize.

The horse cantered through unfamiliar countryside, carrying Elysia from a place of fear to an exhilarating view of the sea. Blue waves sparkled in the late-spring sunlight, beckoning Elysia closer to the rocky beach.

Slowing her horse's pace, she allowed the little mare to pick her footing over the final crest before the shore. Calmed by the time and distance between her and Huntley, Elysia realized the foolishness of her actions.

She should not have run. Confronting him would only be more difficult now. It would have been better to contend with him boldly and accuse him to his face. Leon de Grace would have spoken to the knight about his aggression.

Now, Huntley would probably weave a false tale about her in her absence, perhaps saying she ran off because she was embarrassed at being discovered.

The swine.

It occurred to her that she wasted no time slapping Huntley after his advances today, but she never thought to raise her hand against Conon the day he kissed her in the garden.

Why was it the man was never far from her thoughts? He lurked in the corners of her mind like a shadow in the twilight. It seemed he followed close behind her at all times.

Perhaps it was merely a matter of his good looks. Despite his penchant for thinking the worst of her, there was no denying the fact that the man was physically beautiful. Elysia had played hostess to vast numbers of knights in two countries, and Conon outshone them all.

But surely she was not so shallow of thought that Conon's uncommon handsomeness caused her to permit his kiss when she viciously repelled John Huntley's? Conon possessed some sense of honor, at least, though she did not know that the first day in the garden. And Conon did not maul her with his hands, as Huntley did. Conon was—

Right there. Not even a league distant from her.

Out of nowhere, Conon St. Simeon now stood beside his horse ahead of her, strolling companionably along the shoreline with the dappled gray mare.

"Elysia?" he shouted from his spot on the shore.

Waving her hand, she tamped down a sudden eagerness to join him. She told herself it was merely because she knew she would be safe in Conon's company. Carefully, she picked her way down the last rise to the sea, all the while assuring herself this man was no different than any other man. He craved wealth and power above anything else.

She would do well to remember that.

"Good day, Countess." His grin disarmed her.

"You needn't make a pretense of respect to me, sir, and there is no one else around to impress with your noble attempt at courtesy. You may call me by my given name."

"I couldn't."

She laughed at his feigned expression of shock. "You did when you saw me on the hill just now."

"A slip of the tongue." He reached to help her from the mare. "Although perhaps you could be equally disrespectful and call me Conon."

She slid from the horse and into his arms. "Perhaps I will, Conon." She only meant to rankle him with the bold familiarity, but instead the name hung heavy and warm in the air between them before he released her.

Taking in her rumpled gown and disheveled hair, he frowned. "What is this?"

He brushed from her sleeve a dirty mark the heavy saddle left when she'd hoisted it over her horse's back. The warmth of his fingers pierced the light layers of linen. "Nothing, I—"

"You ride too far by yourself, lady. I thought you were cleaning the herb room today. What brings you here?"

The cold grip of anger tightened her throat as she recalled the embrace that sent her running from home like a scolded child. Huntley's actions humiliated her. "Nothing I wish to speak of."

She could feel Conon's assessing gaze upon her as he secured her horse to a nearby tree.

"Very well, Countess. You are here, and so am I." He bowed low before her and Elysia saw him transform from shrewd observer to carefree courtier before her eyes.

"Let us make the most of this glorious day, shall we?" He offered her his arm and gestured to the path before them. The beach.

Ignoring the proffered arm, she hesitated. "You and I?"

"You would rather return to Vannes?"

The thought made her stomach pitch. "Nay."

"Then I will share with you the magnificent view." He pulled her forward despite her indecision.

A gust of wind rippled through her veils, lifting the light linen from her hair.

"But what will we do?" Elysia reached to secure her wayward head covering, but Conon beat her to it.

He snatched the circlet from her head and carelessly tucked the fabric into the waist of his braies. "Why do we have to *do* anything? Do you always start an adventure with a plan in mind, Elysia?"

She shrugged, fumbling to secure her wind-tossed locks into a small braid Belle had plaited around her head. "The one adventure I can recall having in my life is my trip to France. And yes, it was well planned."

Conon gathered her busy hands and held them still, slowly folding them to his chest.

Elysia felt the slow, heavy beat of his heart. Heat radiated through his surcoat and tunic. The layers of clothing did nothing to conceal the solid strength of his body.

Her pulse quickened at the intimacy, the stroke of his fingers over her hands. She warned herself not to be swayed by his touch. She knew nobles of Brittany were simply much more physical than English lords. Yet Jacques's touch had never affected her thus.

"Today, let us have an adventure that requires no plan." His blue gaze held hers, willing her compliance.

Her late husband's nephew had his shortcomings, but the man's smile was incredibly persuasive. "It is beautiful here."

"So you accept my offer for the view and not the man." Conon laughed, pulling her along the rocky path toward the water, where they let the surf chase their feet. "Perhaps you will surprise yourself and enjoy them both."

Warmth unfurled somewhere inside her. There was a careless charm about him, a determination to enjoy himself that Elysia found difficult to resist.

The notion gave her pause as the wet sand squished beneath her feet. Maybe Conon was popular with young widows for just that reason. She would do well to remember his reputation.

Perhaps sensing Elysia's lingering nervousness, Conon pointed out Vannes Keep in the distance and distracted her with talk about the defensive advantages and disadvantages of a coastal keep. Elysia soon found herself engaged in the topic, contributing bits of discussion and questions that carried their talk over a long stretch of beach and well into late afternoon.

"What will you do with the defenses when you become count?" Elysia picked her way through sharp rocks that lined the sand in the surf. The hem of her gown was wet, but she didn't mind. Just this once she would allow herself to have fun in the carefree way Conon seemed to.

He stiffened at the question, making Elysia regret her impulsive words. "Can I take that as an admission your wedding night was not a fruitful one?"

Elysia felt the flush rise to her cheeks. Once she admitted the truth, she would leave Vannes forever. She would not see Conon again. It took her a long moment to speak the word that would send her home. "Aye."

His face hidden as he reached for a seashell, Elysia could not guess if he meant to ignore her initial question, but after a thoughtful study of the pearlescent prize in his hands, he gestured toward a high rocky outcropping. "Ideally, I would add a tower down here and man it at all hours."

Elysia was relieved not to have to speak any further about future counts and wedding nights. Even if she did find herself wondering what her life might have been like if she'd come to France to marry the count's successor rather than Jacques. What kind of wedding night would she have shared with a man such as Conon? Judging from his gentle touch, she doubted she would have been stabbed in the thigh. For that matter, his reputation gave her the impression he pleased women immensely. Surely it had been the gossip she'd heard that had made her so curious about him.

Shaking off wayward thoughts that made heat rise to her cheeks, she struggled to focus on Conon's words.

"Though we can see the water from Vannes, we cannot detect activity among the trees that line the shore. It is a potential weakness."

"Sounds sensible." Disturbed by the breathy quality of her voice, Elysia shifted her wet slippers from one hand to the other, surprised Conon paid so much attention to matters of defense. Perhaps he was not as frivolous as he appeared.

Elysia began to wonder if she had misjudged Conon when a sharp pain pierced her foot.

Hopping forward with a yelp, she lost her balance and half pitched into the shallow surf. Strong arms plucked her up before she fell, though her skirt was soaked to the knee from the cold sea.

Elysia experienced a brief impression of sun-warmed linen over hard male muscles against her cheek before Conon plunked her down on a sea-worn boulder. Though her foot ached with the sting of whatever lanced her skin, the pleasant sensation of being held to Conon's chest remained.

Stooping at her feet, he tossed the skirts of her wet gown almost to her knees in his haste to examine her injury. She smoothed the fabric back down with nervous fingers and distracted herself from the pain by allowing her eyes to wander over Conon's muscular shoulders, the movement of his muscles beneath his tunic.

Her foot stung with whatever she'd stepped on, but not so much that she didn't notice the smooth play of his warm fingers over her feet.

He muttered a rapid-fire French diatribe under his breath. Though the words were uttered too quickly for her to understand, she gathered he cursed her carelessness.

"I should not have removed my shoes—"

He cursed again, this time loudly enough for her to discern. "I should have never let you in the water with bare feet. It is my fault."

It made her feel marginally better to think he cursed his own carelessness and not hers. His concern prompted her to wonder what exactly she'd stepped on.

"What is it?"

But he was across the beach and to his horse before the words left her lips. She watched as he rummaged through a saddlebag and returned with a skin of wine.

"This will hurt." He knelt before her, handling her foot with infinite care.

She tried to ignore the path of tingling skin in the wake of that gentle touch. She focused on the pain. At least that was a sensation she understood.

"Try to be still."

"What is—" Her skin ripped farther as Conon extracted the cause of her agony and held up the offending object for her to see.

A fishhook.

"Sweet Mary, what do they fish for here?" She fought back tears. Her foot throbbed in fiery rhythm with her heart, but she bit the inside of her lip and concentrated on the tool of her torture. The hook seemed impossibly large for any fish Elysia had ever seen.

"I believe this is a symbolic hook." Conon tucked it safely inside the leather pouch with his wineskin before ripping a section of his tunic to fold into a bandage. "Some of the local fishermen protect themselves from sea monsters by baiting a large hook and leaving it as an offering. I have told the Vannes *villeins* they are not to use such monstrous hooks, but I guess old superstitions die hard." He cursed again as he bandaged her foot. "It is a popular tradition."

Work-hardened hands brushed over her skin as he adjusted the wrappings, piquing her curiosity about how a nobleman of means developed so many calluses.

The pain subsided a bit now that the hook was out. Elysia gladly submitted to Conon's care, surprised at the smooth efficiency of his healing work. Accustomed to taking care of every facet of her life and her linens herself, it seemed strange to let someone else care for her.

And not altogether unpleasant.

She shivered as his hands skimmed her ankles, tying the ends of the linen together to secure it.

"You are cold?" He looked up, frowning.

"Nay."

"You are soaked to the skin, Elysia." His brows knit together.

"It is warm out."

"The water is freezing." He stripped off his light surcoat and dropped it over her head.

"Conon, honestly." Realizing how distorted and undignified her protests must sound through the folds of the garment that swam around her face and shoulders, she reluctantly pulled it on.

Conon grinned down at her, his torn tunic flapping in the spring breeze.

"What?" Elysia asked suspiciously.

Sinking beside her on the large rock, he smoothed a wrinkle from the surcoat's collar, grazing her neck with his fingers as he did. "You called me Conon."

He looked so pleased she found it difficult to argue. "It is hard to be formal with someone who smothers you with his garments."

The wind molded his tunic to his chest as he grinned. "Or mayhap you are growing more fond of your new family."

Fond? Of Conon? She had never made friends easily, and certainly had never shared a sense of "fondness" with anyone outside her family. It surprised her to realize she had conversed more with Conon that afternoon than she had with any other living soul, save her mother.

Perhaps she had allowed her work to consume too much of her life. If she had been home at Nevering, she never would have granted herself permission to abandon her labors for a whole afternoon to indulge in a walk on the beach.

She looked out to sea, unsure how to respond to Conon's words, but relishing the sensation of sharing the beauty of the day with another.

For a long while, they merely sat together, watching the sun sink in the western waters. She did not wish to break the companionable silence, yet knew she could tarry no longer with him. The day had been so enjoyable it frightened her. Conon behaved as the consummate gentleman, treating her with so much solicitous respect she felt every inch a countess.

And a woman.

In all her dealings with knights, merchants and noblemen of all statures, she had never met a man with the power to make every thought in her head evaporate with a glance. But she knew better than to indulge in the kind of flirtation Conon St. Simeon could offer. Hadn't Jacques told her his nephew enjoyed a special affection for widows because they were an easy night's work?

She possessed too much pride to become his next conquest.

"Belle will wonder what has become of me." Elysia moved to stand, striving to ignore the flush that stole over her with thoughts of what Conon did with lonely widows. She could never risk seduction at Conon's hands, no matter how enticing it might secretly be. If Conon ever discovered her virginity, he would learn of her deception.

"We will leave in a moment." With a feather-light brush of his hand, he restrained her.

His touch warmed her where his palm lingered. Blue eyes locked with hers, urging her to stay while her heart fluttered and danced as if it possessed a will of its own.

"About Huntley…" Conon began.

A cold chill replaced the warm flow through her veins. "Yes?"

"You would do well to avoid him."

"He is my guardian in Arundel's absence." No matter how much she resented it. "I have no say in the matter."

"But you can stay away from him as much as possible." The hand on her arm squeezed lightly, as if to imprint his warning. "I do not trust his ability to uphold his vows to Arundel before his personal greed for your wealth."

"My wealth?" she scoffed, remembering Huntley's loathsome kiss. "It is not greed for gold written in his eyes when he looks upon me."

"No?" Conon went very still and seemed to loom closer. "And you think you can discern a man's intentions by his eyes?"

His voice whispered through her, inviting her to confide in him. Elysia felt like a charmed snake, swaying to a tune played by someone else. She suspected Conon's words were leading her somewhere, toward something, but she was too caught up in the music to avoid it.

In fact, his eyes told her something right now, as they loomed closer and closer. Frozen, fascinated, she watched.

When his kiss came it lacked the brutal punishment of Huntley's. Conon's mouth brushed hers gently, teasing her with promise and invitation. Heat sparked through her in response.

His lips hinted of wine and the sea. Elysia moved closer, longing for a true taste. Conon's strength beckoned her all the more for his easy restraint of it. Unlike the brute she'd pushed off of her this morning, Conon allowed her to come to him at her own pace.

Her hands fluttered over his shoulders, landing lightly on his chest. The heat of his body, the unyielding muscle beneath his tunic, fascinated her. She stroked her fingertips over the light linen, reveling in the way his body gave the familiar fabric new dimension.

Elysia's tentative touches seemed to tighten Conon's grip, causing him to flex his fingers into the folds of her gown. Her lips parted on a sigh, providing him with the entry he sought.

His tongue sought hers for one scorching instant, sending waves of heat through her body. A surge of longing stirred in her belly, unlike any hunger she had ever known, pushing her close to the sustenance only he could provide. Her legs weakened beneath her until he halted his advance.

"Do you have any idea what is at stake here, *chère?*" The gentle prod of his voice distracted her when all she wanted was his kiss. For a heartbeat, she hung suspended between reality and the enticing promise of a dream.

Then she opened her eyes.

"Do you, Elysia?" He had moved away from her in the space of that last heartbeat, as cool and reserved as if they had just been introduced. "Do you know how fast a man can take advantage of you when you are so easily swept away by a kiss?"

Cold air rushed between them, a brisk reminder of the approaching nightfall.

She had let her guard down for one afternoon, one small moment when she had foolishly thought she could cast off a lifetime of rigid control for a few moments of pleasure. And it brought her disgrace instead.

Like a cat doused in cold water, she was tempted to hiss

and spit in his arrogant face. Instead she rose unsteadily
on her punctured foot and half slid, half fell down their rock
perch. Dizziness assailed her.

"*Mon Dieu*. Elysia, wait."

Ready to do her own cursing at this point, Elysia prayed
for forbearance as she hobbled toward her horse. In two
steps, he lifted her from the ground and cradled her in his
arms the way one might hold a small child.

"Put me down." Embarrassed, she could hardly meet his
gaze. *How could she have allowed him to kiss her?*

"Not until you converse reasonably with me."

He didn't move. Not toward their horses, not toward the
rock. He just stood there, staring down at her as if he had
all the time in the world.

"If you wish to converse reasonably, you should set an
appropriate example." It proved a challenge to pull her
cool cloak of authority around her while being held in so
ignominious a manner, but she felt determined to try. *The
barbarian.* "Instead, you crossed a line of respect and what
might well have been friendship with your inappropriate
advances, just to prove a point that would have been better made through conversing reasonably." Her voice held
a note of fear that shamed her. "Now put me down."

He flashed her a pleasant smile and ignored her.

Elysia Rougemont St. Simeon was unaccustomed to
being disobeyed. At Nevering, everyone hastened to heed
her. It confounded her that he would still be holding her
after such a speech. In her heart, she admitted she was a
bit grateful, however, as her dizziness made her doubt her
ability to stand.

"I am sorry."

He did not look one bit sorry.

"You might make amends by setting me atop my mare."

Fatigue washed through her, along with the throbbing pain that burned in her foot.

"I cannot. I feel too badly about my behavior to allow you to ride back to the keep by yourself."

As disconcerting as the afternoon's events were, she could not deny her concern about riding with an injury. Blood loss must have made her tired, for she did not have the will to argue. "Fine. But let us depart at once."

She had to return to the isolation of her chamber as quickly as possible. Conon affected her in disturbing ways, and she couldn't afford to care for a man her overlord would never approve of, a man who could discover the truth of her union and rob her of even the small holdings she had now inherited. The first Count of Vannes had provided Arundel with a political alliance. Conon would bring her overlord little more than money, something she already possessed in abundance. No doubt, Arundel would give Elysia's hand to another political marriage, a union to benefit all parties but her.

Conon nodded, blue eyes clouded with something she thought might be genuine concern. He wasted no time lifting her to his own horse and settling himself behind her for the return trip to the keep.

Although she did not want to give in to the lethargy that stole over her, she fought sleep scarce moments after they were mounted. Perhaps the fresh air and all the uncertainty of the last weeks conspired to tire her.

Now, tucked neatly against his chest, she thought she heard him whisper something as they rode away from the setting sun. His lilting accent reached through her hazy dreams as his words finally wound themselves around her.

"Chère demoiselle."

Chapter Six

The kiss haunted Conon.

He stalked the hollow emptiness of his cavernous great hall, momentarily too distracted by thoughts of Elysia to worry about the furniture that Uncle Jacques's creditors had recently appropriated.

A sennight had passed since his brief taste of Elysia's lips, and Conon had yet to send her home. How could he when his memory still conjured every nuance of her tentative touch, every whispered sigh that had shuddered through her?

What the hell had possessed him to kiss his uncle's widow?

Not some harebrained notion of teaching her a lesson, no matter what he'd spouted to Elysia. She'd looked so soft and warm and entirely too vulnerable wrapped in his surcoat. For a moment he had given in to an overwhelming urge to hold and protect her.

A grave mistake, though he had refused to acknowledge it as he rode home with her cradled in his arms.

Obviously, Elysia agreed their encounter had been an

error. She'd been hiding from him all week, confining herself to her chamber or the privacy of the herb-drying room. Conon had been happy to avoid her, but now he'd made plans to send her and her guardian home the following week. He needed to confront her to tell her as much.

He ceased his pacing, staring down at the floor to mull over the idea of seeing her again. In the back of his mind, he took in the fact that the great hall floor still showed outlines of where extravagant woven rugs had lain as recently as last week.

Damn the creditors.

Refusing to give in to brooding, Conon began his search for the countess. Her chamber door was locked, indicating she must be elsewhere. He'd given her the key that she'd asked for after Jacques's death. She had not jested about using it.

He hastened his steps toward the drying chamber. He left the keep to circle around one of the outer towers, then tried the door to the herbarium. Although the knob turned, the door did not open readily.

Conon rapped on the door. "Elysia?"

Her voice returned—halting and formal. "My lord?"

"Yes, it's me. I wish to speak with you, Countess."

"A moment." Her voice was muffled, but Conon heard distinct shuffling noises.

Finally, she opened the door.

She stood, proud and regal with her stiff posture, her dark hair brushing over her shoulders. The scents of the herbarium wafted around her, filling the air with hints of lavender and spices. Framed in the doorway, she was wreathed by dried bouquets hanging from the rafters. Elysia might not have been a famed beauty, but just the sight of her pinkened cheeks, her lush lips, made him forget to breathe. Damn.

"You forget yourself, my lady. Were you unaware that widows do not traipse about with their hair unbound?" The words were hardly worthy of his education in flirtation. In fact, he sounded like an ogre. But he sorely needed the reminder of her widowhood right now.

The flush on her cheeks deepened. "I did not expect to see anyone today."

Her deferential tone reminded him of his new status as Count of Vannes, a title bestowed upon him the day after he'd learned Elysia did not carry his uncle's heir.

Too bad the title would be robbed of all its wealth between the refund of Elysia's bridal portion and the descent of his uncle's creditors. The old lout's penchant for drink and indulgence had effectively impoverished his lands before his death. Apparently he had managed his creditors' forestall with the news he would wed a wealthy English heiress.

None of which was Elysia's fault.

Conon shook himself to stave off his frustrations. No easy task when the tempting countess proved just as dangerous to his sanity as his impending destitution. "It is I who should apologize." He pointed toward the drying room. "May I come in for a moment?"

Elysia nodded and took a step back gingerly on her injured foot, allowing him passage.

And a narrow passage at that. As Conon squeezed through the partially opened door, he realized she'd shoved a heavy chest in front of it.

"You fear for your safety or merely your privacy, my lady?"

"Rumors persist that I had a hand in your uncle's death." She shrugged. "I fear I am not a popular guest here."

Although mollified to think she did not necessarily fear

him, Conon frowned. "None of my people would hurt you. I swear it."

Elysia gazed into his blue eyes, plagued with thoughts of their last interlude. He loomed, large and imposing in the small herbarium, his vital strength a sharp contrast to the fading blooms all around him.

He had swayed her with his kiss so easily, and then had the gall to remind her of the fact. She would not get sucked in by his charm, his lowered voice meant for her ears alone.

"I am usually a very cautious person, my lord." She met his gaze levelly, determined to dispel the awkwardness between them. "Therefore, I must assure you that what happened on the beach last week was highly extraordinary for me—"

His slow grin made her realize her poor choice of words.

The heat of embarrassment and painful awareness pricked over her. "Rather, what happened last week was a horrible mistake, and I wanted to assure you it will certainly never be repeated."

He cocked a brow, his smile never wavering. "Indeed, I fear you are right. I have come to inform you that you will be departing next week."

Satisfied, she nodded. She couldn't leave Vannes fast enough. Between the strange feelings Conon inspired and her lingering fear of Sir Huntley, Elysia longed to return to the safety of Nevering. "Very well. I will begin packing my things."

"No need. You've gained enough wealth from your brief marriage to warrant some help in packing. I will put Huntley to the task."

She resented her circumstances as much as Conon's implication. "Aye. I was not needed to seal the deal, so why should I be needed to settle the consequences? I'm sure I would only be in the way."

She forced herself to curtsy to lessen the rancor of her words. She would never have taunted her overlord thus, but did not fear any retribution from Conon. He might be cruel enough to ply her with false kisses, but he would never lift a hand to her.

He stiffened. She could sense it even with her head bowed to him. When she rose, she noted his clenched jaw and fisted hands.

"I've no doubt if you were the one to write the bridal contract you would have ridden away with the very turrets in your caravan, my lady."

"If it had been up to me, there never would have been a bridal contract." Anger poured through her. "You can keep your dower property, my lord, and save me the trouble of returning it."

"Ah. Ever the independent woman." A scowl darkened his visage as he tipped a hanging bouquet with his finger to send it swinging above her head. "Mayhap I should send you home to the earl with a trunk full of flowers instead?"

Her anger deflated at his cavalier attitude. She crossed her arms over her chest, wishing only to retreat from his presence, his mix of male arrogance and charm that flustered her.

"That would be fine." She didn't tell him a trunk full of flowers would only remind her of him. She'd spent far too many days in the herbal room since their kiss, her thoughts dominated by memories of his touch.

"Stubborn Elysia." Shaking his head, he moved back a step. "You may be successful at running a linen trade, but you cannot escape the influence of men. Sooner or later you must succumb to a man guiding your destiny."

"Experience taught me my brother's guidance only spent the money I worked hard to earn." She tipped her chin at him, reluctant to bow to the notion of a lord and master just yet. "My overlord's guidance tore me from everything important to me in order to further his ambitions. I will not submit to another man's help without a fight."

His blue eyes shifted and lightened. A grin played at his lips as he backed out of the herb chamber. "I hope you will at least allow Huntley to help you home."

She suppressed a small shiver of fear as she watched Conon stride across the courtyard toward the main tower of the keep. She did not answer until he was long out of sight.

"I suppose I have no choice."

A fortnight later, Conon ran his fingers through one of the outgoing chests containing the last of the Vannes wealth. Gold cups and necklaces were stuffed in atop the most precious coins his Uncle Jacques had accumulated in his lifetime.

They had been Conon's for less than a moon cycle.

Some of the wealth would go to his creditors, some needed to be returned to Elysia. And of course, as he packed up Elysia's unused bridal portion, he would include the deed to the dower property. She'd told Conon he could keep the lands, but he would never ignore the stipulations of the bridal contract on the word of a woman.

A wry chuckle escaped as he thought of Elysia's easy dismissal of the Vannes property. She didn't need it. Never would.

Hell, Conon had heard she built her linen trade out of nothing but her own ingenuity. She had amassed a fortune on her own while he couldn't manage to hold on to a fortune that had been accumulated for him. Still, he would not seek the easy solution and wed an heiress, as Uncle Jacques had. Conon would earn his wealth with his sword arm. His honor demanded he win his way in the world on his own merit, no matter how enticing wedding an heiress might be. One particular heiress, anyway.

The memory of Elysia's lips, never far from his mind the last fortnight, floated back to him.

Damn. Slamming the lid shut, he locked the chest and called for a man-at-arms to load it onto the last creditor's wagon. "Is there anything else, my lord?" A man-at-arms stood beside the chest of Vannes's treasures and peered expectantly at Conon.

Conon thought how ludicrous the "my lord" sounded in light of his circumstances. He peered with slow deliberation around the near-vacant hall. "Nay."

"Very well then." The man strained with the effort of lifting the chest onto his broad shoulders. "Sir Huntley asked me to tell you he wishes to depart this morning." The man huffed, his cheeks red with exertion. "He awaits you now in the courtyard."

"The countess, too?" Obviously, she felt no need to part with Conon on any sort of personal terms.

"Aye."

Strange how that notion twisted his gut. The English widow would ride away with the deed to his grandmother's dower estate. Why the hell should he care that she left France forever?

Conon needed to support his people now, and as long as he possessed his horse, armor and weapons, he had all the tools required to ply his trade. He would wield his sword arm as a mercenary so his people would not starve and one day he would be able to provide for a family of his own.

"My horse!" Striding from the keep he moved toward the main gate where the traveling party awaited. He didn't know why he wanted to follow his English guests to their boat, but some niggling sense of honor made him want to see Elysia safely on her journey.

"Good morn, St. Simeon," Huntley called to him from the head of the line, neglecting to use Conon's newly conferred title. Not that it meant much.

"Good day to you, Huntley." Conon nodded in the Englishman's direction, but his gaze fixed on Elysia beside him. "Countess."

"Morning, my lord." She looked agitated, wary.

As befitted his station as host, Conon made a short speech to the English party and ordered the gate to be lowered. He noted Elysia paid him no mind, but kept glancing in Huntley's direction as if waiting for the man to turn into a demon.

Leon had reported Huntley's public attempt to kiss Elysia in the courtyard the day she stumbled upon Conon by the sea. Though Conon had wanted to wring the man's neck, de Grace convinced him to ignore it. Hadn't Conon seen Huntley leave her chambers that night with his own eyes? Perhaps Elysia's rebuff to Arundel's vassal in the courtyard merely signified an end to their relationship.

The matter provoked him, but gave him every reason to view Elysia as no different from any of the other widows he had entertained over the years. It was merely unfortunate he did not find the opportunity to entertain Lady Elysia as much as he might have liked.

After a quick exchange of farewells, she was gone. He should have turned back instead of watching her slender figure sway on her small mount's back, but the longer he gazed, the greater his urge to follow. Perhaps he wouldn't have felt that way if he had important affairs to manage back at Vannes Keep, but the thought of returning to his newly destitute lands only aggravated him. Tomorrow he would venture abroad to win his fortune. For now, it cost him nothing to ensure Elysia reached her boat.

Conon nudged his horse forward, wishing the sense of foreboding he retained since awakening would go away. Elysia was safely on her way home, well rid of his unwanted attentions. There was no reason to stare at her and wish he could claim her for his own.

No reason at all.

Chapter Seven

"Hurry, my lady," Huntley urged Elysia as he maneuvered the lift closer to the boat for her to board. "If we want to sail before the storm, we must be under way."

Huntley seemed to do his best to be pleasant, but Elysia could see the annoyance tickling his mild countenance. The day looked clear and sunny to her, but she did not argue with her detestable guardian. The boat that would sail them to England was huge compared to the tiny vessel she had arrived in.

"Before nightfall, please." Huntley scowled up at her as she debated how to move from the lift to the boat.

"It is difficult to manage this conveyance in a gown," Elysia returned, attempting to maintain civility. Wriggling off the lift, she managed to land on the deck without falling.

A lewd grin played about Huntley's lips. "But you look sorely fetching in the attempt."

When she returned to England, the earl would receive the most scathing of missives detailing Sir Huntley's blatant disrespect and abuse of her person. Until then, she needed to set aside her distaste for the man so she could get home safely.

"I would like to retire to my room, please." She ignored his insulting comments.

"Of course." His smile chilled her. "Just let me help your maid aboard and I will show you to your cabin."

Belle accompanied Elysia to England at Conon's insistence. Ever since he'd discovered Elysia had no personal maid at Nevering, he had been adamant that Belle attend her.

The maid handled the move from the lift to the boat with far more grace than her mistress. Huntley gave instructions to lift the anchor, then showed the women to their rooms.

"Belle, you will be staying here." He pointed out a small cabin already filled with other servants' pallets.

"Won't I room with my lady?"

"Nay, your mistress has her own quarters." Pulling Elysia along with him, he moved away from the maid.

Eager to part company with her guardian, Elysia saw two other doors in the cramped cabin space above deck, but her companion did not steer her toward either one. Huntley's grip tightened around her arm as he maneuvered her to the back of the boat. "If I may have a moment, please."

A warning bell tolled in her mind. Every muscle in her body tensed, waiting for another confrontation. She had done everything in her power to avoid him since the scene in the courtyard, but now she had no choice.

Agreeing gracefully, she hoped that by giving him a chance to speak, perhaps they could set aside their differences for the duration of the journey. There was nowhere for her to run now. No Conon to comfort her as he had the day by the sea.

She allowed Huntley to lead her toward the rail.

"I have reached a decision regarding you and I, Elysia."

Cringing at the familiarity, she bristled at his pompous arrogance. How like a man to announce his decisions with an air of self-importance.

His jaw flexed as he stared down at her. "I am determined to have you for my wife, Elysia. We will wed aboard ship and celebrate our marriage tonight."

By Agnes's sainted slipper, we will not. "It would not be proper to wed without the earl's approval, sir, but I assure you I will broach the subject with him when we return." She would soothe his male pride, attempt to be diplomatic.

As Sir Huntley's brows swooped down in an ugly fit of consternation, Elysia heard the din of the crew preparing to launch the boat.

"The earl approves, lady, let me assure you. I am his right arm. He will deny me nothing."

"He may very well deny you one of the richest prizes in Christendom, sir." Elysia knew her own worth. Her overlord expected her marriages to provide him with important political allies. He would not waste that capability to reward one of his vassals. Curbing her exasperation, she began to lie. "He has already mentioned other potential bridegrooms for me, both of whom will help him gain new lands and rents. I think he will be angry if we disrupt his plans without consulting him."

"Mayhap Arundel should have considered that before he charged me with your care." The knight's sandy hair fell over his narrow forehead, but did nothing to soften the stern set of his angular features. His insolence corrupted any attractiveness Elysia might have seen in him.

Desperation gathered about her like thick storm clouds in April. The look on his face conveyed his seriousness. No matter how irrational he sounded, he meant what he said.

"I cannot agree to such a match, sir, I—"

The furrow in Huntley's brow suddenly smoothed. A smile lit his features. "Fine. If you do not agree to this match the legal and proper way, then I will take you the old-fashioned way." His grin widened. "By force."

Before Elysia could fully comprehend his meaning, Huntley lunged for her midsection, hoisting her over his head. He meant to wed her against her will. To make her his wife.

Elysia screamed.

Shamelessly and as loudly as she could, she cried her displeasure to the heavens. Everyone on board the ship would know this deed was done under her extreme protest.

"Quiet, shrew." Huntley cursed at her and swatted her on her upended bottom, driving her fury to a new level.

Through a swirl of her own hair, she could see Belle's horrified expression as the maid ran toward her to help. Huntley pushed the girl to the deck and continued to the stairs.

No. Yanking the short knife he carried about his waist from its sheath at his back, Elysia jabbed at his hindquarters with the blade. Although she could not muster much force from that angle, she knew she'd succeeded when he howled with pain.

"Stupid wench!" He threw her forward on the deck of the boat, the force of the blow knocking the knife from her hands. He stared down at her with eyes gone almost black. "You think you are too good for me? You think a mere knight is not worthy of your fortune?"

Her body throbbed from the hard slam onto the wooden planking. Elysia wondered if she would be able to move.

"I think I do not wish to be beaten and coerced into marriage." She would never submit to this man. She'd gone meekly to Jacques St. Simeon against her wishes, but she would not heed John Huntley.

"Then I have some unsettling news for your ladyship." He limped close to leer over her like a gargoyle on a church wall. "You won't be getting your wish."

Too late, Elysia willed away the sharp aches throughout her body and scrambled away. Although slowed by his wound, Huntley was still faster and stronger. Meaty fingers sinking into her arms, he secured her easily and headed down the stairs before Elysia could get her bearings.

She screamed again until he knocked her across the temple with an openhanded blow. Head ringing, she kicked, hit and bit any part of him that came near her until he dumped her onto a narrow pallet in a private chamber.

Panting, she could not suck in enough air to fill her burning lungs as she stared at him. Perhaps she would be better off giving in to the inevitable so he did not seriously hurt her, yet she could not command her body to do aught but fight.

The sweaty scent of him assailed her nose as he leered at her, tearing her gown from her shoulder with a yank. Fear coiled deep inside her as the reality of her situation settled heavily upon her.

Perhaps a gently bred woman would cling to the remnants of her torn gown, but Elysia slid from the fabric, leaving Huntley holding the costly silk while she remained clad in a thin shift. Freed from the cumbersome garment, she bolted from the pallet while he released her to shed his own clothes. She raced to the door, but his hulking frame already blocked her exit.

Half-dressed, he stood unrepentant and obviously eager before her. Elysia backed toward the pallet slowly, her arms wrapped around her midsection to shield her body from his avid gaze.

"This is not any way to begin wedded life, Elysia."

"I wholeheartedly agree." Struggling to catch her breath, she tried to hide the tremor in her voice as she faced him. Every muscle in her body tensed for action, Elysia awaited his next move.

"The earl will hear of this abomination," she warned, scrambling for a way to discourage him. "As will the Pope. And the king. You are a knave and you have broken your vows of protection and chivalry. I will see you brought low." By God, she would not let him get away with this.

"Not before I see you underneath me, Elysia, and that is the part that really bothers Countess Haughty, does it not?" Stepping over the pallet, he grabbed her by the hair and yanked her to the floor.

Elysia could not move, suddenly flattened by the full weight of his body.

Pig. Vile, stupid, repugnant pig. She called him every oath and wicked name she could in her mind, but that was as much as she could fight now.

As he reached for the hem of her shift, an axe split the door to the cabin in half.

Hope surged through her. Someone had come to help.

Even Huntley paused to watch the axe fall a second time. Elysia imagined they both looked equally amazed as they faced the man who wielded the weapon.

Conon.

He looked nothing like the beautiful man she'd met in the garden of Vannes last moon. Dripping wet with seawater, his hair was slick and dark and smooth to his head. Blue eyes shone with avenging fury that frightened and thrilled her.

Her champion had arrived.

He pulled her attacker off of her and tossed him to the floor. The English knight screamed protests and curses with almost as much fear and fury as Elysia herself had screamed so recently. With grim satisfaction, Elysia watched Conon's fist break her attacker's nose.

Fighting their way out of the cabin, Conon and Huntley rolled out onto the deck. Clutching a bed linen to her chest, she rushed to the door to watch. Some dormant warrioress in her soul had been awakened by her fight, and with so much fear still churning through her, she refused to miss a moment of his defeat.

When Huntley was subdued and dazed on the floor before her avenger, Conon hauled him up the short steps and over the rail of the boat, into the sea.

Apparently, that roused Huntley, for the whole boat could hear him shouting epithets and predictions of Conon's fate at his hands.

Relief flooded through her, leaving her so weak she fell to her knees. Conon tucked the blanket around her more closely and guided her back to the cabin, as the boat moved steadily through the water, toward England and Nevering.

He seated her on the chamber's lone bench, then kneeled before her, dripping wetly on the bed linen she clutched.

"Did he hurt you?"

"Not seriously." Not so much on the outside. But the inside…she could not think about what might have happened.

"But he hurt you?" Conon's voice raised a notch, body tensing. Elysia wondered if he would leap overboard to murder his enemy if she said yes.

"He hit me," she acknowledged. "But I will be fine." As that notion settled into her mind, gratitude washed over her. She would be fine because of Conon.

Still caught in the whirlwind of emotions the day had wrought, Elysia reached for him. Squeezed his hands.

Threw herself into his arms. "Thank you. My God, Conon, I cannot thank you enough."

"Elysia."

The strangled tone of his plea penetrated her overwhelmed brain, making her aware of her actions. Her blanket forgotten, she clung to Conon with nothing but her shift on. The fine linen was now soaking wet because of her heartfelt hug. For a moment, she held on to him, afraid to let go and have her whole body exposed, but mortified to remain fastened to him.

"I—"

"Let me get you a blanket."

His breath hovered warm and wonderful against her cheek. Elysia recalled their kiss and its dizzying effect. Just now she welcomed Conon's protective arms again.

So much.

For all that she had inwardly railed against the male penchant for assuming control of women's lives, Elysia had never been so grateful that a man had provided the protection and strength she was incapable of furnishing herself.

"Madame?" Belle appeared in the doorway, her voice tentative and scared. "Are you all right?"

"Aye."

"She needs a blanket to wrap herself in, Belle." Conon's words rumbled through her, his chest brushing hers in a way that sent pleasure curling through her.

How could she feel such heat, nay, *desire* for a man after what had just happened with Huntley?

The maid hurried to bring a linen sheet for her mistress and discreetly plucked Elysia from Conon. Gratefully, Elysia turned in the woman's arms.

As she did, something snapped inside Elysia. After a lifetime of maintaining absolute control over her emotions, her self and her business, she found herself overpowered by a jumble of unfamiliar feelings. A sob broke from her throat and from there, she could not stop the hoarse cries or the tears.

When the maid left and the remnants of the hacked door were closed behind her, it was Conon who held her in his arms. She sobbed on his shoulder, still so grateful and so scared and so wretched from Huntley's touch she couldn't put two words together. "Belle?"

"I told her to keep everyone away and bring you something to eat. She will return soon."

"It was so awful. How did you know to come?"

"I wanted to assure myself your boat departed safely." Conon stroked her hair and kissed her. "I heard you scream all the way from the shore." The rough edge in his voice, the angry tension in his body, soothed her.

Elysia wondered why she should feel so comforted by Conon's touch. She knew she should extract herself from his embrace, but her fears were too fresh, her body too shaken, to refuse his gentle protection.

She lost track of time as he held her, his strong arms providing a sense of security she had never felt before. Dusk fell by the time he murmured something about finding Belle and a meal for Elysia.

Watching Conon depart, she mourned the loss of his strength, his warmth. It occurred to her that in the course of her brief time at Vannes, she had come to rely on him.

The notion disturbed her. She was immensely thankful that he had saved her today, yet it worried her to realize she needed a man's protection so desperately.

When Belle arrived with her meal, Elysia had regained a measure of calm. As the night shadows lengthened, her tears dried, her backbone strengthened and her resolve returned not to let any man make decisions for her again.

None of this would have happened if she had not been forced to come to France and wed a man she did not wish to marry. Or if she had not been forced to accept any lusty old man her overlord chose.

She was long bathed and dressed and fairly recovered from the day when Conon called to her through the broken cabin door.

"Come in, my lord."

Slowly, the door creaked open. He stood framed in the narrow opening, his body too large and too looming for the confines of the tiny chamber.

"You look much improved, Countess."

She nodded her thanks, not sure how to behave with him anymore after she had exposed herself to him in so many ways today. He'd seen her half-dressed, had held her in his arms when she'd been in nothing more than her shift, yet that physical intimacy had not frightened her as much as the way she'd broken down in front of him.

Her feelings toward him puzzled her. She had little experience with men in her life until arriving in France, and then her few encounters had not been pleasant. Her husband had been roughly demanding before he died in their marriage bed. Huntley had been obnoxious and brutal until Conon saved her.

Conon St. Simeon had been both utterly rude and strangely gentle with her. Which Conon was real—the one who accused her of greed for wedding an ancient count or the one who had pulled a fishhook from her foot and held her while she cried?

"I am in command now," he continued, striding forward to kneel in front of her. "I will see you safely to your home, as I trust none of Arundel's men to do it."

His confident words reminded her that Conon was not as gentle as he sometimes seemed.

"That is the way of the world, is it not?"

"As much as you might not approve, Elysia, it is."

"At Nevering, I made all the decisions. But everywhere else, I am a mere woman, incapable of deciding anything for myself, let alone commanding a keep or a boat or another person. Men, on the other hand, can bid anyone to do whatever you like."

"Do not group me with Huntley, *chère,* because we are not of the same breed." His blue eyes turned stormy, reflecting a dark swirl of emotions.

"Nay, but you both have the power to do as you please while my fate is cast upon your fancy. If you had not followed me to the boat today I would be as good as wed to that beast now."

Conon fell back on the pallet, arms flung wide. "But you are not wed to him. You are free. On your way home to this precious Nevering. I will see you safely there, and then we shall part company. You will return to your old life, while I will return to the life of a mercenary. All shall be well."

How could he make it sound so simple? Her old life of independence had been illusory…and now it was far behind her. "But for how long will I be free? A fortnight? A moon or two? How many days before I am once again a pawn for the earl to make a good alliance?"

Her gaze strayed over his masculine form, remembering the way his body had felt against hers. There could be no denying he was an attractive man. A dangerously enticing man.

"That is the curse of an heiress, I am afraid. But you must know your worth, Elysia. No prospective husband will hurt you or beat you. You are far too valuable."

"How comforting."

"'Tis more assurance than many a lesser noblewoman

has to comfort her." Conon stood, staring down at her as if she were naught but a spoiled girl. His fists clenched at his sides. "After I see you safely home, I will leave you to reclaim the independence you value so highly. I will be traveling widely to peddle my sword arm this year, but if you have need of me again, send word to Vannes."

Bidding her good-night, he left her to her thoughts. She had angered him, she knew. Probably because she had dared to voice a complaint about her lot in life. Her brother had often been frustrated with what he saw as her lack of gratitude. Outsiders looked at Elysia's prosperous household and wondered what else she could possibly want.

Was it so difficult to understand? After all her hard work, was it so much to ask for a bit of autonomy?

Her trip to Nevering brought little solace when she knew it was just a brief respite from her most lucrative occupation of all—marriage making. She stared down at her idle hands, wishing there were something she could do to change her fate. Her body still throbbed with the painful bruises Huntley had given her, while her heart ached to think of a future dominated by another husband.

Yet what grieved her most as she crawled into bed was the loss of Conon's warm embrace.

Chapter Eight

Conon shook his head as he watched Elysia stare out to sea two days later, unsure what to make of her distant demeanor. She gripped the rail of the small boat with white-knuckled fingers, her dark eyes trained on the coastline with as much concentration as a knight strategizing his next battle. Although her midnight-blue surcoat fluttered in the breeze to outline a decidedly feminine form, her bout with Huntley seemed to have filled her with a warrior's spirit.

He was just thankful she was safe. His heart nigh erupted when he heard her screaming that day Huntley attacked her. Without thinking, he had leaped from his vantage point in the thicket and started swimming, oblivious to how he would get aboard the ship once he arrived at it. Like a nightmare that wouldn't end, it seemed as if his swim to the boat took forever.

Never in his life had he felt such an overwhelming urge to protect someone. Feelings beyond chivalric impulses swamped him, sentiments he had not known he possessed. Whatever the cause, he had made Elysia's safety his vow. She would arrive home unmolested.

Too bad he would have to stay away from her in order to keep that pledge. It almost killed him when she flung her half-naked body around him to thank him for saving her. Every nuance and subtle curve of her form was imprinted on his brain. He would never forget that sweet softness if he lived to be one hundred.

"I see it!" she cried, moments before the captain shouted down the same message from his perch at the wheel.

"England." Conon strode to the rail to join her, studying the horizon. Cold drops of water hit his face as the boat sped toward land under a sudden gust of good wind. "Your mother will be surprised."

Elysia smiled for the first time Conon could recall since their shared afternoon on the beach at Vannes. "She will be delighted, I am sure. My mother did not relish the notion of running the linen trade by herself."

"It is sizable then, this venture of yours?"

"Aye." Unmistakable pride lit her features while her gaze lingered on the coast of her homeland. "Our only competition is Flanders's linens. Nevering cloth is the finest quality and it is produced in relatively large quantities."

"It is remarkable that you run such an undertaking on your own."

She shrugged as if it were a matter of no great import. "The labor is both a pleasure and a necessity. At first my mother and I wove our linens for extra income to buy winter stores after my father died. Now we have almost fifty women sewing at all times."

"You do not encounter resentment among your customers? Do not some men refuse to do business with a woman?"

"Aye." She laughed, a joyful, mischievous sound Conon relished all the more since she hoarded it like gold. "But thank the Fates, women purchase most of the linen for their households, and they are most willing to deal with me."

He could not help but admire her industry even as he looked forward to claiming his worth in the world, as well. Now that he no longer owed his sword arm to his uncle, he would reap the rewards of his warrior skills. Once he reestablished Vannes's fortune and prominence, he could found the family he had dreamed about.

As he thought of the future, he realized he envisioned his home as the Vannes dower estate. He glanced over to Elysia, who seemed absorbed in the view of the English coastline. "My lady, just what do you intend to do with your French lands now?"

Her brown eyes widened as if she had forgotten about the holding so dear to him. She appeared thoughtful for a moment, a stray lock of hair dancing across her cheek. "Truly, I do not know. I do not feel entitled to your family lands and would gladly return them to you, my lord."

Conon bristled. "They are not to your liking?"

She shook her head, dislodging the curl that had wrapped itself about her neck. "Nay. The property is beautiful and I should enjoy residing in such a keep—"

"Not grand enough to support your linen trade, I suppose." Fuming inwardly, he remained offended to the core she would think he'd take the keep back. Did she somehow learn of his empty coffers?

Or worse, did she feel sorry for him?

"I would merely like to give you the deed back because my overlord would never let me retire there anyway." She frowned, shuffled her feet about the deck of the boat. "Besides, I've hardly served your family enough to have earned such a gift."

"It is no gift, but part of a contractual agreement." Annoyed, he ground his teeth. "Your overlord would not allow you to make such a transaction anyhow. I am certain he will have plans for the lands even if you do not."

Stiffening, she allowed the barrier of her frosty demeanor to settle between them. "I'd forgotten I'm not allowed to make any decisions on my own. I will speak to Arundel about the property as soon as possible."

Satisfied, he nodded. Despite his sentimental affection for the holding, he did not want Elysia's charity. Frustration warred with grudging respect for her. Apparently he and Elysia shared something in common—neither wished to be rewarded with something they did not earn.

He expected her to storm off, but she remained beside him at the rail to watch the waves slap the side of the boat and scan the horizon for activity on the shore.

When a gust of wind blew her skirts like a blue banner behind her, she wrapped her arms about herself and Conon could not help but wonder what she might feel like wrapped in his arms instead.

"Thank you for escorting me home," she said finally, keeping her eyes trained on the coastline. "I know you must have other matters that call for your attention."

"None so important as you." He realized with a jolt those weren't just idle words. "No matter where you go next, or whom you wed, you will always be the dowager Countess of Vannes. I shall be bound to protect you."

"Once I return home I will not need any protection." Her voice rang with conviction, revealing her love for her home. "Nevering has always been a safe haven for me."

"I hope it remains thus, my lady." If her keep was secure, Conon would have no need to linger. He could return to Vannes so that he and Leon could begin their quest for fortune. And he would never see Elysia Rougemont St. Simeon again.

Odd how the thought unsettled him.

* * *

A day later, Nevering beckoned from its low rise, the small turrets decorating its corners more than defending them. Somehow humble and proud at the same time, it remained a beautiful keep, though small and awkward to defend. Although it lacked the grand façade of Vannes Keep, the smaller structure possessed squat rounded towers and arched entryways that somehow seemed more inviting, even if it lacked many arrow slits or fighting galleries on the crenellated outer walls. Elysia peered over at Conon as they rode closer on horseback, anxious to know what he thought of her home, but preparing herself for typical male scorn of its defensive inadequacies.

"It is a unique holding," Conon remarked with diplomacy.

She could almost see his mind proposing ways to improve it, strengthen it. His instincts to protect lurked close to the surface.

Glancing back to shore she thought about all the good reasons to be home—the chance to visit with her mother, the opportunity to check on the progress of her flax plants, and of course, she would finally be able to speak to the earl about her unconsummated marriage. She'd carried her secret for too long and looked forward to unburdening herself soon. But as they neared the keep she noticed something out of place. Something most unwelcome.

A small red flag flew over the highest turret.

"What in Hades—" Squinting for a better view, she leaned forward over her horse's head, her brain refusing to comprehend what she spied.

"What is it?"

"My neighbor's flag flies over my keep, my lord." Sir Oliver's flag, in fact. Another of Arundel's detestable vassals.

"Just what does that mean?" His gaze swept the high walls, his warrior's eye searching for weaknesses.

She had heard Conon enjoyed a reputation as a fierce mercenary knight. If he were confronted with an enemy, he had the option of fighting. Elysia had no such option, and she had to admit his presence lent her strength today.

"I cannot imagine." Elysia's mind already buzzed with scenarios as they rode down the hill into view of Nevering. Her trunks and belongings, including the bridal portion of her dowry, had been left at the boat. Some of it would be brought later by Arundel's men, the rest she planned to send back to France with Conon once she confessed the truth of her marriage to the earl.

Now she and Conon raced over the final hills to Nevering, their horses kicking up clods of lush green sod as they ran. Barely noticing the small duck pond or the tiny hermit's cottage beside it, Elysia did not take her usual pleasure in riding up to her home.

Waved through the keep's rough-hewn stone gate by a man she did not recognize, she felt her apprehension grow.

"You are welcome, my lady!" a villager called out, but Elysia did not pause to converse. It would be undignified to ask one of the crofters what went on at Nevering.

"Where are all of your tenants?" Conon peered around the near-vacant crofters' cottages.

"The men are in the fields and the women are sewing." She hoped. Elysia gulped back her increasing unease.

"What of the children? Does no one have children?"

"The women take turns watching them on the lawns near the sewing hall." She flung herself from her horse, ignoring a nimble young groom who rushed to help her. "I imagine they are there."

Though she did not pause for Conon, he was beside her before she crossed the courtyard stones.

"Wait." Yanking her back, he stepped in front of her. "When we do not know what we might encounter, I go first."

Nodding, she peered around at the silent stone walls. Where was everyone? There were usually at least a few servants from the keep milling about. But today the courtyard was still as death, as if everyone were in hiding. Perhaps holding their breath to see what would become of their former lady. She had assumed everyone at Nevering knew of her disastrous marriage since some of Arundel's men attended the wedding and would have told the tale.

Not bothering to wait for the servants, Elysia waved Conon ahead as they reached massive oak doors at the main entrance. The door creaked, echoing eerily off the silent limestone walls. Stepping into the keep, they paused.

A maid observed them, and, forgetting to greet the guests, ran with all speed into the hall.

"Peculiar behavior." Conon peered around the entry hall, his blue eyes dark in the dim interior that smelled vaguely of a sweetly scented hearth fire. "Does your overlord live nearby?"

Not near enough, apparently. "His keep is just over the next rise, some three leagues distant. He has always protected our holding in the past."

"Welcome, Lady Elysia!" A man's voice boomed with the affable familiarity of a great friend, but as the speaker stepped into the fading light admitted by a high window, Elysia could see it illuminated no ally of hers. "I hear your marriage came to a rather abrupt end."

Oliver Westmoor stood before her in an elaborate scarlet surcoat that swirled about him as he bowed to her. He had always fancied himself a man of great intellect and refinement, and he had never understood Elysia's work ethic. The man didn't know the meaning of toil and he was quick to boast of the fact.

"I do not understand." Elysia made no pretense at polite conversation with him. She needed answers.

"What is to understand?" Tall and reed thin, Oliver laughed a nasal bray and slipped his arm about Elysia's shoulders with feigned fatherly affection. Her senior by some twenty years, Oliver had never been tolerated by Elysia's father, but since the elder Rougemont's death, he'd made himself an unpleasant fixture around Elysia's mother. "I am merely happy to see you have returned."

"Where is my mother?" Skin crawling from his touch, Elysia turned out of his grasp. Something had to be terribly wrong for Oliver's flag to be flying over Nevering. "And where is the earl? Is he not in residence this summer that you have weaseled your way into Nevering?"

"Arundel is still abroad, I believe. I have not seen him since he accompanied you to France for your marriage." Oliver fixed his gaze on Conon. "Surely, my dear, you have not taken a lover so soon after the good count's death."

"This is the count now—"

"You will apologize to Lady Elysia for that remark." Conon stood implacable as a mountain, an expression of calm assurance upon his face.

But Elysia did not care for a battle of wills, she simply wanted to know what on earth was going on. She thought Arundel would be back in England by now, and she surely never expected to see Oliver here, residing in her keep as if he owned it. "It is all right, if I could just know—"

"It is *not* all right." Conon's tone brooked no argument. His gaze never left Oliver's face. "Sir?"

With a derisive sniff of his hawkish nose, Oliver waved

an indifferent hand. "Very well then, my noble young lord. I am sorry, Lady Elysia."

"You are forgiven." Unsure whether Conon would let the "young lord" remark pass uncontested, she hurried to blurt, "Perhaps you could tell me where to find my mother?"

Oliver smiled with a superior smirk that filled her with dread. He looked as if he were savoring the moment with great relish. "My lady wife is indisposed today."

Vaguely, she became aware of Conon's arm sliding beneath her elbow to lend support.

"Wife?" She wavered on her feet but did not fall. Bless Conon.

"Lady Daria and I wed last week, Elysia. I am sorry you could not be here for the ceremony. We will move to Westmoor Keep next fall, but for now we will reside here while I develop a more profitable linen trade."

He droned on about his plans for Nevering, but Elysia could comprehend no more.

"I must see my mother."

Frowning, he dismissed a manservant from the hall, leaving the three of them alone. "She is indisposed. I am afraid I cannot allow that."

"But she is my mother. She will want to see me."

His expression tightened into disapproval. "She is my *wife,* Elysia, and she will accept visitors when I say she is well enough to do so."

"Perhaps you were unaware that your new stepdaughter is a countess, sir." Conon's intervention kept Elysia from screaming the hall down in growing frustration. "I would ask that you respect the title."

"So you are count and countess now." Oliver sneered as he beckoned a household page. "Shall I have the boy put your things in the guest quarters, Countess? I assume you will stay with us long enough to share a few meals at least."

"What generous hospitality, my lord." Elysia seethed. She would lose her tightly stretched control soon if she did not escape his gloating presence. "I would appreciate the opportunity to stay long enough to visit my mother, but I cannot presume upon the count to do the same."

With every fiber of her being, she hoped Conon would stay for at least a night or two. But he had delivered her safely home as he promised. There was no reason for him to remain now. For a long moment he stared down at her, peering into her face as if plucking her thoughts from her head. Slowly, he nodded.

"I think it would be best if I remain for a short while at least."

Thank you. Elysia hoped he read that thought as clearly as he seemed to divine all her others. How peculiar Conon seemed to be her closest ally at the moment.

"Very well." Oliver nodded in brief acknowledgment of his guests' noble rank, no doubt to appease Conon. "The household has already eaten, but our sideboards are still full. Avail yourselves of whatever refreshment you like."

Elysia watched him depart in silence, willing herself to maintain her temper and quell her fears until she escaped to the privacy of her own quarters.

Conon urged her forward toward the stairs. The page's blond head bobbed like a beacon in the fading light as they proceeded.

"Hullo, my lady." The earnest little boy's face peered up at her as he struggled to heft the heavy bags up the stairs.

"Good day, Eadred." Elysia ruffled the boy's hair, grateful for the sight of a friend in a keep grown cold and unwelcoming in her absence. "I see you are growing strong and tall."

"Aye, my lady." He looked furtively down the stairs in the lord's direction. "Lady Daria says I will be serving her soon."

"Good for you. She would not accept you unless you were well ready." Distractedly, Elysia watched a maid light the torches at intervals down the long corridor they traversed.

The lad beamed. "She says I'm a big help since he came here. I help her keep him away."

Reaching the guest wing, Eadred set the bags down with a thud. Conon's blue gaze met hers over the boy's head.

"My mother does not wish Sir Oliver near her?" Elysia asked in her most casual voice.

Eadred grinned, revealing two missing front teeth. "Things haven't changed *that* much since you left, my lady. It has been two moons."

Laughing, Elysia hugged the boy impulsively and then scrambled into her room before the tears fell from her eyes. The day would overwhelm her at any moment and she was determined to have no witnesses.

Through the maelstrom that crashed through her, she barely heard the words Conon spoke to the boy outside the door, though she discerned the jingle of coins pass between them.

Conon should have been moving to his own room, but he was inside hers. After shutting the door, he seated himself beside her on the wooden bench near the hearth.

"I cannot see you just now." She could ill afford to appear weak in front of Conon again.

She had scarcely shed a tear in her life until Huntley's attack. With all of her responsibilities and work, crying had always been an indulgence she did not have time for. Now it seemed she had no control over the well of tears inside her.

"I will stay to help you." Conon's voice, though soft and low, was resolute.

The lump in her throat made speech impossible. She shook her head. Tomorrow, when she had recovered from the distress of Oliver's underhandedness, she would devise a way to deal with him and see her mother. But just now, she didn't have the will to fight.

"You still have your bridal portion if not the keep, Elysia." The kindness in Conon's voice nearly undid her. "You remain a coveted heiress."

As if mere wealth could restore the thriving linen trade she'd cultivated with wit and cunning. Besides, the bridal portion was not truly hers, either. Arundel would simply use the gold to lure another strategic marriage for her.

"Please go."

"You may win back your keep if you appeal to Arundel. He might not like this situation any better than you do."

This was more in line with what she hoped to hear, but she was not prepared to plot her strategy just now. She needed strength. Patience.

And heaven help her, she wanted a few moments alone before she dissolved into a tearful flood in front of Conon once again.

Conon watched the poised, headstrong dowager countess fight valiantly for self-control when most women would have screamed or cried or otherwise raged at the heavens.

But she was not the average woman, he'd come to learn.

Instinct told him she would refuse any comfort he offered, so he did not warn her of his intention before pulling her into his arms. A dangerous move for him, no doubt, since his uncle's widow tempted him in ways no other woman ever had. Yet he could no more walk away from her now than he could have when he first heard her screams on the boat departing France.

Protecting her had become second nature.

He realized as he stroked her satiny smooth hair that he would gladly slay dragons to help her. But would she ever willingly call upon him to do so again? No matter how bad things got for Elysia, she still had a fortune at her disposal, easing her way at every turn. She would wed an equally wealthy man, bear him healthy children, and dominate his household with her strong will and perfect efficiency.

A perfect wife.

Elysia would make the perfect wife for him. Her bridal portion could restore Vannes enough to ensure his people would not starve. Heaven knew, she could provide him with a nursery full of healthy, headstrong children who would be as smart and determined as she.

Perfect.

Except Conon's honor would never allow him to win a fortune that way. And no matter how much Elysia appealed to him at times, she was not the woman of his dreams— not the gentle beauty who would gladly devote herself to home and hearth.

"I am sorry." She stirred in his arms, her feminine softness scrambling his thoughts all the more.

She blinked up at him with a wealth of sadness in her dark eyes while a lock of black hair escaped its wrinkled linen covering.

"You have returned to a very unhappy situation." Conon could not resist the urge to tuck the strand back into place. "It is no crime to need help."

He knew it was not his place to offer her aid, however. He needed to leave Nevering as soon as possible if he hoped to supply Vannes with the income it required. Still, he found himself saying, "I will stay at Nevering until I am certain you are well settled here."

Where had that come from? Conon could not call the words back now, but he wondered what madness came over him in the presence of his uncle's widow. He was rewarded when Elysia's face flushed a charming shade of pink. Conon realized he had never felt so needed in all of his life.

"Thank you."

An answering surge of male pride crashed through him. She looked grateful, so uncharacteristically vulnerable, Conon found himself leaning closer to the allure of her eyes.

And he kissed her.

Not to show her he could, although he would bet what was left of Vannes that he could persuade her to open those lips and cry out for him in the space of a few heartbeats.

No, he kissed her to show her tenderness since she had not been the recipient of much compassion in her life lately.

"I am happy to serve you, Elysia."

Departing her chamber before he kissed her for far more selfish reasons, Conon savored the softness of her skin on his lips and knew he would never forget her taste.

Chapter Nine

"You have been here a sennight and I was not told?" Daria Rougemont Westmoor paused her embroidering in midstitch as she looked up at her daughter in her solar a few days later. After covering Elysia with kisses and hugs upon her arrival, Daria had settled into her sewing while they talked. "That miserable bastard."

Accustomed to her mother's candor, Elysia ignored the comment and gazed upon Daria, thinking she looked well for a woman who had been abed for weeks. Her green eyes were as brilliant as ever, her dark curls shone with health and her gestures were animated.

Sixteen summers older than her daughter, Daria still managed to look as young as Elysia. Thirty-four years and bearing two babes only succeeded in adding voluptuous curves to her figure. Her waist remained slender, as did her shapely legs and arms. The energy with which she moved, the vibrancy in her voice contributed to the youthful impression.

"I am sorry, Mother." Elysia did not wish to upset her. Stretched too emotionally thin herself, Elysia couldn't cope with someone else's anger. "I know he is hateful, but I thought he was at least honest about the fact that you were ill."

"Ill to him, anyway." Sitting back in her chair, Daria allowed her stormy frown to fade, replacing it with an impish grin. "I have made quite a disgusting pretense of being too sickly to join him in the marriage bed. I am a convincing performer, you know."

Elysia laughed. She had spent too many years rising and falling with her mother's turbulent temper not to know the full scope of Daria's dramatics. "I only hope Oliver does not learn the truth of it. How long do you think you can hold him at bay?"

"The deed is done, in case you are wondering, sweeting, so don't think you can save me." Daria stabbed the needle through the cloth with angry force. "Oliver insisted on his wedding night and saw the thing through despite considerable resistance."

Recalling John Huntley, Elysia felt her belly roil, her throat tighten in empathy. Conon's support in the face of her recent trials had taught Elysia the value of simple comfort. She hated it that he had become such a friend to her while her deception about her wedding night remained between them. If only the earl had been in residence so she could have spoken to him and cleared up the matter.

Shoving aside the worry for later, she squeezed her mother's shoulder to comfort her. "I am so sorry."

Daria's eyes narrowed. "Is that melancholy I detect in your voice?"

Embarrassed by the emotions she used to be able to control, Elysia waved away her mother's concern. "I have come to realize the utter humiliation of having a man command you completely."

"I knew you were not suited for Jacques St. Simeon," her mother scoffed. "He was too old for you."

"I do not refer to him, although that was wretched, too."

"You have been defiled?" Daria tossed her sewing aside and leaped to her feet. "Who was he? We'll have his head, by God—"

"Nay." Elysia scrambled after her mother, comforted by Daria's vow of vengeance even as she knew it would be futile to seek justice for Huntley's thwarted attack. "The count's nephew saved me at the last. But it was a near thing. I can imagine how awful it must have been for you to allow Oliver near you."

"Who is this nephew?" Daria tapped her well-worn velvet slipper on the cold stone floor of her solar.

Sighing, she knew Daria would misinterpret her relationship with Conon. "Conon St. Simeon, the new Count of Vannes since Jacques died. He escorted me home."

"You brought a *man* to Nevering?" Her mother clapped her hands together in delight. "How wonderful!"

"No mother, it is not wonderful," Elysia snapped. "He merely escorted me when the guardian Arundel gave me turned out to be a knave."

"But that was three days past." Girlish mischief danced in Daria's sea-green eyes. "Why is he still here?"

Elysia asked herself that question the past two nights as she lay in bed, knowing Conon slept in the next room. She saw him only sparingly since her arrival because she had been preoccupied with her flax plants. For his part Conon had been making plans to hire himself out to a neighboring lord as a mercenary knight before returning to the continent to seek fortune in yet another lord's service. The life of a mercenary was lucrative apparently, but did not allow Conon much time at Vannes.

She did not want him to leave yet, though she prepared herself for the inevitable. But no matter what wayward feelings he had inspired with his kisses, she knew she could never think of him as anything more than a friend.

"He just wants to see me settled, I think. He does not feel it is safe to leave me with Oliver, perhaps."

"He feels responsible for you."

Elysia gazed out her mother's solar window, unwilling to discuss Conon anymore. Her feelings for the knight confused her too much. "But what of you, Mother? If I send to the earl about your marriage, do you think we could get it annulled?"

"No." Black locks flying in urgent disapproval, Daria shook her head.

"But you were wed against your will and without your overlord's knowledge."

"What can we possibly do about it besides stir up trouble? I have no wish to bring Oliver's wrath down upon my head any further than I already have." She hugged her arms more tightly to her, as if chilled by the mere thought. "He has warned me in the most dire terms about seeking annulment, and I believe his revenge would be painful, if not fatal. Not to mention, our chances of getting the marriage annulled are less than nil."

"It is unfair," Elysia insisted, surprised her passionate mother would refuse to fight and unwilling to believe Oliver would be so foolish as to threaten Lady Daria. The Rougemont women had always been beholden to the Earl of Arundel, even when Elysia's father had lived. Oliver had no right to steal away her mother without his overlord's blessing. "This is *our* home, our profitable trade that we started with hard work."

"Aye. But we are women, Elysia. Our voices are ignored. Our pleas are meaningless." Daria touched her daughter's cheek to encourage her gaze. "Although Arundel will be furious that Oliver did not consult him about the marriage, the earl will ultimately give his approval to a strong knight he favors. Oliver will have to pay a special fine perhaps, or add more men to Arundel's troops, but he will be forgiven."

"Mayhap." Realizing this was one battle she would have to wage on her own, Elysia peered out the casement to where Sir Oliver sat in the orchard among at least fifteen attendants. As if he were holding court, his entourage fell over themselves to please him. "But I refuse to believe I cannot make myself heard, Mother. One way or another, Oliver will do penance for this injustice."

Strains of the lute and lyre provided a sharp contrast to Oliver's nasal donkey laugh the next day as Elysia approached the idyllic scene in the orchard. A plump upstairs maid fed him sugared summer berries from chubby fingertips while a traveling jester entertained him by juggling apples, a short torch and what looked to be the maid's worn leather shoe.

Thistles snared Elysia's gown as she tromped through the high grass toward the group. The heat of the day worked her ire with Oliver Westmoor into a flaming fury.

At the discreet nod of the juggler, Oliver turned about and spied the newcomer.

"Ah! Elysia. How nice of you to join us, my dear. You really must see the tricks Ragnar here knows—"

"I seek an audience with you, my lord." The simmering emotion behind her words was unmistakable, yet Oliver's expression indicated he chose to ignore it.

"Finally. You have been here for days and not sought me

out. You do not even bother to grace my table at mealtimes. I am feeling neglected indeed."

While they talked, Oliver's attendants went about their merrymaking. Elysia noticed the juggler's hand disappear under the maid's skirts as he replaced her shoe.

She tried not to think about Conon's hands on her leg that day at the beach. If she had smiled as warmly as the maid, would Conon's fingers have strayed farther? Heat seized her belly, making it difficult to focus.

Fortunately, Oliver's insipid expression spurred her on, reminding her of her purpose.

"There is a matter I must discuss with you." She folded her arms.

"As you can see—" Oliver gestured with a grand sweep of his hand "now is not a good time."

"Since your companion is already eyeing another man, I would say it is a fine time."

Glancing over his shoulder, Oliver made a clucking noise in his throat Elysia could only interpret as mild disapproval. "Very well then. You have my undivided attention."

"Your marriage to my mother is not valid because you forced her into it. I wish to see it annulled and you barred from Nevering after I appeal to the earl."

Oliver stiffened. "Did Daria tell you as such?"

"No. My mother refuses to work against you because you have threatened her. But I will not allow you to steal Nevering out from under us and make my mother's life miserable." Elysia rose to her most imperious stature, the posture that had always sent the women in the sewing room scurrying to work faster. "I appeal to your adherence to a knightly code, Sir Oliver, and your commitment to what is right and just. Renounce this marriage and free my mother."

"You cannot be serious." He shook his head dismissively, appearing more interested in the blatant flirtation of the maid and the juggler who now lay back in the grass to tangle limbs about one another.

"I am *very* serious." Her mother's happiness was at stake. And although Elysia had her share of differences with her mother, the two of them had seen each other through some hard times.

"You are much less clever than I gave you credit for if you think for a moment your woman's shrewishness can send me packing." His eyes narrowed to thin slits. "I suggest you hie yourself back to the keep and find your chambers lest I forget to treat you as an honored guest."

"I am a countess, sir." Praying fervently that would sway him, she could not help but think her message would make more of an impression if she had Conon at her side right now to force this man to listen. "I am not without resources for turning you out."

"Your word means nothing compared to Arundel's, my lady, and you only show your naiveté by confronting me with hollow womanly babble." He popped another berry into his mouth and moaned enthusiastically over the taste. "I think what you need, Elysia my dear, is another husband. This conversation makes me realize I am not prepared to host you for long as an unwed, and shall we say…untamed…relative."

Indignation curled through her even as the reality of her own powerlessness hit her full force. Oliver couldn't have been more confident of his authority, while Elysia was only just beginning to learn the limitations of her own.

Her mother had been right. Arguing further with Oliver would be pointless. Seeking a way to depart with what little remained of her dignity, she pivoted on her heel and prepared to retreat.

For now.

"But never fear, my dear." Oliver's voice halted her, calling her to turn back. Another berry flew through the air to land in his mouth. Ignoring Elysia, he took in the half-naked scrambling of the maid and juggler with an avid gaze. "Your stepfather has a solution to all of your woes."

Struggling to ignore the bawdy spectacle herself, Elysia was surprised when the image of Conon returned in vivid, breath-stealing detail.

She closed her eyes against the blatant sensuality of the scene, unsure if she fought the view of the maid and juggler or the more dangerous vision of Conon and herself entwined in that same way. "Oh?"

"Aye."

She could hear the grin in his voice, which she assumed was for the maid's now-naked breasts, though Elysia did not peek. Her heart sped as her mind supplied an equivalent image of Conon making love to her.

"I am holding a tournament at summer's end in your honor, Countess. The prize of which will be none other than your hand in marriage."

"What?" Her eyes flew open. Oliver might succeed in wedding Daria behind their overlord's back, but he could not be so audaciously stupid as to play guardian to Elysia.

"Don't look so startled, my dear. I have already discussed the plan with Arundel."

Elysia didn't believe him. It couldn't be true. Could it?

"I am looking to increase my store of knights," Oliver explained, as reasonably as if he were discussing the weather. "The chance of winning your hand will attract the best warriors across the land to Nevering."

"But I am no prize." The world swayed before her in a swirl of disbelief and summer heat. She raised a hand to her temple to still its pounding. "I do not even hold Nevering anymore. My wealth is sorely decreased by your marriage to my mother."

Oliver snorted. "Your bridal portion still makes you wealthy beyond most women's dreams, Elysia. And now you hold a French dower estate. Believe me, the suitors will flock here for you."

Elysia massaged her aching forehead. "You have no right to wed me off without the earl here to approve the husband. I am Arundel's responsibility."

"As my stepdaughter, sweeting, you are now *mine,* and I say you will be wed to the tournament's winner at harvest time." His brief interest in her finished, Oliver turned his eyes to the more frantic movements of his plump maid.

Arundel would be furious with Oliver's blatant manipulation. Lesser infractions than this had led men to war. "But—"

Oliver no longer bothered to mask his anger. "Now away to your chamber, my dear, before I miss the best part." With steely warning in his measured words, Oliver dismissed Elysia.

Her attempts at dignity forgotten, Elysia ran with all haste from Oliver, the tangle of naked limbs in the orchard and her new, wretched fate.

"Have you seen the count this sunrise, Eadred?" Elysia asked as the boy bounded past her on the stairs the next morning.

"Aye, my lady. He helped Cook make a rabbit in some sort of sauce." Eadred pinched his nose closed at the memory. "Yuck."

She must find him before he left England. If he would seek the Earl of Arundel on her behalf when he returned to France, there remained a slim chance she could extricate herself from Oliver's scheme.

Although she questioned the wisdom of becoming further indebted to Conon, Elysia could see little choice. She had to stop the tournament, and Conon was her only hope of accomplishing that goal. Odd how much she had grown to depend on him. Would he try to collect on that debt one day? As an experienced seducer of young widows, would Conon try to sway her to his bed by playing on her guilt?

An answering shiver tingled through her body, a common enough occurrence lately whenever her thoughts strayed to Conon.

Hurrying into the kitchens, Elysia found no one but Cook and her assistant.

"Have you seen my lord the count this morn, Cook?"

"Oh, aye, my lady." She blushed and smiled. "He has a grand way with food."

"Do you know where he headed when he left?"

"He said something about wanting our gate closed at all times," the cook's assistant offered. "I think he went to speak to the guardhouse about it."

Since arriving, Conon had conducted several training sessions with the men-at-arms and Elysia's former knights, who were demoted and ignored by Oliver's troop of warriors. In addition, Conon created a workforce of village men to repair places along the parapet that needed reinforcing.

All of this, Elysia knew, was accomplished without Oliver's knowledge. Because the new lord of Nevering was absent much of the time in his quest for self-indulgent pleasures, his men grew lax and lazy. She wondered why Conon would bother, but it seemed she could never locate him to initiate a conversation.

Arriving at the guardhouse harried and out of breath,

Elysia found the guardsmen busily polishing their blades, but no sign of Conon. "Good morning, sirs. Have I missed the count?"

One of them looked up but neither paused in their efforts. "Aye, my lady. He went riding, I believe."

Elysia gave up, hoping she might see him in the evening hours. Surprised at the depth of her disappointment, she walked back to the keep, distracting herself by admiring the proud walls of her home with sad nostalgia.

It had never really been hers.

The knowledge ached inside her. For years she'd deceived herself, thinking if she worked hard enough, she would grow and gain something of value all her own.

As she neared the sewing lodge from the lawns, Elysia's musings were interrupted by the sounds of shrill shrieking and children at play.

The children's area was housed in the low building beside the sewing lodge, but the little ones were not allowed to shout and carry on so loudly after their luncheon break. Thinking perhaps one of the attendants in the children's area was absent from her chores, Elysia hastened her pace. As she neared, she saw the children out of doors and romping in playful frolic with—

Conon.

The man she'd sought all morning rollicked at the center of the melee. Swinging a wooden sword with the same deft care as if it were the real thing, Conon parried thrusts with three of the older boys, much to the delight of the young onlookers. Other children ran for sticks of their own, anxious to emulate the blue-eyed Frenchman who towered over them like a god.

Soon mock battle broke out among all the children.

For a moment her heart warmed to see his genuine affection for the little ones. He seemed to enjoy the shouts and play as much as they did.

She had not realized how much she missed seeing his ready smile, hearing his quick laughter. Yet Conon's carefree attitude toward life differed so greatly from hers. He could afford to have fun, to play while Elysia struggled to be taken seriously. Forced to remain aloof and reserved in her business, she found it helped people take her more seriously.

And right now Conon's fun disrupted the well-ordered labors of Nevering's workers. In an attempt to quell the chaos, Elysia opened her mouth to yell.

A profusion of feminine giggles snapped it shut again.

Mothers and sisters, grandmothers and aunts poured out of the sewing lodge to watch. The keep's linen workers idly enjoyed the joyful shrieking and raucous romping of their little ones. And of course, they enjoyed the playful Count of Vannes, whose innate sense of fun never disappointed a crowd. Elysia watched him bow to his opponents and his spectators before resigning his post as head knight to join her.

"They are quite the little hellions once you get them started." Good humor vibrated from him. Leaning his wooden sword against a tree, he grinned down at her.

"They never quit once you get them started, either, my lord." Her voice conveyed more annoyance than she'd intended. She knew she was being unfair but couldn't seem to help herself. "I suspect the nursery attendants will be beside themselves trying to restore order."

Conon's brow swooped down as he studied her with a shuttered gaze. "Mayhap they will allow the children to enjoy themselves first."

"So that their mothers can idle the day away to watch their antics?" She gestured toward the assembled crowd, and was appalled to realize she was the subject of several curious stares. Lowering her voice, she continued. "It is unwise to cease labor in midday."

"Do not fret over it, my lady. 'Tis no longer your trade to run anyhow." Spinning on his heel, he stormed down the incline to the stables before she could speak.

He was right of course. Elysia felt utterly ridiculous—more childish than any of the little sprites who romped and played on the keep's lawns.

She did not begrudge the children their playtime. She was angry for reasons that had naught to do with how much time the linen makers spent watching the little ones cavort. Perhaps her frustration stemmed from seeing Conon so at ease among her people. Even after a lifetime of keeping her family and tenants well fed and prosperous, Elysia had never been embraced the way Conon seemed to be within a matter of days.

A soft voice called from behind her. "It is good to have you back, my lady."

Turning, Elysia found Anna Weaver at her shoulder, a shy young mother of three with one more babe on the way.

"Thank you, Anna." Elysia was somewhat surprised any of the women noticed her return.

"We have missed you these past moons. The new lord knows nothing of making cloth or sewing, thus he rarely comes to our lodge. And with your mother hiding herself away from him, she does not come, either. The women have grown rather lax."

This did not in the least surprise Elysia, who found the sewing lodge ran most efficiently when she made two random visits to oversee the work each day.

"It is to be expected, I guess," Anna continued, steadying an overeager young jouster who backed into her legs.

"But it is more difficult to work when the slackers are gibbering nonstop or initiating foolish games around the rest of us who do not wish to play. More than once the elders among us have bemoaned the loss of our disciplined Lady Elysia."

Sighing, Elysia cast a wistful glance toward the horizon, wondering where Conon went. "I was beginning to think I was the only one in the world who appreciated a little hard work."

As if following the wayward direction of Elysia's thoughts, Anna raised a curious brow. "The count seems as industrious as you, my lady, if I may be so bold."

Elysia would never have thought so if she had not seen him in action the last few days, but now she was forced to agree.

"It is unfortunate his efforts are lost on our hedonistic new lord. I fear he wastes his time."

"Mayhap he hopes to win it back for you one day, Countess."

Elysia mustered a smile as she departed, the ludicrous words lingering in her mind. Conon did not covet Nevering or her, for that matter. He merely wanted to lend his expertise. Yet throughout the remainder of the day, Elysia was struck anew by the thought of Conon winning back her home in a grand gesture of chivalry.

Ridiculous.

Even more ridiculous, Elysia thought as she sought her chamber to change, were her sudden and vivid memories of his kiss. She consoled herself with the notion that Conon had played havoc with more experienced hearts than hers. Besides, there would be no more kisses. Conon was angry with her and rightfully so. Her behavior toward him today ranked somewhere between churlish and childish.

And, she'd failed to confront him with the favor she so desperately needed.

Now she would have to brave the meal in the great hall tonight and hope Conon chose to attend. After she apologized, would he find it in his heart to grant her favor? Taking deep, calming breaths she assured herself everything would work out.

All would be well as long as Conon did not somehow sense the seductive weakness she sometimes felt in his presence.

Chapter Ten

"Leon de Grace is here to see you, my lord." Young Eadred announced the news with wide-eyed enthusiasm just before dinner.

In his chamber, Conon finished penning a letter to his steward and nodded at the boy. Thankfully, some people in this godforsaken keep still found things to enthuse over. Lord knew the blasted countess never would.

"Is he alone?" Conon liked Eadred. Smart and determined, the boy soaked up knowledge and affection as if he could never gain quite enough of either.

Conon had been that eager once, but with three older brothers to ensure the future of his father's small holding, he often went overlooked and unnoticed throughout his childhood and foster years. He made sure to praise Eadred and take note of the boy's accomplishments for that very reason.

"Two men attend him, my lord." Eadred hurried to where Conon sat and took up the boots.

"Do you know why I ask, son?"

Shaking unkempt blond curls, the boy laced Conon's

boots. Eadred should have been serving Elysia's mother, but Lady Daria seldom had need of him and was only too glad to loan the spirited lad to Conon.

"More men means trouble. Now, I may have need of you later to deliver a message to de Grace."

"Aye. I will stop by your chamber before bed."

"Good lad. Run and ask Lady Daria if she wishes to attend dinner. I will be down shortly."

Whistling a happy tune, the boy departed in a whirlwind.

Watching him go, Conon wondered why the boy's father consented to have him fostered in a keep full of women. Before Oliver came, Elysia and Daria had been responsible for the boy. It did not bode well with Conon, and he made a note to learn more about the young page.

Strapping his short blade to his waist, Conon's thoughts turned to Leon as he puzzled over what had taken de Grace so long to reach England. When Conon departed Vannes to follow Elysia, he assumed his friend would be only a day or two behind him. Why had Leon waited over a sennight to sail north? News of Conon's guests hastened his step toward the hall.

Torchlight flickered. Jesters juggled and danced. A minstrel wailed a pitiful tune. Oliver Westmoor drank from a huge horn at the center of it all, his court a motley mass of traveling troubadours, peasant girls and grizzled knights.

Much to Conon's surprise, Leon de Grace already sat next to the newly convalesced Lady Daria, who looked amazingly fit after her extended illness. In fact, she looked beautiful. And very captivated by whatever Leon said at the moment. Surprised to see his old friend engaged in such intimate conversation with a woman, Conon noted the way Leon gave Elysia's mother his full attention. Surely Leon knew better than to pay court to another man's wife? Especially when the other man in question possessed a temper well known among his men-at-arms.

Conon had not taken much note of Elysia's mother before, other than to observe she was as different from her daughter as the sun from the moon. Although they shared the same raven-dark tresses, all resemblance ended there. Where Daria smiled and beguiled, Elysia cloaked herself in chilly reserve.

"Fun and games after the meal everyone," Oliver shouted out in a drunken slur, his arm cast about the neck of a serving maid bent to pour him more wine. "Be sure to stay and hear the grand announcement I will make."

Elysia sat to Oliver's right. Daria and then Leon to Oliver's left. There would be no personal discussion with de Grace at the meal this eve. Instead his dining companion was his countess. Elysia.

He hoped she found the strength to restrain her viperous tongue.

"Good evening, *chère*." He kissed her hand with what he hoped was his standard aplomb. She may have made him furious, but he was a Frenchman, after all.

Her cool greeting did nothing to alleviate his annoyance. But what could he expect of the proud dowager countess?

Despite her reserved demeanor, however, Elysia radiated beauty. The longer he spent in her company, the more appealing she grew. Tonight, sapphires and tiny white beads circled the neckline of her elaborate gown, ending in a large sapphire set in the fine white taffeta that covered the place between her breasts. Yet had she been attired in sackcloth, Conon would have thought her exquisite.

Although she lacked the pronounced high forehead that was so popular at court, her heart-shaped face boasted a small, straight nose and the most perfectly shaped lips he had ever had the pleasure of admiring.

"I believe I owe you an apology, my lord."

The words, spoken with her usual brusqueness, surprised him. She turned wide, dark eyes upon him and waited. When he made no reply, she raised her cup to her lips for a dainty sip of wine, then patted her mouth with a small linen.

The gesture tied him in knots and reminded him he needed to get away from Nevering with all haste. His gaze remained on her lips long after the linen square rested again in her lap. But still he said nothing, refusing to allow her a graceful escape from an apology he well deserved.

Sighing, she began again, forced to raise her voice above the din of minstrels. "My behavior this afternoon was inappropriate, and I am sorry if I offended you."

Conon took up her hand and squeezed it—quickly enough to be discreet, hard enough to convey his sincerity. "No doubt you have been struggling to come to terms with the new developments here. Your misplaced anger is not difficult to excuse."

Her smile, though little more than a lifting of the corners of that perfect mouth, pleased him. At that moment, he forged a new mission in life—to make her laugh uproariously one day.

"You are too generous. I—" She flinched as Oliver pulled one of his endless parade of female servers into his lap. The upended woman's feet missed Elysia's arm by a hair's breadth, forcing her that much closer to Conon.

Her sweet softness brushed against him so briefly, he almost wondered if he truly touched her, or if he was merely experiencing one of the multitude of pleasant daydreams he found himself immersed in since coming to England. Must have happened, he thought. The daydreams were much more explicit.

Struggling to rein in his thoughts, he stared toward Oliver. "He certainly fails to attend your mother."

"The man does not even make a pretense of respecting her." Elysia shot the lord a derisive glance, which, coming from her, could freeze a normal man to near death. Oliver Westmoor, however, remained happily oblivious, tickling the serving girl until she begged for mercy.

"You will notice Lady Daria is not at a loss for attention this night, nevertheless."

When she turned to look, Conon thought he spied a hint of excitement in her face. "Your friend is here."

"This pleases you?"

As she colored slightly, a surge of jealousy pounded through Conon. A man of Leon's somber temperament might appeal more to someone like Elysia. But how the hell would Elysia have come to know anything about Leon, let alone take a liking to him?

"Nay. But I assume this means you have plans to leave Nevering?"

The anticipation in her voice was unmistakable. She wanted him to leave. If Conon had not kissed her for himself, he would think the woman possessed no shred of human warmth or compassion. "You are eager for me to depart?"

Elysia shook her head, flustered, and sent the soft black curls dancing about her shoulders. "Nay. I wish to ask a favor of you, and seeing your friend here makes me think you might be more predisposed to undertake this favor."

"You have need of me?" Through her small measure of dependence, Elysia bestowed upon him a very flattering amount of trust.

"I have no right to ask it of you—"

Pride forced him to interrupt. "Ask me."

He picked up her hand again, less discreet than before, and pressed his lips to her fingers. The ensuing blush on her cheeks gave him a rush of satisfaction.

"Oliver plans another marriage for me."

He would kill the bastard. Conon smothered an oath and prayed that was the favor she sought.

"And I had hoped that you would intervene on my be-half with the earl when you returned to France." Her brown eyes loomed brilliant as the sapphire glimmered at her breast.

"Of course. I hear he has not moved his troops far from Brittany." It was a simple task, really, and one he would un-dertake with pleasure. The thought of her in another man's arms made his skin crawl.

While running her prospective groom through with his sword might have been more satisfying, Conon saw the practicality of her request for diplomacy.

"Really?" A full-fledged smile spread across her face. "I am unaccustomed to asking favors, Conon." She waved a flustered hand through the air. "Thank you."

In a moment of warm appreciation, she reached for his hand and squeezed it, as he had done to hers earlier. Conon had never seen her so pleased and animated. It made him want to sing and juggle for her. Anything to keep that glad light in her eyes.

Before he could respond, a nasal bray trembled through the hall.

"Noble company, honored guests, may I have your atten-tion please?" Oliver Westmoor wavered on his feet, yet his eyes remained cunning and bright. Conon sensed the man was more clever than he appeared since he had masterminded the scheme to usurp Nevering out from under its mistress.

The hall stilled.

"In honor of my stepdaughter's return, Nevering will host a tournament to rival London's best at harvesttime. The most illustrious knights of the realm will compete to demonstrate their prowess on the field and to capture the magnificent prize I have to offer."

Conon smirked, knowing there was nothing a man of Oliver's means could offer to entice knights from far and wide. It was all empty bragging.

"One of our country's wealthiest heiresses—"

Conon felt the smirk slide from his face. Oliver couldn't possibly mean…

"Lady Elysia."

Elysia paced her small guest chamber, wishing she could go riding or walking, or anything outside the confines of the narrow room. The uncommon heat did nothing to alleviate her nervous unease.

Although the mounds of melted candle wax assured her it was long past nightfall, the hall still rang with the drunken songs of its inhabitants. She could not go back down there. Neither could she sleep. The strange events of the night played themselves over and over in her mind.

Conon had left the hall shortly after the announcement. He had bid her such a terse good evening that Elysia could not help but wonder if she had overstepped the bounds of friendship by asking her favor.

Even more disturbing was the clandestine embrace she spied her mother indulging in with the newly arrived Leon de Grace. Not that she begrudged her mother happiness, but the scene outside Daria's solar made Elysia fear for her mother's safety. Oliver would have no mercy if he learned his wife had been in the arms of another man.

And, too, the kiss she accidentally witnessed stirred

memories of she and Conon, similarly engaged. The more she tried to forget their kiss ever happened, the more vivid her memory of it became. She could not look at him now without recalling how his lips had breathed a fire into her soul, a hungry ache unlike anything she'd ever known.

Since she'd met him, she hardly knew herself. She acted more and more like her theatrical mother with her emotional highs and lows. She didn't trust her emotions, only her logic that told her to forget about Conon. He would squelch her independence like any other man. Still, her heart raced when she thought of his arms about her, and at this rate, she would never get any sleep tonight.

Giving in, she pulled on a light cloak. If she moved with stealth, perhaps she could pilfer a loaf of bread or pinch of cheese from the kitchen. With a bit of food for comfort, perhaps she could sort out the muddle of her life.

Carefully slipping past the hall, Elysia made her way down the familiar darkened passage. As she leaned against the heavy door to the kitchen, soft voices from within froze her where she stood.

"You can touch it, *chère*. It won't hurt you."

Conon.

Feminine giggles followed. "Hold still."

Ice ran through Elysia's veins where blood recently flowed. She should turn and leave. Retreat to her chamber.

She commanded her feet to do her bidding, but they remained rooted. So traitorous was her body, in fact, that it leaned forward to push more forcefully upon the door. She could not tamp down the curiosity and perhaps even jealousy that seized her emotions. Without one more thought to the consequences, she stepped into the kitchen.

"Elysia?"

Ignoring Conon's question, she took in the scene.

Conon's golden head was inclined toward a server's auburn one where the two of them crouched on the floor. The object of their interest pranced around Conon's feet, rubbing its feline body against his leather boots in time with its happy purring.

"Excuse me, my lady." The maid blushed at being discovered, hastily curtsying as she backed out the door.

Still Elysia did not move, now feeling a bit foolish for her intrusion.

"Elysia." This time Conon's voice rang sharp in the stillness.

"Yes?" Her head snapped up in annoyed and embarrassed response.

"What are you doing?" His brows knitted together. He had not looked so forbidding since the first time they met.

"Only attempting to find something to eat. It seems I have interrupted your evening entertainment. I am sorry."

"Nay, *chère*, my evening entertainment has apparently only just begun." His eyes settled on her breasts, which suddenly felt much too exposed by the sheer fabric of her night rail and haphazardly tied cloak.

Pulling the cloth more firmly together, Elysia attempted to march past him to peer into the larder. "I will not dignify that with a response."

He caught her by the arms before she could edge past him. "You will most definitely give me a response, Elysia." He whispered the words in her ear, sending unwelcome shivers down her spine. "But it may not be as withering as you hoped."

He turned her in his arms to face him and, for a moment, Elysia lost herself in the exquisite feel of his body.

"Chère demoiselle."

That refreshed her annoyance with him. Stepping back,

she retreated as much as his arms would let her. "Do not call me endearments you squander thoughtlessly on any passing maid."

Releasing her, Conon's eyes looked heavenward as if seeking relief, but Elysia ignored him. She went about the business of finding a snack.

"I call no one *demoiselle.*"

"That is not what I refer to."

"I call you no other endearments, *chère.*"

Whirling on him, she slammed the recently located cheese onto a large worktable. "Of course you do, but you use the word so unthinkingly, it means nothing to you."

He thought so long, Elysia went back to her search for bread.

"I call you *chère,* as I often call women."

"Precisely. And no woman likes to be called by a common name except for 'lady.' So please do not use your insincere endearments with me anymore." Victorious, Elysia emerged with the bread and a fresh plum and began to look for a basket to put it all in.

Opening the larder for himself, Conon found another plum and added it to her pile of food. "I called the little maid *'chère,'* and you are annoyed with me." He sounded so pleased with this revelation Elysia wanted to throttle him.

"I am *not* annoyed." Basket now in hand, she handed the plum back to him. "I can't eat this, too."

"You are irritated because you secretly enjoy my endearments." Stuffing the plum in the basket, he informed her, "It is not for you, it is for me."

Dropping the fruit none too gently on the table, she snatched up her food hamper and headed for the door. "Good night, my lord Count."

Quicker than she could blink, he plucked the basket off

her arm and commandeered her elbow. "Not so fast, Countess."

Closing her eyes, Elysia tried to regain her composure while he pulled her toward the back door of the kitchen.

"We need to talk."

"I am not dressed to talk." She halted, refusing to be yanked along with him, even if it meant losing her snack. It had been a wretched day from start to finish. She wanted to escape from it. From him.

From the warmth he stirred inside her.

That hungry look in his gaze had abated somewhat since she had tied her cloak closed, but Elysia could see the traces of lingering heat. It was dangerous for her to be around him. The man could be as persuasive as the devil himself, and she found herself disturbingly attracted to him.

That combination of feelings could only lead to trouble. Especially when he was going to save her from a wretched marriage. She needed his aid, not his remaining lust for the auburn-haired kitchen maid. For the first time in her life, Elysia realized she was disappointed that she had to be so logical all the time. Wouldn't it be nice to occasionally do the things she *wanted* to do, instead of what she should?

"No one will see you." With possessive hands, Conon straightened her night rail and cloak at the neckline to be sure she was adequately covered. "And you owe me an explanation for tonight."

"Explanation for what?" Distracted by the tingling heat that skipped through her at his touch, she allowed herself to be pulled through the kitchen and into the warm night air before she realized what he was about.

"For not revealing to me the extent of your stepfather's plans for your nuptials." Directing her toward a large wooden bench near the well that served the household,

Conon set down the basket and began dividing the horde. "You misled me when you said Oliver planned a marriage for you."

"He *does* plan a marriage for me."

After slicing the cheese into thin slabs, he offered her a bite from his fingers. Wary of the intimacy of that act, Elysia took the cheese in hand to feed herself.

"But I am not sure your overlord will object. It is not as if you already know your suitor and detest him. Your husband could be any knight of the realm."

Sighing, Elysia looked up at the stars, amazed at the beauty of the night sky. How long was it since she had ventured out-of-doors at night? For as long as she could remember, her life consisted of work and more work. There was never time for anything so frivolous as stargazing.

Conon found time. And, since Elysia became acquainted with him, it seemed he made sure she found time, too. Like their walk on the beach, when he kissed her.

Licking lips gone suddenly dry, she focused on his words.

"Don't you see the problem? If *you* were the one being wed, wouldn't you want to know your bride ahead of time? I can't imagine marrying someone whose name I will not know until a day before the wedding." Tearing at the bread with a vengeance, Elysia broke off a piece.

"But you will have to wed someone eventually, Elysia." He caressed her with his gaze, his blue eyes as unfathomable as the starry night sky. "Why not wed a strong man who can beat back a field of the best competitors? A man who is well qualified to protect you and your fortune?"

"What fortune?" she muttered crossly, shivering in the night air. "Oliver is doing his best to usurp Nevering's assets, and my bridal portion may well be lost considering how long it is taking to be delivered."

"Your belongings from the boat have not yet arrived?" Pulling his surcoat over his shoulders and off his body, he dropped it down around Elysia's neck in a gesture that brought back a wellspring of pleasant memories.

She shook her head.

He frowned. "Then I shall make inquiries after them on my way to France. Oliver should have already sent men."

As he cleared the bench of leftovers, Elysia admired the efficient work of muscles beneath his thin linen tunic.

Cradled in the warmth of his garment, lulled by his sweetly accented voice, Elysia wanted to remain there forever.

"You have already done so much to help me, my lord. I would not inconvenience you any further."

"I need to see you safely settled."

Was it her imagination or had he moved closer? His warmth spanned the gap between them, curling around her body and her heart. The scent of Conon—something akin to pine and the sea—permeated her senses. Knowing she wore the surcoat that so recently clothed his body sent a surge of longing through her.

"But I am less certain now about what I can do for you in terms of forestalling your wedding."

Shaking off the lazy peace of the moment, she straightened. "Have you changed your mind?"

"Nay. I have every intention of speaking to the earl, but I am not certain that he will disapprove of your stepfather's tactics."

"But you will at least try to dissuade him?" She could not—would not—marry again. At least not so soon after the debacle of her first marriage. And certainly not to a stranger who sought her hand in combat.

Conon stared at her for a long moment, and it seemed

to Elysia that he chose his words with caution. "I will press my suit in the most strenuous of terms."

She should be happy with that, but somehow his words left her uneasy. "That is the best I could hope for."

For a long moment, Elysia counted the stars in the sky, wondering if she should speak to Conon about the other concern that preyed heavily upon her mind tonight.

"I saw my mother embracing Sir Leon after they departed the hall tonight." Conon would only find out from his friend anyway. And it might put her mind at ease if she knew more of Leon's character.

"You must be mistaken." He shifted subtly away from her, allowing the air around her to chill once again.

"I am positive. I sought my mother's advice tonight, and thought to find her in her chamber. When I arrived at her corridor, she was in front of her door, holding your friend in a most affectionate embrace."

"Most affectionate?"

Though the night was dark, her eyes were long adjusted to the light of the moon, and she spied Conon's grin. He leaned back into the bench again, his closeness sending sparks of desire tripping through her veins.

Warmth suffused her cheeks, yet she continued to meet his eye. "Yes. They were…kissing."

"Ah. Kissing is a very affectionate thing to do." Voice lowered, the intimacy of his tone wound suggestively around her imagination. Conon thought of *their* kisses, devil take him, and that was completely different. In those instances, the kissing had been one-sided.

Almost.

"In this case, it looked it." Elysia spoke sternly, but only earned a laugh from her companion.

"You are such an expert on kissing, after all."

"Just what is that supposed to mean?" Indignation bubbled.

"You would probably think a brother kissing his sister good-night looked passionate if you did not know their relationship. You do not know a thing about what goes on between men and women, Elysia."

"I am a widow." Now her cheeks burned. His audacity knew no bounds and his all-too-accurate remark made her fear that he somehow knew the truth of her wedding night.

"Of one night," Conon scoffed. "And initiated into passion by a drunken old man to boot. Trust me, *demoiselle*, you probably misinterpreted what you saw going on with your mother."

The sensual knowing in his gaze flustered her. She distracted herself from the heat it generated by shifting frustrated desire into annoyance.

"I know very well what I saw. I saw one of your friends feasting upon my mother's mouth like she was a starving man's last meal."

"I find that difficult to envision." Conon studied her thoughtfully, as if he had all the time in the world to ponder the matter.

"Ha!" Her anger peaked, pushing her to argue the point. "My mother was fair bent backward." In a grand theatrical gesture worthy of Daria herself, Elysia threw her head back to expose a broad expanse of her neck. "And your friend leaned forward—"

In an instant, Conon's mouth was on top of hers, capturing her words in a hungry kiss. Her heart hammered out a furious rhythm, pressed tightly to Conon's chest. In perfect mimicry of the embrace she described, Conon bent over her, his lips slanting over hers.

Elysia raised her hands to push him away, or maybe to pull him closer. She couldn't remember her intent when she fell captive to the fascinating play of his mouth on hers, his tongue seeking entrance with a seductive stroke.

Pleasure, dark and thick, coursed through her veins with more potency than any wine. Elysia's heart sped, pumping the heady intoxicant throughout her insides until she swayed beneath him like one enchanted. All hope of logic drained away, replaced by hunger for the thrust of his tongue against hers, the gentle caress of his hands beneath the cloak she wore.

His palm skimmed her waist and spanned her belly as if he could sense the wild flush of heat racing over her skin. She edged closer, sinking into that touch, delighting in every new caress.

He reached her breast, cupping its softness through the negligible barrier of her muslin night rail. Her hands fluttered at his chest, confusion and passion warring within, then settled on the hard breadth of his shoulders to pull him closer still.

"Conon." Elysia breathed his name like a whispered prayer while he trailed kisses down the column of her throat. She floated in a sultry world where feeling ruled thought and, for once, passion ruled Elysia.

Scooping her off the bench, Conon settled her across his lap. The coarse fabric of his braies chafed her skin through her shift, but the hard warmth of his thighs beneath her filled her thoughts with steamy visions of twining limbs with him. Heat suffused her while gooseflesh tickled her arms and legs.

"Mon amour." Conon whispered the words between kisses, his voice ragged with passion as intense as her own heightened emotions.

Mon amour...my love. Though Elysia knew he did not feel the full sentiment behind the words, the endearment melted her heart, turned her legs to liquid.

Breasts already aching from his teasing touch, Elysia arched back as his finger traced a path down her belly to the top of her thigh. The moan that escaped her sounded foreign in her ears. Surely she wasn't responsible for that hungry cry.

His touch left her for a moment, leaving her more bereft than she would have thought possible. But then her shift stirred around her legs as Conon reached beneath the hem to skim up her bare thigh.

"No." Some last gasp of logic must have pushed the word from her mouth in spite of the pleasure his hands inspired. She forced herself to meet his gaze in the moonlight, her eyelids heavy with sensual hunger.

Although his fingers ceased their upward trek, Conon did not retreat.

"I must leave on the morrow, Elysia." He peered at her through eyes as dark as the midnight sea. "Would you deny me one glimpse of heaven, 'ere I am shut out forever?"

His words tempted her. She would likely never see the Count of Vannes again. She would wed another rich man who was too battle hungry to care about his young bride. Whereas Conon could show her pleasure most women only dreamed of... What on earth was she thinking?

She slipped off his lap to land on the hard wood of the bench with a soft thud.

"I cannot. It is immoral and it is wrong." By the saints, she hated sounding so self-righteous.

But it wasn't so much the immorality of being with him that made her cease. Conon seemed to hold himself responsible enough for her already, and if they continued in this vein, he might feel even more obligated.

His hands vanished from her body, but not the memory of his touch. Elysia knew the imprint of Conon St. Simeon would stay with her long after he was out of her life.

"I understand, *chère*. It is *I* who ought to know better. You are my family, the one I vowed to safeguard." Gently, he smoothed her hair behind her ear, gazing into her eyes as if she were the most cherished of creatures.

Her resolve swayed. Her body cried out for his touch, screaming at her confounded common sense for interrupting this first attempt to follow her heart. Could she resign herself to a life beside another aged lecher, never having known the heated touch of true passion? And yet, sharing any intimacies with Conon would be dangerous. Impossible. He could discover her secret and unveil her deception.

As her inner battle raged, Conon knelt before her. "I swear by all that is holy, I will speak to Arundel. In this I will not fail you." He seemed ready to depart.

"Must you go?" She wanted to linger by his side a bit longer, commit every detail of him to her memory so that she could resurrect this moment on dark, lonely nights.

"I must find Leon. If we are to leave tomorrow, we have many preparations to make." He curled his fingers about her fisted hands. "Besides, I cannot linger in the moonlight with a beautiful maid and expect to retain my status as a gentleman for long." He squeezed her hands in his. "You tempt me, my lady. Too much."

Elysia did not want him to go. She knew they would not speak again before his departure and she would never have the chance to tell him how important he'd become to her. Now she couldn't bear to see him leave. Forever.

"But—"

He sealed her protests with one calloused finger laid

over her lips. "I will not fail you, Elysia. I promise." He cupped her cheek in his palm.

It required all her strength not to close her eyes and lean into that strong palm.

"Goodbye, *demoiselle*."

"Godspeed, my lord." She straightened, needing to escape the temptation of his touch. "And thank you."

Elysia burrowed more deeply into the folds of his surcoat as she watched him walk away, praying he possessed the deep sense of honor she'd glimpsed in him.

By granting Conon her favor, Elysia had also given him a dangerous weapon—all the power he needed to break her heart.

Chapter Eleven

Nevering overflowed with life at harvesttime. Two full cycles of the moon had come and gone since Elysia had implored Conon to help her, but still she had heard no word from him or her overlord. She'd attempted to reason with Sir Oliver and she'd sent letters to the earl abroad, but nothing had affected Oliver's plans to see her wed.

Now Oliver's tournament attracted more men and women than Elysia had ever seen gathered in one place. She squeezed past the crowd around a vagabond trickster who juggled fire while balancing a jug of ale on his nose. For the hundredth time, she marveled at the crush of humanity.

Beggars and thieves pitched their pallets near knights and nobility. Prostitutes abounded. Elysia gaped as every manner of jongleur, minstrel, troubadour and bard congregated in throngs, vying for thick-pursed patrons by hosting impromptu concerts or storytelling competitions.

Across the marketplace lay Elysia's current destination. The jousting field. Her steps grew heavy with dread as she and Daria approached the reviewing stand.

"I cannot bear to watch today." Hitching up her skirts

on one side, she leaped over a broad expanse of mud between the horse stables and the seating. "The thought of wedding the tournament winner makes me ill."

Conon had obviously neglected to intercede with the earl on Elysia's behalf. She still could not believe it. Her faith in him had not faltered, even when the merchants' tents and the reviewing stand were erected the week before the tournament. But now, on the last day of Oliver's grand event, Elysia had to admit it: the earl would not come.

Conon had broken his promise.

Her heart ached with the knowledge that he'd left her to this fate without so much as a word. Now, after three days of varied contests, the undisputed leader in the tournament standings was John Huntley, newly returned from Arundel's forces in France. Apparently the earl's most valued knight was scarcely reprimanded for his brutal overtones toward Elysia.

"I don't know why you insist I be here." Elysia had not determined what she would do if Huntley won, but she could not wed him no matter what threat Oliver spouted.

"If I did not accompany you out here, my husband would." Daria jumped another patch of mud, then smoothed her gown. "And I am certain you would prefer my company."

The unusual serious note in her mother's voice surprised Elysia, calling her from thoughts of her own miserable future. "Is he becoming more difficult to bear?"

They climbed into their box and settled themselves on a narrow bench. The wooden reviewing stand held only enough seating for the nobility in attendance.

Daria flipped her veil over her shoulder and straightened her skirts. "Only since I met Leon de Grace." With a furtive glance around, Daria leaned closer. "For one moment of lunacy, I considered trying to annul my marriage and free myself for him."

"You spoke with the man for naught but the course of an evening." Elysia lifted an eyebrow in disbelief. Her mother had always been impulsive, but she had never been completely impractical.

"Aye." Mischief danced in her mother's green eyes. She looked winsome and beautiful and much too young to be tied for the rest of her days to a wretch like Oliver. "But trust me, 'tis enough when you meet the right man."

Elysia found that difficult to believe, but said nothing, her gaze straying to a juggler warming up the crowd before the first joust of the day.

"Then again, maybe I don't know." Daria pouted as she twisted a curl about her finger. "I thought he felt the same, but he ran off with nary a word."

"I am afraid that is my fault, Mother. I asked Conon to speak to the earl, so he probably left sooner than he intended." It pained her to recall how abruptly he'd announced his departure. Just when she'd come so close to relenting—forfeiting every shred of her pride and honor to chase that nameless desire he stirred in her soul.

Regret lingered even now. To think she had never surrendered to that sweet longing when she would soon be wed to a man who could make every day of her life a living hell. She might never know a tender touch again.

Chère demoiselle.

As spectators trickled into the reviewing stand, Daria lowered her voice to a whisper. "Leon de Grace may have been trifling with me to steal a few kisses, because it certainly does not look like he had any intention of spiriting me away in the night."

The pain in Daria's gaze, though well hidden, hurt Elysia, too. "Maybe he will be back—"

"He has no reason to return."

"I am sorry, Mother. Truly, if I can—"

"Good morning, ladies." Sir Oliver suddenly stood before them, several of Nevering's noble guests around him.

Had he overheard their conversation? Elysia panicked for her mother's sake. She did not doubt a violent streak seethed close to the droll surface Oliver Westmoor presented to the world. Yet his eyes gave away nothing.

After exchanging polite greetings, however, Oliver and his guests settled in the box next to them and turned their attention to the first match. Because the first contenders included no one of note, the spectators gossiped and chattered more than they followed the contest for the early rounds.

"You must feel proud." A stout gentleman seated nearby addressed Elysia later in the day. "It is fortuitous that one of Arundel's favorites leads the field for your hand, Countess. The earl will be well pleased."

"I am rooting for one of the others, my lord," she said, displaying more boldness than normal. The hopelessness of her situation made her less careful of her tongue and her manners. Fancifully, she thought maybe some of Conon's carefree approach to life had rubbed off on her.

"Oh?" The gentleman puffed up with indignation. "And which young man has caught your eye, Countess?"

"Any of them but Sir Huntley, my lord."

The nobleman nodded coldly before he turned away. Soon her comment was whispered throughout the seating in a visible wave.

"Fie!" her mother hissed at her. "Your wedding night will be harsh enough as it is. You needn't draw more of Huntley's wrath upon your head."

"It is not over yet. Perhaps some struggling young knight will catch wind of my fervent wishes and that will spur him to beat Sir Huntley." A foolish, romantic notion she would have never entertained a year ago.

Unwittingly, she timed her words with the downfall of Huntley's current opponent. The knight fell to the ground, motionless. Fear knotted in her belly. She had fought against despair all summer. Faith in Conon had given her so much hope. If only he could have convinced the earl to spare her this marriage.

Huntley circled the arena amid cheers. Before clearing the way for the next match, he paused before Elysia's box. Built at horse level, the raised reviewing area put Elysia and her adversary eye to eye. Pulling off his helm, he confronted her for the first time since that day in the boat cabin. "I think it is past time the good countess granted me her favors—er—favor."

His deliberate slip was accompanied by a flourished presentation of his sword, the tip of which he held a finger's length from Elysia's face. Much too close.

"I would not offend the field, sir, by favoring you alone." Elysia found herself frozen with panic now that she sat so near to him, though she spoke passively enough. She had forced the memory of his brutality to the darkest corners of her mind. But she had not forgotten.

Every spectator within sight craned their necks for a better view of the scene.

Huntley leaned closer so only Elysia and those sitting nearest could hear. Lowering the tip of his sword to barely lift her wimple from her neck, he whispered, "But I have seized your favors before, Elysia."

A flutter of breeze against her bared neck chilled her. Any retort she might have formed fled her mind. The icy grip of fear and humiliation choked her. He replaced the folds of her wimple about her neck and trotted from the field to make way for the next contender.

Even with the restored cloak of her head covering, the chill remained.

"My God." Daria squeezed her daughter's arm in unspoken empathy.

The other spectators seemed too startled by the exchange to even gossip about it, though Elysia guessed their tongues would loosen soon enough. Two new men rode to their starting points. One, Sir Godfrey of York, ranked third behind Huntley. The other man, devoid of standard or colors, was a new knight unknown to the crowd.

A rumble of confusion rippled through the throng of eager viewers.

"Can he do that? Join the tournament four days into the contests?" Daria spoke Elysia's thoughts aloud.

"In an open tournament such as this," the plump gentleman beside them piped up, "a knight can join the lists at any time."

Oliver leaned over from his box. "The first few days are more for winning horses and armor and such. Some of the most successful knights don't make an appearance until the last, though I have never seen this particular knight."

The tournament master announced the undecorated newcomer as the Black Knight. A rush of excitement swelled through the crowd at the presence of the stranger. Elysia experienced it most keenly of all.

The match began, horses running full tilt. After a crash and a thud and another crash, Elysia dared to look.

The Black Knight remained on his horse.

As cheers shook the reviewing stand, Daria leaned close. "Here is your last hope, Elysia."

"Perhaps he does not identify himself because he is an outlaw. He could be just as bad as Huntley."

"Nay." Daria shook her head, sending black curls flying. "I feel it in my bones. This is a better man. Shh! Here he comes."

Elysia never failed to be amazed at how frivolously her mother would pin all her hopes and dreams on something so insignificant as a "feeling."

The man in question did indeed ride toward them. A nervous quiver skittered up her spine. She did not want to marry anyone, but if forced to wed, she prayed it would not be to Huntley.

Stopping in front of Elysia's box, the stranger bowed from atop his horse. "Countess," he intoned, in a soft voice meant only for her ears. "It is for you I ride."

Because the mysterious knight did not remove his helm, his voice echoed eerily within the armor, sending an answering shiver through Elysia. His words, controlled but impassioned, disturbed and stirred her at the same time. Was it merely her fanciful imaginings, or did his voice sound vaguely familiar?

"I pray you a safe day, good sir."

Once again, every eye fell upon the exchange between knight and lady. The heat of embarrassment warmed her cheeks.

"The day will be mine, but only by your leave, fair one." With a grand sweep of his arm, he laid his sword before her to rest on the edge of the box. His way of asking for her favor.

He spoke like a gallant, anyway. Elysia pulled a length of sheer silk from her head covering and wrapped it around his proffered sword. The Black Knight might turn out to be as cruel a man as Huntley, but at least he would not enter into marriage with revenge in mind.

Arcing the silk-tipped sword high above his head, the Black Knight silently declared himself her champion before all. The crowd went wild with shouts and cheers. Now the fun began, as far as the average spectator was concerned. For Elysia, the nail biting would commence while her future rested in a stranger's hands.

The knight lowered the sword and replaced it at his waist. As the crowd applauded, he whispered, "In this, I will not fail you," then rode from the field.

The words remained to haunt her.

His parting declaration, a common enough way to phrase a pledge, called to mind another leave-taking with a man full of promise. A man who'd disillusioned her.

The thought lent an ominous cloud to an already dismal day. She tried to stay calm as one man after another fell before either Huntley or the Black Knight until it seemed inevitable the two would face each other at day's end.

Having placed all her faith in Conon, she had not prepared herself for the consequences of this tournament. What would her new husband think when he learned of her virginity, in spite of her reputation as a widow? Would he be pleased? Or angered that she misrepresented herself? After all, no man wanted a wife who would lie to him, but her absent overlord had presented her with no opportunity to amend the lie.

"It seems it has come down to just the two of them," Daria noted as the afternoon grew late.

Huntley and the Black Knight. The devil she knew and the devil she didn't know.

She would opt for the latter, but it vexed her to think of being sold off to the highest bidder once again. Oliver had won fame and reputation for himself through hosting the tournament, gathering a force of knights to rival the king's, thanks to her. Men gained what they wanted while women must quietly submit to whoever would pay or risk the most for them. Or so they thought.

Elysia vowed no matter who she married, she would find a way to carve out a small measure of independence. She would begin a new linen enterprise of her own, perhaps. But she would not quietly submit this time.

After three passes on the jousting field, the Black Knight fell from his horse. She cringed as her champion hit the dirt, armor colliding with the ground in a discordant crash. The crowd leaned forward to see the condition of his helm, hoping to catch a glimpse of the mystery contender, but he rose to his feet instantly, still protected by the armor that covered his head.

Had Sir Huntley been an honorable knight, he would have dismounted to level the playing field. But he made no pretense of honor. Instead, he turned his horse and lined up the beast's nose with his downed opponent.

Elysia clenched her mother's hand, loathe to see the mystery nobleman ridden down in such ignominious fashion.

Huntley galloped forward while the Black Knight did nothing to remove himself from danger's path. Was he a fool that he did not attempt to evade certain death?

Resisting the urge to squeeze her eyes shut, Elysia watched the battle of wills until the bitter end. Just before Huntley would have trampled his opponent, the Black Knight lurched to the ground and reached for the rider's foot. As he yanked a surprised Huntley from his mount, the unknown knight rolled away from the horse's hooves.

For what seemed like hours, Elysia watched them circle, swing, block and thrust with their weapons. The Black Knight fell twice, each time from a blow to his right leg, which bled profusely.

The second time the injured knight rose, Elysia complained to her mother, "Why doesn't Oliver halt the match? Does he want to see one of them killed?"

"I think they must fight until one admits defeat or is pinned at sword point. The contestants decide when it is over."

"They will kill each other."

"I hear they do, sometimes."

"Sweet Jesu, Mother—" Elysia's outrage dissolved in a sea of gasps from the crowd. Huntley lay on the ground.

She clapped her hands, though she felt like a bloodthirsty heathen doing so, and prayed for Huntley's capitulation. The Black Knight pinned his opponent at sword point. All waited for the downed man to admit defeat.

They heard naught but silence as he refused.

"Dear God," Daria muttered.

"Pray don't kill him." She wanted to see Huntley lose the match, but she certainly did not want to see him dead because of her. "Please."

All waited with bated breath. The Black Knight lifted his sword.

"No!" Elysia cried out, though her words were useless against the blow. The sound vanished in a roar of violent cheering from the crowd.

The Black Knight had knocked his opponent on the head with the blunt edge of his sword, rendering him unconscious and, therefore, defeated.

It was over.

The Black Knight reigned supreme on the field. Meaning, Elysia slowly comprehended, he would win her hand for his prowess. Her marriage loomed now—inevitable and tangible.

"I am praying he is a wonderful man."

Her mother's whisper echoed Elysia's thoughts with

uncanny accuracy. Together, they watched the victorious knight approach the reviewing stand for his prize.

"Pray he is already wed and wants no part of Oliver's ludicrous reward," Elysia returned, her heart growing heavier with each step the man took.

She had favored him to beat Huntley. That did not mean she wanted to wed him. Elysia did not want to wed anyone. Once more she wished Conon had not failed her, that he could have urged the earl to stop the whole farce. That he could have been the one to introduce her body to pleasure.

"Good Knight," Oliver greeted the champion with hands extended, ushering him up the steps to stand within his box.

The knight drew off his glove to accept the handshake.

"I offer you my heartiest congratulations, and with it your prize." Oliver turned toward Elysia, drawing her forward.

Although she forced her feet forward to meet him, fear nipped at her with sharp teeth. What if her future husband turned out to be a heartless mercenary knight—a deadly hired blade? The Black Knight could be a one-eyed toad beneath that helm, and she had blithely granted him her favor.

"May I introduce you to the dowager Countess of Vannes, good sir?" Oliver prompted. "And to all who long to know your identity?"

Elysia's heart slowed down to a heavy *thunk, thunk* against her ribs as she waited. The knight lifted his helm. A familiar face was revealed.

Conon.

Betrayal personified.

"My God," Daria gasped in unison with her husband.

Elysia could not speak. Surely there must be some reason for his secrecy. Some grounds for his actions, even though he had never shared them with her.

"My lady." Conon's deep blue gaze pierced her, familiar and yet dangerous at the same time. "I am honored." He reached for her hand.

Startled by this mercenary side of Conon she had never fully comprehended before, Elysia found she could not offer him her hand in return. Like a small animal, too paralyzed by fear to move, she stood immobile.

Conon ventured closer and plucked up her fingers for himself. He kissed them tenderly, chastely. Not at all as he had kissed the rest of her before he left.

As the crowd once again took up its joyful noise and appreciation, Elysia searched his eyes, confusion jumbling her thoughts.

"What of the earl? Why didn't he come?"

She waited to hear the hardships and struggles Conon had faced trying to get her message through to Arundel. He had made her a promise, after all.

Yet Conon's visage revealed no hint of apology. In fact, Elysia noted an unrepentant set to his jaw, an icy determination in his eyes.

"I did not ask him to."

"You vowed to speak with him." Betrayal stung her anew as she withdrew from his grasp. Better a one-eyed toad than a man who abused her trust. She stood dazed. Snatches of conversations buzzed in her ears. All around them, the noble company discussed the surprise identity of the knight and how he came from France to compete for the coveted countess.

"I did speak to him." Conon ran a weary hand through his hair. "But I did not ask him to halt the tournament, I merely informed him of my intent to win."

"How could you?" Her heart ached. Conon had been the one man she thought she could count on.

But the enthusiastic crowd soon surrounded them, giving him no time to answer. Sir Oliver pulled the tournament champion away to show him off to his noble friends despite his obvious resentment that Conon had won the day.

Elysia watched Conon accept congratulations from everyone around them, his powerful presence obvious in the throng of spectators no matter where he moved. Could this lethal warrior be the same man to whom she'd foolishly entrusted her future?

Although grateful to have been saved from marriage to Huntley, Elysia could find no pleasure in wedding a warrior knight who tricked her into marriage. Especially after she had allowed him to take liberties with her person. Shame filled her when she recalled the way she had clung to Conon the night before he left for France. In the few moments she had allowed herself to relinquish her rigid control of her life, Elysia had made an utter fool of herself.

"How soon will you claim our heiress, my lord?" Oliver asked a few feet away, his question deliberately loud to attract as much notice as possible.

She held her breath as she awaited the answer. Not only would she be marrying a man who deliberately deceived her, she would also be wedding the man who would soon discover her for the virgin and liar she was. As that icy realization washed over her, she wondered how she could be angry with him at all. Hadn't she perpetuated an even more grievous deception of her own? She could not wed a man who would one day come to despise her.

Saints forgive her, she'd made a mess of things.

Conon's height allowed him to peer above the heads of other men around him, his gaze settling on her with an unspoken warning and—it seemed to Elysia—a palpable heat. "On the morrow. I am most anxious to take her home with me."

When the cheers came this time, Elysia did not stay to listen. Confused and fearful of marriage to the new Count of Vannes, she turned on her heel to flee the reviewing stand.

The wet slap of Elysia's retreating footsteps lashed Conon's heart. He closed his eyes to obliterate the vision of her evading him, knowing he had just traded her blossoming trust for a small fortune and a bride who would resent him forever.

Damn.

He hadn't wanted to hurt her. He stalked away from the curious stares and hearty congratulations of the tournament arena, needing a moment to consider his next move. He'd spent the summer in service to any lord with a fat purse. What he didn't win in gold and armor and horses, he extracted in high ransoms from his noble captives. He'd been determined, ruthless and invincible enough to win sufficient fortune to settle Vannes for another two years.

He'd meant to return to Nevering triumphant, to win his bride with his sword instead of wooing an heiress for her money since Elysia was too proud and too stubborn to marry him of her own volition. Yet she *needed* his protection. Between Oliver and the earl, she would find herself wed despite her protests. Conon had somehow convinced himself that she would be more content with him for a husband than another lecherous old drunkard.

Maybe he'd been wrong and he'd sorely misjudged her needs.

Perhaps, despite all his carefully laid plans and ruthless battles to win his fortune, he'd just lost the most valuable tournament prize of all.

"Elysia, you're acting like a child," Daria called to her daughter through the door to the guest chamber. "Let me in."

"The lock was bolted for your own good," Elysia muttered as she slid open the bolt and allowed her mother to enter. "I am not fit company for anyone, nor do I have any desire to be."

"Then you're throwing an old-fashioned fit?" Her mother promenaded about the room, inspecting the simple furnishings and spare decor with roving fingertips and inquisitive eyes. She looked over everything as if seeing the room for the first time.

"You could say that." Elysia flopped back onto the bed. She had no intention of entertaining her mother when her own world had disintegrated before her eyes.

"Good for you, Elysia." Daria grinned. "You're usually much too serious. In all the years you worked like a peasant to support Robin and me, I never once saw you cry."

Elysia focused on the wooden beams in the ceiling. She didn't wish to discuss the hard times. They had survived. Prospered, even.

"I haven't seen this chamber in ages." Daria smoothed one of the tapestries.

"Because you don't supervise the care of your keep, Mother. I've never known you to venture far from your rooms or the hall." Rolling onto her belly, Elysia plucked at the elaborate coverlet on the guest bed, one she had sewn as a girl. The embroidered pattern depicted a flower garden with a tall fruit tree in the center. Elysia recalled spending painstaking hours completing the design by candlelight. There had never been enough time in the day for all the things that needed doing.

"Yet my home always looks lovely." Daria smiled in spite of Elysia's obvious dark mood.

"You've always had someone else to take care of things."

"Like you, you mean." Daria plopped herself beside her daughter. "I suppose I have relied heavily upon you, but it is your own fault for being so damn capable."

"Mother." Elysia frowned at the oath as much as the sentiment.

"You think I cared what the guest bedchamber looked like all those years we struggled to survive?" Palming Elysia's cheek with her hand, she held her daughter's gaze. "I am not the sort of woman to fret over trifles. I could never understand all the chores you forced yourself to accomplish, day in and day out. To what end? I only wanted us to be well fed and happy."

"I wanted our home to be prosperous and secure," Elysia countered. Was it such a silly wish? She had grown accustomed to certain refinements in their keep while her father lived. Elysia never understood why her mother allowed it to deteriorate.

"And as beautiful as your coverlet is, my dear, I would have just as soon let the moths eat the old one to pieces before I lifted my needle a moment longer than I absolutely had to."

"I felt responsible for—"

Daria held up an intrusive hand and completed the thought. "Everyone. And everything. But you bring that upon yourself, Elysia. Truth be told, I think you like the responsibility because it gives you the independence and sense of worth you crave. Recall, sweeting, no one forced you to shoulder the burdens you have."

Regret stinging her eyes, Elysia wondered how she could go for eighteen years of her life without crying and then turn into a waterfall over the course of a few moons. "I know."

"'Tis why you struggle so hard against marriage." Daria released her hand and stood to look out over the balcony onto the western courtyard. "You cannot relinquish your freedom."

"Nay." Elysia joined her in the small terrace. "That is not it. Not only did Conon fail in his promise to halt the tournament, he used it as a way to win me." Although, even as she said it, she knew that's not what bothered her. She could forgive his deception, as she had not been honest with him, either, in claiming widowhood.

What niggled more was a fear that Conon had only wed her out of a misplaced sense of duty.

She stared out over the courtyard in the falling darkness. Fires were lit all around the marketplace and tournament tents, which still rang with activity. All of the contestants indulged in a night of whores and drink now that the contest was over.

"He saved you from a wicked fate at Sir Huntley's hands."

"Aye. Perhaps that is why he did it." The notion depressed her. Conon was so honorable, he probably competed in the tournament just to ensure she would be safe. She ducked back into the chamber to light the torches and shore up emotions threatening to break free.

"Do you love him?" Daria's voice startled her.

Slamming the torch in the wall sconce, Elysia spun to face her. "How could I love him after what he has done?"

"Those we love have the power to hurt us most." Daria smoothed her daughter's hair in a gesture of maternal affection. "What about before today?"

"I had come to trust him. He saved me from Huntley." She did not mention Conon's kisses. They only muddled the picture.

Sighing, Daria paced the room with slow, measured steps. "I will have to take matters into my own hands."

"What?" Elysia's nerves fluttered and jumped.

"I will set things right, my dear, just you wait and see." With a flounce, she sidestepped her daughter and headed for the chamber door.

"Oh, no you don't." Elysia hurried to plant herself between Daria and the exit. "You're not going anywhere until you tell me just what you have in mind."

"You won't like it." A wicked smile spread across her mother's face.

"I'm certain I won't, but you must share it with me anyway."

"I'm going to see the earl myself, Elysia, and I will show you how a woman goes about getting what she wants in this world." Daria crossed her arms and stood as tall as her slight frame would allow.

"And just how is that?" A tic pulsed in Elysia's eye as her mother's plan washed over her.

"By appealing to men's sensitivity, which they've all but forgotten they possess until a clever woman reminds them." She lifted her chin in self-defense. "You think I am not as sharp as you, Elysia, but you will see your mother is not as dull witted as you thought. I may not know much about running a trade, but I know a great deal about human nature."

"My God, Mother. Arundel is in France. You cannot travel abroad by yourself."

"I will travel in disguise." Perhaps she heard Elysia's scoff, for she hastened to continue. "And I will take Eadred."

"You'll get him killed, too!" Elysia panicked. Why would her mother do something so drastic now, when she had been so complacent about her fate at Oliver's hands when Elysia had first returned to Nevering? "You can't go. I won't let you."

"I am stuck in a far more miserable marriage than you will make, Elysia, and I plan to extract myself without delay. We have suffered enough for Arundel's lack of attention, and I plan to do something about it." She turned to grasp the doorknob. "With the earl's help, there's a chance I could still get an annulment. So could you, for that matter."

"Wait." Elysia held the door closed with her hand. Her eye still pulsed with the tic, and now fear pounded through her, too. An annulment? *Mon Dieu,* did she even want one?

Daria Rougemont Westmoor had never been an overly ambitious woman, but once she set her mind to do something, Elysia knew it was virtually impossible to keep her from it. She might as well try to avert as much danger as possible. Someone had to be practical.

"Please. How can I help?"

"I'll go right after your wedding." Warming to her idea, Daria chewed her lip thoughtfully. "Just tell Oliver I'm sick again. Do whatever you have to do to keep him from discovering I've escaped. Even a day or two will get me far enough away where it won't matter."

Elysia wanted to cry and hang on her mother's skirt, but she took a deep breath instead. "Don't take Eadred— He's a mere child." *Barely eight years old.* "Bring one of the knights in training. Gryffyth, mayhap. The two of you will look like young knights on an adventure and he can fight for you if necessary."

"Done. Anything else?" The words were a challenge, daring Elysia to stop her.

"Please do not do it for my sake."

"I owe you the world, Elysia, but I am not doing it just for you." The green eyes that so often reminded Elysia of a child's looked sage and wise for a moment. "My time with Leon made me realize I don't want to waste away as Oliver's bride. I want a chance at happiness."

The desperation in her mother's eyes told Elysia just how much Daria regretted Leon de Grace's departure.

"It is Conon's fault he left, you know."

Daria shrugged with studied carelessness. "No matter. Though I've always been curious about those French men."

Her throaty laugh flustered Elysia who merely scowled at her mother's impertinence.

"What? They are reputed to be fabulous lovers, you know."

Perhaps because Elysia's own thoughts had trod down a similar path in recent weeks, she could not jest about the subject. Instead she found herself wondering when she could seek out Conon and speak to him about their impending marriage. She could not afford to share his bed until she confided the truth of her first wedding night.

"Be careful." Elysia hugged Daria, squeezing her eyes shut tight against the flood of childhood memories that assailed her—the scent of lemon verbena, the little hurts made better by a gentle embrace.

"Do not worry, Elysia." She smiled, an astounding grin that had made Daria the most sought-after woman in all of southern England when Lord Rougemont snatched her up twenty years ago.

Still Elysia held the door. "If Arundel will not champion your cause, Mother, come to Vannes."

"And risk running into Leon de Grace? No thank you."

"I mean it. You would be safe from Oliver there. You always have a home with me."

"Thank you." Daria kissed her. "I will keep the offer in mind."

"If I do not get to speak to you in private before you go, Godspeed, Mother. Good luck."

"Watch and learn, Elysia." Her mother winked. "Your mother has not forgotten how to handle a man."

Daria disappeared into the corridor, leaving Elysia to worry and wonder if she should have offered to ride with her mother. Yet she knew without question that if she disappeared from Nevering, Conon would find her. Oliver Westmoor, on the other hand, could hardly bestir himself from his daily self-indulgences to exercise his knights in the practice yard, so he did not seem likely to ride all over the countryside in pursuit of his wife.

Still, the notion of her mother on the road upset her. Too worried and restless to seek her bed, Elysia vowed to look for Conon and confront him about their imminent nuptials. Although, thinking back on his arrogant means of winning her hand, perhaps she should not be so quick to smooth over matters between them to facilitate Conon's plans. If she learned he had won her hand merely as a matter of honor—or worse, out of a sense of duty—she would gladly accompany her mother to France, consequences be damned.

Elysia had struggled too long to maintain her independence, only to have it snatched away by a man who saw her as nothing more than an obligation.

Or worse yet, a battle prize.

Chapter Twelve

Elysia and her few attendant women approached Never-ing's small chapel the next morning, the sun shining cheer-ily on the huge throng of guests crowding the door. Only the highest-ranking nobility and family members actually got inside, but that did not deter the merrymaking villagers who sought to see the wedding.

Apparently, news of Elysia's stormy departure from her future husband after the tournament had spread like wild-fire. Now everyone wanted to see if the wedding would be equally good fodder for gossip. But Elysia had a stern talk with herself before leaving her chamber, and resolved there would be no more Daria-style theatrics. If she could not halt the wedding, she would at least proceed with a modi-cum of dignity and good grace.

Dressed in a modest pink surcoat and matching tunic, Elysia did not feel like a bride. Although she usually en-joyed the rare ritual of dressing for a festive occasion, today she did not want to invest too much of herself in the ceremony that would tie her to Conon forever.

Or until he discovered the truth of her maidenly condition.

She'd spent most of the night worrying about the wedding. And the wedding night. She had even gone so far as to search for Conon in the village where revelers lit balefires to honor their tournament champion, but she had found no sign of him and did not have the chance to share her secret. Now she had no choice but to tell him after the ceremony, when they could at last be alone.

"Pardon. *Merci.*" A man's voice drifted through the crowd.

That voice. The laughing good humor. The unmistakable accent. It could only be one man.

"Please, dear lady," he pleaded with an anonymous woman in the crowd. "I must get to the chapel to wed my bride."

Surely Conon wouldn't just be arriving *now* to his own wedding? He could not be so relaxed and at ease when her heart beat so fiercely she feared the whole assembly would hear.

"I am not too late." He carried a small cluster of wildflowers in his hand, a riot of color next to his spare black hauberk and surcoat. With a flourish, he presented them to her. "For you, *chère demoiselle.*"

He spoke more to the eager-eared crowd than to her. As she plucked the offering from his hand, he bowed low. When he arose, she expected a pretty speech for the benefit of the gossip-hungry attendants, but he merely looked her in the eye. In the soul.

What he saw there must have silenced any witty rejoinder he would have made, for he settled for a chaste kiss on her other hand, then stalked into the nave.

"He adores our lady!" shouted one of the village women. "See how he plays the gallant for her?"

The sea of well-wishers crowded close, won over by Conon's charm like a flock of swooning women. They did not know the deceit behind those incredibly blue eyes. She needed substance behind pretty words. Why then did her heart race like an overrun mare's?

The midday bell tolled as the chapel doors creaked open for Elysia. She was probably the only unwilling bride in history to show up early for her wedding.

Cursing her rigid punctuality as much as Conon's carefree late arrival, she stepped into the nave. Dark gloom descended upon her, dispelled at long intervals by narrow panes of colored glass. Behind her, the heavy chapel doors fell shut and the exclamations and joyous shouts of the outdoor attendees grew muffled.

Within three moons of her first husband's death, she was a bride once again. Only now, the man beside the priest was no aging lecherous drunk. This time, Conon waited for her.

She watched him through the screen of her lashes as she walked to him. Young, strong, handsome—Conon epitomized every maiden's dreams. Garbed all in black, he looked more somber than usual. Truly, his whole appearance lacked its usual merriment. His eyes grew dark sapphire in the dim light.

Reaching his side, she paused. He lifted her hand to cradle it between his own, and Elysia's heart caught in her throat.

No. As the priest began his words of welcome and blessing, Elysia promised herself she would not be swayed by Conon's touch. He had only wed her out of a sense of duty.

She would ignore that tremor that passed through her at the sweep of his thumb over the back of her hand.

"In nomine Patris…"

Under the continuous current of Latin, Elysia noted that the summer months had altered Conon. He looked harder, if such a thing were possible. More determined. Stronger.

The planes of his face were more sharp and well-defined. His skin reflected the warmth of endless days spent in the sun's rays. His mouth lacked his perpetual grin.

Not that she would be affected for a moment by his touch or his physical beauty. Conon just happened to be the kind of man that drew a woman's eye and trifled with her heart.

She tried to listen to the mass, but Conon turned over her captive hand and now stroked the palm with subtle but insistent pressure. The warmth started in the region of her heart and soon suffused her belly and limbs. A wave of heat spread through her cheeks but it constituted more than a simple reaction of embarrassment. This flushed warmth had everything to do with the night he kissed her on the kitchen bench outside the keep and her body teetered on the verge of something glorious.

Elysia heard Conon acquiesce to the marriage somewhere in the back of her mind. Her real attention remained on that thumb and her determination not to give in to the sensual power he wielded over her so effortlessly.

"And do you, Elysia Theresa Rougemont St. Simeon promise to…"

Conon watched her now. Her skin tingled with the weight of his gaze before she even met his eyes.

He whispered to her in the silence that fell, though Elysia couldn't be sure of his words until he repeated them.

"Say yes."

Her mother's unmistakable giggle somewhere behind them brought her to her senses.

"Yes," Elysia snapped, vaguely annoyed with herself. "I—um—do."

And then the smile came.

Brilliant as the sun on a May morn, Conon's grin softened his features, calling to Elysia's mind the man she thought he was before he left for France.

Her words obviously pleased him.

Warring with herself throughout the rest of the ceremony, Elysia did not hear a word until the priest instructed Conon to kiss her. Of course, it was her wedding day. She owed her husband a kiss. Too bad a kiss would surely steal her will.

Lifting her hands up in an awkward denial and a plea for mercy, she found her fingers resting on his broad shoulders. If Conon saw confusion in her eyes, he ignored it.

His arms went around her in a fierce embrace, reminding her this was the knight who battled a field of the best warriors to wed her. The strength in his arms crushed her against him, while his lips took hold of hers in an act of definitive possession.

Heat coursed through her. Elysia's head swam with the heady delight of his lips upon hers. Her hands, captured between them in his onslaught, relaxed and fell in limp surrender.

"You will not be sorry." His gaze held her for a moment after his lips departed.

No! She stepped back out of his grasp and nearly lost her balance. She could not allow herself to care for a man who would never return her affection.

The chapel doors were flung wide and daylight flooded the dark sanctuary. Conon steered her up the aisle and into the sea of people tossing flowers and seeds. Everyone shouted their wishes for a long and fruitful marriage.

Fruitful. That was all Conon cared about.

Tears stung Elysia's eyes.

"It is not that bad, Elysia," Conon whispered as he escorted her over the lawn to where the wedding feast waited.

Plucking a flower from the bunch she still clasped in nervous fingers, he tucked the blossom into the narrow circlet about her head. "I have more surprises in store for you."

"I only hope you are not disappointed with what you have wrought." She kept her voice low in deference to their guests. Seating herself on the trestle Conon pointed out, she settled her skirts around her. "After all, you have paid a high price to win me, Conon. Are you sure marriage to an independent woman will be worth it?"

She tried not to notice his furrowed brow as she spoke. He seemed genuinely concerned for her happiness, but never once had he offered his heart. Would he entertain himself with lonely widows while Elysia slept alone? She did not forget his preference for experienced women.

A sumptuous banquet had been prepared for the wedding feast. Around them, musicians played joyful songs on every manner of harp and lute. Villagers crowded the wine servers as Oliver bragged to everyone within shouting distance how many casks awaited their consumption.

All the tournament participants, except for John Huntley, remained to share the last day of revelry with the new couple. The merchants, the prostitutes, the noble attendants flooded Nevering's lawn to eat and drink their fill.

Conon and Elysia sat alone on a high dais, apart from the happy laughter of guests all around them. Elysia searched for a safe topic of conversation to break the cool silence between them.

"Congratulations, my lord." She raised her cup in salute to her husband. "I have not yet complimented you on your tournament prowess."

Conon nodded. "Thank you. I know, however, you would have preferred the tournament have no winner. I am sorry to have disappointed you."

"Nay." She shook her head, toying nervously with the lace about her wrist. "If I had to wed, I would have chosen you above the rest of the field."

The admission had been difficult, but she was rewarded with a gentle touch of his hand over hers. "When you first asked me to intercede for you with Arundel, you told me Oliver had plans to marry you again, against your will." He smoothed her wrinkled sleeve and squeezed her restless fingers. "I thought you merely objected to a man he'd chosen and wanted to halt the wedding. I had no idea you wanted me to call off a whole tournament."

Elysia frowned, thinking back to the day she asked Conon her favor.

"I would have made certain you did not wed another man, Elysia. *That* is the promise I intended to keep." He picked up her hand where it rested in her lap and squeezed it. "I had toyed with the notion of wedding you myself, so it would have been an easy thing to keep my word and prevent you from marrying."

If only he had wanted to wed her because he cared for her. But Elysia knew that was not the case. She had never been a great beauty. She lacked the soft-spoken gentleness men seemed to appreciate in a wife.

Perhaps Conon sensed her doubts because he caught her chin in one hand and commanded her gaze. "It was not until Oliver announced the tournament that I realized the enormity of what you asked. How could I halt an event that I wanted most desperately to win?"

So close he nearly embraced her, Conon's breath warmed her cheek as he spoke in soft, persuasive tones. Elysia willed herself to be strong and was saved from the lure of her husband's eyes when the servers put food on their trenchers for them.

"Oliver's tournament was a way to win you without confronting your stepfather." Conon's countenance grew fierce along with his words. "By my own strength and sword, I have earned you."

Elysia withdrew her hand. "Earned me?"

"*Aye.* Earned. I fought for you fairly and I won." His eyes glittered with a dangerous light, as if challenging her to refute his claim. He lifted one hand to cradle her face. "And it will not be such a bad marriage, Elysia. You cannot say our shared kisses have left you unmoved."

She willed away the shiver that threatened to trip down her spine at his simple touch. He thought of her as little more than a fat tournament purse. "One does not wed for kisses, my lord."

"Then mayhap it had more to do with the way your eyes get dark and hungry when you look at me." Undaunted, his calloused palm trailed down the column of her throat, drawing a gasp from her. "And the way your lips part when I touch you."

Breathing became difficult. She wondered how she could prevent herself from falling in love with her husband when he touched her with magic in his hands. No matter how much she told herself he would break her heart, she found herself leaning toward him, wishing for a taste of him.

"Congratulations, Vannes." Oliver's nasal shout interrupted them. The lord of Nevering approached their table with his arm slung about an overblown noblewoman who was thrice widowed and eager to celebrate her latest status as a free woman.

Elysia pulled away from Conon, disgusted that Oliver could be so openly rude to her mother with his antics.

Conon nodded stiffly. "My thanks, sir, for the extravagance of the day."

"It will not be money tossed to the wind if you join my ranks, Vannes." Oliver released the woman with a little shove to send her on her way, then turned serious eyes to Conon. "I am amassing a powerful force of knights for Nevering."

"And who do you anticipate battling? I have no wish to cross swords with Arundel no matter how grateful I am for my bride."

Elysia admired the way Conon spoke to Sir Oliver with cool authority. Westmoor never failed to rankle her, and it was one pleasant benefit to marriage to be out from under the man's control.

Oliver bent down so as not to be overheard. "And I would not be surprised if you found yourself in closer service to our king under my ranks. With the men we are gathering, I may appeal for my own vassalage directly to His Highness."

Elysia smothered a gasp with a bite of salmon. Oliver's greed knew no bounds. To gain direct service to the king meant Oliver would break his vow of loyalty to Arundel and fight under his own banner.

"Are you saying there are knights here today who are willing to fight for a man who would forswear himself?"

Oliver drew himself up to his full height and glared down at Conon. "There are plenty of men who want to improve their station in the world. I would think you, of all people, would appreciate that."

Conon turned to Elysia and lifted a speculative brow. "But is the loss of honor worth it?"

"You would insult me after I have gifted you so generously?" Westmoor peered down his nose at Elysia.

"Elysia's hand was earned, not given. And while I am grateful to the lady for it, I owe you no more."

Her mother's husband stepped back, smart enough to read Conon's warning. "Then you will excuse me, I presume?" He nodded in a mocking show of respect. "Elysia, dear, have you seen Daria? I seem to have lost track of her."

"I…" In her worries about the wedding, she had forgotten about her mother's plan to leave. "The closeness of the chapel air made her feel faint, sir. I encouraged her to find her bed and rest." Elysia swore the lie must be evident as the nose on her face.

"She is a delicate thing, I suppose. Very well then." Oliver moved away, apparently satisfied with her answer.

Conon observed her with lazy eyes as he sipped his wine. "You do not lie very well."

Her sharp intake of breath gave her away before she could weigh her response.

"You need not explain yourself, Elysia." He waved away any excuse she might have come up with. "It is of no import to me."

They ate in silence then. Or at least, Conon and Elysia remained silent. All around them, revelers ate and drank, sang and danced, leaving the newly married couple to their thoughts.

As Elysia finished her salmon and picked at the wedding cake, she prayed for her mother's safety. Would Daria convince Arundel that Oliver had treachery in mind? Even if Arundel did not intervene in Daria's marriage, there was still a chance he would act upon Elysia's. Politically, her marriage would be more important. Would Arundel contest her union with Conon?

Sneaking surreptitious glances at Conon, Elysia thought the new Count of Vannes did not seem like the kind of man who would give up his wife without a fight.

Yet, after Conon discovered her virginity, mayhap he

would be anxious to be rid of her. How would her husband react once he discovered her treachery in the marriage bed? She had to tell him before it was too late. Once they were alone she would explain her reasons for deceiving him.

Surely Conon would understand why she had allowed the world to think her a widow. Wouldn't he?

The thought filled Elysia with foreboding. Now, more than ever, she dreaded the upcoming night.

Chapter Thirteen

Daria allowed herself a moment to catch her breath, amazed at the ease with which she had escaped. Now that she was two leagues from Nevering, she could make the coast by nightfall, then worry about how to cross the sea in the morning.

Running her hands over sore thighs, Daria noted with wry amusement she wasn't as young as she used to be. The exertion of the ride had taken its toll upon her.

Still, she was exhilarated.

Feeding off the fresh air with more joy than she could remember feeling since her first husband died, Daria reveled in her freedom. She had announced her idea of going to France before she had even thought it out, but as soon as she spoke the words, the plan took root in her mind as if it were the single most important act she would ever accomplish.

Why it was so important to her, she still couldn't say, but adventure beckoned and Daria answered with all the secret longing in her soul.

She had left Gryffyth at home. In fact, despite what she

told Elysia, Daria never intended to ask anyone to accompany her. What if they betrayed her by telling Oliver of his wife's clandestine plan?

The sound of hoofbeats moving toward her broke her reverie, shattering her one moment of happiness.

Could Oliver have already missed her?

Slapping the reins against the horse's back, Daria spurred her mare forward and ran for cover. Having made it this far, having experienced this one shining moment of freedom, she would not go back.

The sheltering trees hovered—so close—but the drum of a horse's gallop grew so thunderous she knew her pursuer must be on her heels.

In the space of a heartbeat, an impossibly strong arm plucked her from her horse. Instantly, she let go of her reins, not wishing to harm the mare because of her folly.

But that did not mean she would go down easily.

"Bastard wretch!" she screamed, clawing and pushing at the immovable muscular limb that secured her effortlessly to her captor.

The wretch slowed his horse.

"Daria."

The man's French accent flowed over her like a caress. Her gaze flew to his face. *Leon.*

Even now his nearness staggered her. Her outward struggle halted, but the inner battle began.

"What are you doing here?" She adopted her best ice-queen posture, refusing to let him see how much he rattled her. How dare he remove her from her horse?

With measured movements, he stopped the huge destrier they rode and vaulted down, then lifted his hands to help her off.

Ignoring him, she slid down on her own, determined to

show him she did not need him. Her short legs did not come anywhere near the ground from the height of the animal's back, however, and she promptly fell into his waiting arms.

To his credit, he did not laugh.

"Well?" She crossed her arms as she pulled herself away from that hard masculine body, as much in an effort to control her reaction to him as an attempt to communicate her anger.

Had he been that insanely handsome the last time she saw him? He stared at her with infinite calm while her heart beat like a rabbit's.

"I was worried when you left the wedding feast."

He spoke with such matter-of-fact distance, Daria wanted to strangle him. Didn't he remember what they shared?

Unaware of her growing ire, he continued, "I could not imagine what—"

"Wait a minute." Her hands moved to her hips. "You were at the wedding?"

He paused. Daria watched the muscle in his jaw flex and tried not to remember how the hard planes of his face felt beneath her fingers.

"Yes."

Of all the unmitigated gall. "You mean you have been *here,* watching the goings-on at Nevering without revealing your presence?"

Nodding, Leon stroked his nervous horse as the beast reacted to Daria's angry tone.

"In other words you've been spying on us?"

"No, Daria—"

Defying the tall man and his immense warhorse, she straightened her spine to her own less-than-intimidating height. "That's Lady Daria, to you, sir."

"Sometimes I find it easier to watch over Conon from a discreet distance," he continued, unperturbed.

She wondered what it would take to rile his exemplary temper.

"When I am not among the crowd I notice unusual things, such as Lady Elysia's mother riding off in the middle of her daughter's wedding feast." Crossing his arms, he looked forbidding as a snowstorm in March and twice as cold.

She did not want to address that one yet. She had not thought of a good excuse, but given time, she would. "But you were not in hiding to spy on me, sir." She moved closer to him, just to see what would happen.

For a moment, he remained perfectly still. Then he inclined his head just a fraction, and Daria could see the subtle flare of his nostrils.

Interesting.

"Just what were you looking for from your secret position today?" She lowered her voice, drawing him closer still to listen.

Dear God, but he was a handsome man. Not so wildly attractive as Conon St. Simeon, but full of bold confidence and maleness. Her fingers itched to comb themselves through the long, coal-black hair he kept tied at his nape. Or test the softness of his perfectly trimmed moustache with a kiss. Tall and lean, he carried himself in a way that conveyed he would be a formidable opponent.

Or mayhap a powerful ally....

"Conon believes Arundel will come to retaliate against Oliver's growing insurrection, and we want to be certain that doesn't happen until Conon is safely away with his new bride." Leon grinned. "On that count, he is most adamant. Lady Elysia is not to be separated from him, no matter what."

The mention of Arundel's name brought to mind Daria's impending mission. If she did not get away from Leon, she would never make the coast tonight.

"So you have been watching for signs of the earl…coming here." Who was she going to see in France if the earl was already on his way to England? She'd never anticipated this.

"What is it?" He moved closer to take her chin in his hand.

"Nothing." Daria flashed him her best smile. "Now that the air is cleared here, I had better retrieve my horse." She whistled to the mare.

Gently, Leon laid a finger over her lips, halting her call. "Nay. I think not."

Heat flooded her limbs at his touch. The man strained her senses. Daria stepped back, hoping she was not too obvious. "Really, sir, it is my daughter's wedding day. I must be heading back—"

"I will escort you."

Of course that wouldn't work. She tried another approach, calling upon her skills as a rather gifted truth-twister. "Well, honestly, I needed a little time to myself today. 'Tis why I came out here alone to begin with." She gave him a soulful look.

"The truth, Daria." Without warning, he stepped closer to stand scarcely a hand span from her.

Her name on his lips nearly turned her inside out. How could she think of a good lie when he did this to her?

"I was—"

He loomed near.

"Yes?" The word was barely a breath across her mouth for a moment before he kissed her. And dear Lord, did he kiss her. Slow and deep and warm until Daria thought she would die of the pleasure wrought by that simple act.

"Please," she sighed, not knowing if she wanted him to let her go or lure her closer.

Stepping between her feet with one of his long legs, Leon pulled her intimately against him. A beam of sharp pleasure coursed through her. Although Oliver Westmoor had stolen a night in her bed after their wedding, his repugnant hands had not come close to truly touching her.

Leon touched her.

Her body. Her heart. Her soul.

Eagerly, her fingers wound themselves into the tie that constrained his hair and pulled it loose. Soft black hair fell over her hands.

"The truth, Daria." Leon whispered the words into her lips. "Where are you going?"

She wanted his kisses, not his conversation. She needed him more than the air she breathed. "France," she muttered impatiently.

The kiss stopped.

Her eyes drifted open, confused, until she saw the look on Leon's face. Warily, her fingers released his hair. She slid back down his body to stand on her own feet.

"What?" Like thunder in the distance, his voice rumbled, low and ominous.

Damn. Daria threw her arms over her head in disgust. "France, all right? I'm going to France, Leon, and there is nothing you can do to stop me." She ruined everything in the space of a heartbeat because Leon de Grace was too tempting by half. Elysia would be so disappointed.

Leon's smile bordered on condescending.

"Don't you dare look at me like that." She pointed her finger in his face. "I will go if I want to, de Grace." She whistled again for the mare, stomping down the short hill toward the trees.

"Oh, no, you don't, lady." Leon grabbed her by the arm and turned her to him. "I want to know what in the name of all that is holy you think you are doing going to France by yourself?"

Pasting her most wicked grin on her face, she lifted her chin. "Mayhap I sought the man who stole my heart and broke faith with me to return to his homeland without telling me."

"No." Leon shook his head. His hair fell about his face since Daria's curious fingers had loosened its tie during their kiss. "You won't torture me out of my quest. I want to know what you were planning to do in France."

Happy she found a place to dig in her heels, Daria had no intention of budging. The faithless liar had run off and left her. Let him squirm for a little while.

"You have no right to hold me, kiss me or otherwise detain me, Leon the Faithless. I am leaving."

"You're serious."

"Very serious." She pivoted on her heel.

"Wait." He did not restrain her, but the desperation that edged his voice halted her. "Bargain with me."

Daria hoped it involved a quick tumble behind the trees. "I'm listening."

"I am going with you."

"Nay."

"I can help you." Silver eyes beckoned her. He looked sincere enough. "No questions asked."

"Really?" A trip with a handsome man who would do her bidding without getting in her way. She would have leaped at the chance if she was not married. Daria had been forced to wed Oliver at knifepoint, but that did not take away the tie that bound her to him. Strangled her.

"You have my word on it, lady."

Daria frowned, having been left high and dry by this man before. How could she believe him so easily?

But she did. If Leon de Grace gave his word, Daria knew he would not break it for anything. His sense of honor was one of the most compelling things about the man. Heaven knew that nobility was completely lacking in her treacherous husband.

And Daria really could use his help if she were to succeed in her mission for Elysia. After all the years Elysia had dedicated to their family, Daria felt she owed her daughter this much.

"It will be a hell of a lot easier for me to get us across the sea than for a woman on her own," Leon urged.

Since when had she ever played it safe? Oliver would probably lock her away for the rest of her days when she returned to Nevering anyway. Why not allow herself a few weeks of freedom before she submitted to whatever cruel punishment he devised?

She twirled a lock of hair in pretend thought. "Will there be any more kissing?"

Elysia's maids giggled and twittered as they fussed over her hair and garments late that night. Other women plumped pillows, sweetened the rushes and lit candles everywhere.

Conon's chamber looked like a shrine to his bed. The mattress was already strewn with flower petals when they arrived after the feast, although the women all swore up and down that none of them had committed that particular romantic deed.

Had Conon arranged for the gesture? The flower petals matched the color assortment of the posies in the small bouquet he gave her at the chapel. He certainly knew how to make a woman weak in the knees. Elysia could not begin to imagine how she could maintain her cool distance tonight, when he came to claim her as his bride. Her only hope was to confess her virginity to him. No doubt, that would quell all romance between them.

"Ow!" Her hair snagged as the brush caught.

"Sorry, my lady." The maid bit her lip in concern. "Do you want any rose oil brushed through it?"

"No, thank you, Belle." She fiddled with the long ribbons on her sheer night rail, wishing she'd found time to speak to Conon before now. "I am just nervous."

"He will be gentle as he would be with a first-time bride, my lady," Belle confided low enough so the others would not overhear. "He knows you had less than a night of experience as a married woman."

"You are not nervous, are you, my dear?" One of the elder maids paused her errands to pat Elysia's shoulder. "My stars, but he is the most gallant man I've ever seen. He will treat you like a queen, I'll wager."

The room overflowed with feminine laughter as Elysia wished her mother could have been here instead. When the door flew open, her attending women scattered like leaves in the north wind, rushing out the door and shushing each other.

"What have you ladies done with my bride?" Conon bellowed the good-natured threat.

Giggles floated back to Elysia's ears from down the corridor as her ladies responded. Her heart caught in her throat now that her husband had arrived along with her opportunity to speak to him. Finally. She would be able to unburden herself of her secret and hope that Conon would understand her silence.

Either way, tonight the truth would be unveiled.

Conon searched the dim room for his bride, disappointed she was not already in bed, where she should be.

That just added one more step to his already lengthy list of things to do before he could consummate his marriage.

She sat stiff and straight near the washstand, hair streaming down her back and over her shoulders like a black waterfall. A gossamer gown floated around the rest of her, revealing more than it concealed through pale-pink silk.

Patience.

Conon drew in one ragged breath after another, doing everything within his power to stay focused on her fair face. Her lips beckoned him, soft and shimmery and rosy in the candlelight.

Deciding those lips were his ticket to torture, he focused on her eyes. Nowhere else. Elysia's eyes.

"You are beautiful." He cursed the growl that seemed to dominate the words. She looked ready to flee.

"Thank you." She toyed with a slender ribbon that remained undone on the sheer shift she wore. Only then did he notice the nervous movements of her fingers on the silky tie.

Nervous? Elysia? Her hesitant glance seemed a far cry from the intrepid countess he knew.

Refusing to allow any fear into their marriage bed, he vowed to make her forget any apprehension she might have. He might not have as much gold to his name as some men, but he had learned a few things about pleasing a woman. In this, he would not fail.

"You are nervous." He crossed the room and knelt before her to see her eye-to-eye. Her soft lavender scent lured him closer, but not half so much as the creamy temptation of her exposed skin. Oh, yes, he would ensure she would not think long enough to be nervous.

"I would like to speak to you, Conon." Her words dissolved away in a sigh as he dipped into the neckline of her night rail to kiss the delicate arch of her collarbone.

"There will be time to talk, but first, I have a surprise for you." Hellfire, what bride thought her husband wished to speak on their wedding night? Still, he did not wish to argue. He would simply find ways to tempt and distract her from her cause.

Her fingers stilled on the ribbon a moment as she met his gaze.

Grinning, he picked up her hand and planted a kiss on her palm before turning to gather up the bed linens—flower petals and all—and a jug of wine.

"What are you doing?" she squeaked, though Conon did not miss the excitement in her voice.

Next he hoisted her up into his arms and cradled her like a child across his chest.

"Conon!" Her cheeks flushed as he strode toward the door, and he relished the wriggle of her curves as she twisted against him as if to free herself. "Where are you taking me?"

Squeezing her gently, he peered into her wide, dark eyes. "We're going outside to stare up at the stars. I have no intention of taking a frightened woman to my bed, and from the looks of you, sweet *demoiselle,* you were scared to death when I walked in here tonight."

"Truly, we must speak first, and—" She seemed to search for some way to dissuade him, her teeth sinking into her lower lip for one delicious moment. "And I cannot go out-of-doors dressed like this."

Pulling a corner of the bed linens from his shoulder, he flung a length of it over her slender form. "There."

Not giving her any more time for protest—or idle conversation—he pushed the door open with his foot and carried Elysia down the back stairs, through the southern wing and out of the keep.

They passed a maid indoors, and a boy who swept the courtyard, but Conon merely nodded and maintained his pace, as if spiriting off a noblewoman were a common enough occurrence.

Let the people of Nevering talk. He intended to woo his bride as gently as he knew how. Elysia had suffered too much at the hands of her first husband and then in her close call with Huntley for Conon to besmirch their wedding night with clumsy impatience.

He would banish the fear in her eyes and soften her heart just a little with a night of stargazing. Heaven knew, the woman never took the time to indulge in such things on her own.

"Where will we go?" Elysia peeked out of the crook of his arm where she had hidden from the eyes of passersby.

"The night is warm and clear. I thought we would go to the top of the southern hill where there is no water and no bugs." A half moon shimmered through a thin cloud, lighting Conon's way as the keep grew small in the distance.

The chirping, buzzing silence of a summer night surrounded them in welcome.

"The view is fine there." Her approval, though typically understated, pleased him. "And then we must speak about the wedding—"

"Shh." He climbed a narrow path that wound around the profusion of flowers and sought for any topic except their wedding. Or their wedding night. "Tell me, did you ever take midnight treks to the southern hill as a girl?"

"Nay." Her mouth hardened in a flat line of disapproval. "It was a favored pastime of my brother's."

Reaching his intended destination, he set Elysia on the

soft grass, then laid out the thick linens like carpet. Flower petals flew in every direction.

He plunked himself down and opened the jug of wine. Holding it out as an offering, he patted the place beside him. "Come here."

She looked like a pagan Venus in the moonlight, every inch of her a testament to grace and beauty. A hint of creamy skin tantalized him above the neckline of her night rail. With tremulous steps, she joined him, taking the jug and raising it to those perfect lips.

Feeling his body respond with painstaking urgency, Conon focused on her eyes.

When that didn't help, he busied himself removing the long, formal surcoat he wore for their wedding and balling it up into a prop for his head. Stargazing looked like a good idea, at least until he gained some control of himself. "How did your brother die, *chère?*"

She tensed for a moment before she replied. "In battle." She sighed, a soft, resigned sound that told Conon she was not completely ill at ease with him now. Perhaps he had succeeded in distracting her. "He was completely unsuited to be a knight. My mother and I did not have the money to have him fostered and there was no one here to train him." She chewed her lip thoughtfully, then shook her head. "Rather, there were other knights here for him to train with, but Robin thought that beneath him. He quite resented our lack of wealth after my father died."

Conon thought of his own childhood—impoverished and lacking the opportunities that fostering allowed a young nobleman. Eadred would fare no better if Conon did not think of some place more suitable than Nevering to send the boy.

His children would not suffer the same fate. The fruit of Elysia's womb would be well cared for. Cherished.

The bitterness in Elysia's tone as she spoke of her brother surprised him. "You two were not close?"

"Robin deemed my penchant for real labor disgusting. I believe he saw me as belonging to the peasant class but for an accident of birth." She lifted the jug again, then settled down beside Conon, cushioning her head on her arm. "Earning money was beneath Robin, though he quickly spent every farthing Mother gave him."

Conon moved his surcoat pillow under her head to share it with her. Elysia looked wary, but dutifully laid her head beside his. Strands of brown velvet caressed his cheek. How easy it would be to grow accustomed to this familiarity with her.

"Conon, I must speak with you about our—"

"My family could not afford me, either," Conon interrupted, unaccustomed to sharing his humble upbringing with anyone, but determined to share a bit of himself with her tonight. "I know the hardship of a noble life without the necessary accoutrements to support it."

Frowning, she settled herself deeper into the blankets, her arm propped beneath her head where she lay.

"But you would never rely on others to fill your coffers as my brother did. To this day, you do not throw money away, but pinch excess candles to save it." She pointed to his chest with her hand. "Look at how hard you have worked to establish yourself. You must be a tremendously accomplished knight to beat back the whole field at Oliver's tournament, and—"

She stopped herself, wide-eyed, as if embarrassed to reveal any admiration of him.

He could not wipe the grin from his face, even if it would have soothed her embarrassment. Few people in his life had ever found him praiseworthy. Furthermore, positive words coming from Elysia were worth more to him than gold. She was not the kind of woman to waste compliments that were not deserved.

"Pray, do not stop on my account." He could not keep the husky note from his voice as his hands skimmed the soft skin of her shoulder. Hadn't he exhibited the patience of a saint to wait this long to have her? He meant to enjoy his wedding night. Enjoy Elysia.

The time for talking was over.

She flushed crimson in the moonlight, her skin suffusing with warmth he couldn't wait to feel for himself. "I only mean to say, you are *nothing* like my brother."

Conon pulled her closer. The rush of male pride she instigated made his hands greedy for her. Stroking her pink cheek, he whispered across the narrow, heated space that separated them. "*Mon Dieu,* I thank Heaven you do not think of me in a brotherly way."

Chapter Fourteen

Elysia held her breath, wondering if Conon would close that last gap between them. Truth be told, she wanted him to.

Memories of another eve of stargazing assailed her. The sweet fire he sparked in her that night on the kitchen bench had abated in his absence, but it flamed bright with naught but a whispered word, a warm look from him.

In the mesmerizing thrall of that one look, she forgot her reasons for resenting him, her need to speak with him. The sultry summer night conspired to woo her, though it was not responsible for this unsettling heat within her.

His lips grazed hers with no more force than a butterfly's wing, teasing her with her own want, enticing her to come closer and discover the taste of this man who appealed to her in so many ways.

"You must know I would not hurt you." His voice curled around her in the darkness, melting her heart and softening her insides.

"Aye."

He kissed her again, nipping at her lower lip before soothing the place with a sweep of his tongue. He skimmed a touch along her waist, hard enough to stir her need, but not nearly enough to please her. The night air cooled her swollen lips, reminding her of the unfulfilled ache she experienced deep inside whenever he touched her. He was so different than Jacques. So different from any man she had ever known in that he could be unspeakably gentle. Tender. She did not know that a warrior who had long served as a mercenary knight would appreciate such a description, but she knew no other way to express the way Conon treated her.

Even now, on his wedding night, he took care to sift his fingers through her hair lightly, to nudge her silken gown from her shoulder slowly. He planted a kiss there, right in the hollow beneath her collarbone. An answering shiver danced through her, awakening her to pleasures she could not fully imagine. Oh, but she had faith Conon would be able to deliver them. Any man who could call up such a shiver with only a brush of his lips on her shoulder could surely make her see more stars behind her eyelids than she'd ever find in the late-summer sky.

"Conon." She hoped her voice conveyed the longing of her body and soul, because she was powerless to put her need into words. "Please."

He emitted a hungry growl as he covered her body with his, apparently understanding the gist of her plea. And though his lips met hers gently once more, his tongue soon sought entrance into her mouth, tasting and teasing in equal parts.

Tentatively, she mimicked his movements, and was rewarded by a deepening of his kiss, a slow, sweet fusion that left her clinging to him with both arms. The heavy weight of him pleased her, even though he levered himself above her enough to ensure she did not bear the full brunt of his taut muscles and strong frame. His thighs brushed hers, his one hip grazing hers enough that she could feel the heat of him through her shift. Her own hips twitched in response, eager for more of this. Of him.

He whispered incoherent endearments and heaven knows what else in her ear; a low catch in his throat made Elysia all the more eager for the fulfillment his kisses promised.

Clutching handfuls of his tunic, she could not be still under his touch. She gloried in the moment he pulled the tunic over his head, exposing his body to her view.

Pulling him back down to her, she marveled at the hard expanse of his lightly furred chest against her breasts. The prick of the hair through her sheer silk gown tormented her, adding to the increasing ache that pooled inside her.

As his mouth moved lower to the neck of her night rail, Elysia arched her back in blatant offer.

Then the kisses stopped.

Dismayed, Elysia looked down at his golden-blond head to find him in serious contemplation of her breasts through the silk. Her nipples tightened even further at his scrutiny.

"Conon?" She whispered his name uncertainly.

"Yes?" His reply hissed through gritted teeth.

Peeking through her lashes, she spied him unlacing the ribbons on her night rail with his teeth. Laughter bubbled up in her throat.

"What are you doing?"

"Seducing you." His grin was shameless.

All thought of laughter fled as his mouth unerringly sought first one taut peak and then the other. Exquisite pleasure rushed over her in waves, her senses overwhelmed with the liquid warmth that seemed to fill her veins. The blanket beneath her chafed through her thin gown, but the minor discomfort helped anchor her against the sea of hot sensation wrought with a flick of expert tongue; the soft draw of full lips.

Elysia tunneled her fingers through his hair, pulling him closer still. Wrapping herself tightly around him, her restless hips rocked against his thigh, her hips meeting the hard length of his manhood as he pressed her fully against him. The solid weight of him provided welcome relief from the hunger within her, her body seeming to understand what she needed long before her brain comprehended those wants. She trailed a hand over his back to slide over his hip. So strong.

His head came up as if she pained him. Blue eyes burned into hers.

"Elysia, *chère,* you're killing me."

As if drawn to her lips, his gaze locked upon her mouth. He kissed her again, feasting upon her with undisguised hunger.

Her breasts cooled to the chill of the night air, leaving her body bereft until she felt his hand slide up her thigh to gather the silk of her gown at her waist.

Any lingering fear was cast to the four winds as his touch lingered on her belly then fell to the heated center of her.

Elysia kissed him. His shoulder, his cheek, his chest. With her kisses and her sighs she begged him for nameless pleasures.

She could not stifle the little cry that came when he tested her warmth with his finger. Her thighs squeezed together reflexively, but then the lush wave of feminine response rolled through her, her legs easing apart again. Her breath came in short pants, the sound of it rasping in her throat as she fought for a deeper breath, or even some small sense of self-control as her inhibitions slid away. She wanted this, wanted him with an ache so deep it unsettled her. He touched her until she writhed beneath him and her hands clutched his shoulders in desperate need.

Although he paused only for a moment to divest himself of his braies, Elysia's eyes widened. The moonlight through the trees cast shadows on his form, but what she spied had naught to do with a trick of the shadowy night.

Conon fell onto the blankets beside her and rolled her on top of him, grinning, "Countess, your praise has done much to please me this day, but not so much as that sweet expression on your face."

Embarrassed, Elysia hid her face in his chest, refusing to meet his eyes. How could he tease her at a time like this?

Squeezing her to him, Conon rolled her once more onto her back and forced her chin up to meet his eyes.

"Elysia, I adore you."

Her heart fluttered with hope. With an answering exclamation. Could he harbor some feeling for her besides a sense of duty? "I—"

He kissed her silent. "Give yourself to me. I want all of you now."

With a tentative nudge, Conon sought to take her—rid her of the maidenhood that clung to her long after her first marriage.

A wave of panic flooded through her, reminding her of the discussion they needed to have, chilling her former rapture.

She did not want to be caught in a lie of her own. How could she have forgotten her own deception, perpetuated the night her first husband died? She and Conon were getting along so well. More than anything, she wanted another chance to tell him before it was too late. "Wait, Conon—" Her ill-timed words coincided with his sudden movement.

One hard stroke and he broke the maiden barrier to sheathe himself within her.

Pain seared her heart.

Conon's eyes went wide with clear disillusionment. He stared down at her utterly still. Stunned.

"Conon, I—"

He kissed her savagely. Angrily.

And he drove into her with a force that pained her heart far more than her innocence. In an instant, he howled a heathen cry to the heavens and it was over.

Elysia felt the warmth of him inside her long after he slid from her body to leave her cold and shivering in the sultry night air.

Pulling one of the blankets around her, heart catching as the soft flower petals cascaded around her body, she waited for Conon to say something.

Anything.

The silence hammered through her with more angry accusations than Conon could have ever expressed. Her own guilt—her deep sense of responsibility for her deception—lashed and upbraided her with every barbed cruelty her morality could devise.

Conon dressed. Slowly and deliberately. Elysia watched him, waiting for his pronouncement of her sins.

"You lied." It was not an accusation, but a statement of fact.

"Only by omission, I…" Elysia faltered, recalling what an excuse maker her brother had been. She hated excuses. "I'm sorry." Inadequate though the simple utterance might be, it was more than Conon had offered her for his own deceit.

His eyes were upon her. Their utter condemnation weighed on her shoulders more heavily than any burden she had borne in all the years she toiled to build the most successful linen trade in England.

"You purposely allowed the world to think you consummated your marriage to Uncle Jacques, even going so far as staying at Vannes an extended fortnight just in case you were with child."

That hadn't been her idea. "I wanted to tell the earl the truth the very night it happened. But Huntley refused to let me see him."

He swiped a tired hand through his hair. "You could have told *me,* Elysia. I came to your chamber that night."

She clutched the fabric of the coverlet more tightly around her. Conon had a way of making her feel completely exposed. "I did not feel comfortable speaking of such intimate things with you." Her face burned.

"Yet you related the other events of your wedding night to me." His jaw flexed in hard angles. "You told me he bade you undress and—"

"And every bit of it was true," Elysia flung back, unwilling to relive the night of the count's death. Her whole world seemed to have been turned on its ear from that day forward. Maybe she had been ill-advised to hide the truth of the wedding night, but Heaven knew, she had been a bit overwrought. "I just hadn't completed my story when your mistress pranced in to scream down the keep. By the time the whole wedding party arrived in our chamber, I felt uncomfortable relating the sordid details."

Conon shook his head. "What of the blood, Elysia? You obviously didn't feel 'uncomfortable' pricking your own finger to stain your bridal sheets."

"Nay." Her mouth fell open in mute disbelief. He believed that? "It just so happens your oafish uncle stabbed me in the thigh with his eating knife. I never said the blood was from…"

She did not bother to complete her thought. From the

expression on Conon's face, it was obvious he would not be convinced.

"Nay, you never did lie outright, did you? You just allowed everyone to assume your wedding night had been consummated. And for what?" His icy blue eyes seemed to coax an answering chill in Elysia. "So that you might retain your precious independence and fend off the eager suitors for another few months. Widowhood has distinct advantages, doesn't it?"

Elysia could think of nothing to say. Conon made her motives sound petty, but she could not argue the truth of his words. Still, she wondered why he found her deception about widowhood so much more damning than the way he had deceived her into marriage.

"But I guess I did not seek your hand for your trustworthiness." Conon laughed without mirth.

The barb stung, making a mockery of the tender feelings Elysia had experienced that eve. "Nay, my lord. I understand you only wed me for my womb."

He stiffened as her jab apparently found its mark, as well. "No, Elysia. I wed you to protect you." He picked up the jug of wine and took a long swig.

Elysia understood why he was the country's most celebrated knight as his final blow summarily defeated her. Shame flooded her to think he had, in his own high-handed way, only tried to safeguard her by giving her his name. And she had repaid him with her girlish anger and deceit for his trouble.

The rapidly cooling night air wrapped her in its chilly embrace, but it did not come close to the deep freeze of Conon's distance from her. Elysia vowed to make it up to him somehow. If there was one thing Elysia knew how to do, it was to make herself useful.

Although she might never feel the warmth of his ten-

derness again, she would at least have the comfort of knowing she would take naught from him. She was nothing if
not self-sufficient.

"I will haul your sorry carcass before the king, if I have
to, Oliver, but by the Blessed Virgin, I will not go home
empty-handed." Conon's angry voice echoed through the
courtyard and up to Elysia's balcony.

The yelling woke her from a sound sleep, although
bright daylight already seeped in through the heavy window coverings. She must have overslept after her wedding night.

"And King Edward will be in such a hurry to help a
Frenchman, I've no doubt." Oliver's sarcasm was thick
and evident even two floors away.

She crept from her bed, pulling the rumpled and dew-
damp blanket from the chair where she'd flung it the previous night. Bits of leaves and flower petals littered the
floor in her wake.

Her body protested the movement. Sore from the unaccustomed activity of the night before, Elysia's aching legs
reminded her of the deeper pain in her heart.

"He is eager enough to marry his English heiresses to
French noblemen of Brittany, sir. He may indeed be anxious to see the Count of Vannes well pleased."

Elysia looked down from her balcony to where the men
stood. Conon, all golden and muscular, dominated the
courtyard in his wrath. Oliver, wiry and reed thin, faced
him with his usual bevy of constant hangers-on and power-
hungry young knights. He probably could not encounter
the avenging angel before him single-handedly.

Oliver shrugged lazy shoulders. "Then ask the king
about it, my lord. I have no idea what your wayward wife

has done with her bridal portion. I have not seen a farthing of it since she arrived."

Perhaps she moved then, because Conon chose that moment to look up at her window.

Elysia froze. Embarrassed to be caught eavesdropping, she felt the heat blaze in her cheeks. All eyes in the courtyard turned to her as Conon stared upward in silence.

Pride forced her to stand there and face them.

"Good morning, Countess," Oliver called up amiably, then turned his attention back to Conon. "Really, my lord, why not ask your wife where the money went? She is the only one who can retrieve it for you."

Amid muffled titters, Oliver's group moved out of the courtyard and down toward the marketplace, where the tents and carts were being taken down and packed for moving to the next fair or tournament.

Still Conon remained, scowling up at her.

Elysia hated calling down to him like a shrew, but what choice did she have? If he would not converse with her at a closer distance, she had no option. "I thought you were going to inquire after the bridal portion at the boat before you went to France, my lord." Elysia crossed her arms, feeling exposed and unkempt with her bed-rumpled hair falling about her shoulders.

Conon crossed his arms in a reflective image of her. He rocked back on his heels and cocked his head to one side. "Oddly enough, they told me the inheritance had already been sent to its rightful owner."

"That is all?" Elysia began to worry, just a little. What if her wealth had been stolen or lost? By rights, Conon deserved it as part of their marriage.

"*Aye, chère.*" He smiled. A false, mocking sort of smile.

Odd how even his sarcasm and anger did not detract from his appeal.

Elysia tried not to think about the things he did to her last night that had left her breathless and wanting.

"What more did I need to know?" he continued. "You have it, and now I would know where you have secreted it."

Dear God. "No one has delivered anything to Nevering in your absence." He would think she really *had* hidden away the dower money.

The smile slid from his lips, replaced by a stony glare. "So that is the way of it, wife? You would go so far as to cheat me of your dower?"

Their animated conversation attracted attention. Gossipmongers flocked to the courtyard, busying themselves with any silly chore to hear the nature of the newlyweds' quarrel.

Realizing argument proved futile, Elysia lifted her chin and peered down at him with cool detachment. Or at least she hoped she did. "I have cheated you of nothing, sir. You have no one to blame but yourself if you could not keep track of the bridal portion until it arrived safely at my gates. If I were you, I would waste no more time beginning the search."

She swept from the balcony in her trailing blanket with the flourish of a queen. Mother would be proud of her daughter's newfound affinity for theatrics. Too bad they gave Elysia no pleasure at all.

Sighing, she plunked back down onto her bed and stared at the ceiling. Conon's face still appeared before her eyes, as it had all last night in her dreams.

Like a dangerous poison in her blood, the man infected her. He did not trust her now—believed the very worst of her by thinking she would be so petty as to hide her bridal portion from him. She resented his reasons for marrying her, and she feared he would try to dominate and control her.

Yet, she did not hate him.

Conon would forever be her savior for halting John Huntley's attack on the boat. And marriage to Conon saved her from a repeat performance with Huntley as his legally wedded wife, had he won the tournament.

But like every other man in her life, Conon St. Simeon had let her down. This time the knowledge hurt more, somehow.

Elysia had remained on the southern hill into the wee hours of the morning after her wedding-night debacle. Hours of stargazing forced her to think about her marriage and what lay ahead for her as the Countess of Vannes. Again.

She would accept her fate until she heard from her mother. Maybe Daria would have good news from the earl, and Elysia would be able to annul her marriage to Conon when Mother annulled hers to Oliver. Then everything in her life could go back to the same way it used to be, before she met Conon or went to France. Much as the idea saddened her, she knew it would be for the best.

Elysia dressed slowly, resolved to face Conon with polite reserve and distance today. She would clear her mind with a brisk walk to the marketplace to see if she might strike any good bargains with peddlers hoping to pawn off leftover wares.

Fastening her girtle into place and smoothing her skirts, she couldn't shake the niggling doubt in her mind that nothing in her life would ever be the same again.

Conon tossed a rotten apple for as far as the eye could see in the dense orchard near Nevering. The pointlessness of the act pleased him. He picked up another apple and threw, following its progression above and beyond the trees.

Where the hell was Leon when Conon needed him?

Leon's cool voice of reason would be welcome now that Conon found himself in the most humiliating position of his life. Heaven knew, this did not constitute Conon's first brush with ignominious circumstances. Inheriting nothing from his father had devastated him. That memory deserved an apple tossed in its honor.

Arcing his arm, Conon heaved it with all his strength.

Showing up for his first battle as a mere foot soldier so he could win a dead man's horse and armor to become a knight ranked among the low points of his life. That called for two pieces of flying fruit at least. Conon's arm throbbed with satisfying soreness.

Enduring taunts of all kinds at the French court when he arrived, knowing absolutely nothing of decorous manners or speech didn't bode well, either.

But the latest humiliation of his marriage took the prize for the most abjectly humbling. After a lifetime of striving to achieve some status in the world, he had been duped by a gorgeous set of wide brown eyes.

Placing a new twist on his game, Conon dropped a rotten apple and kicked it. The brown fruit smashed to bits in the air before the core sailed even higher than those he had thrown.

The situation galled him.

At least if Leon would make his presence known, Conon would have someone to fight with. He itched for a good fight.

Or a good roll in the sheets with his treacherous wife.

Plucking up yet another apple, Conon swore as his thumb smashed through the outer skin in his tense grip. Last night did not begin to cure his hunger for Elysia.

Mayhap he was ten times a fool to want her, but the small taste of passion he extracted from her yesterday only whet his appetite for more.

It amazed him how easily she came to him. He expected more cold resistance from his reserved countess, but her sensual urges seemed to run as fast and furious as his own. When he'd hovered over her last night, ready to claim her, he'd congratulated himself on his incredible good fortune to find such depth of passion in practical, efficient Elysia.

Then all hell had broken loose.

His world had crumbled around his ears when he breached her maidenhood. For one shimmering instant, he'd gloried in that barrier's presence in a primal, male way. But just as quickly, his rational mind realized the truth of his wife's deception.

And at that moment a hope he had not even realized he had been harboring was crushed. It seemed that despite Elysia's bristly exterior and cool manner, Conon had nurtured a wish that their friendship would lead to a happy marriage and a close family. All his life, he had wanted that kind of security for himself—the true sense of home and belonging he had only experienced with his *grandmère* as a small child.

But Elysia's perfidy had proven him a fool. She would never forsake her independence and devote herself to a family.

The sounds of the marketplace closing down drifted on a breeze through the orchard. Everyone else was packing to leave the tournament. Tromping through the wooded area, he headed in the direction of the activity.

Conon couldn't wait to leave Nevering. At Vannes he would put plenty of space between himself and Elysia. She could start a linen business in France and earn the blasted money that seemed to please her.

He couldn't believe she had hidden her bridal portion from him. Did she value her independence so greatly that she would set it aside for herself? It seemed a foolish thing to do, because if anything happened to Conon, the dower wealth would revert to her anyhow.

So just in case Oliver hid the money and not Elysia, Conon had decided he would turn Nevering upside down looking for it before he took his bride to France. If he could not find it, then he would know Elysia had given it to Lady Daria to steal away. Why else would Daria disappear right after their wedding?

If such were the case, Conon planned to make life a trial for his new bride. Setting aside his dark thoughts, Conon stepped through the last thicket around the orchard and arrived at the marketplace. People still milled around in large groups, chattering and trading goods before they went their separate ways.

"Conon, *mon amour,* is that you?" The heavily accented English caught his attention amidst the rumble of the crowd. A stunning woman beckoned him, her voluptuous curves shown off to their best advantage in a slim-cut, split-side surcoat. Her eyes danced with a mischievous light.

"Marguerite." He was in no mood for the frivolous widow but Conon strode to her side and kissed her chastely upon the mouth. Though he took no pleasure in the kiss, he could not deny that attention from her soothed his wounded pride just a little.

"I heard you won the tournament, my love, but I have had one of my wrenching headaches these last two days and missed all the fun. It is a pleasure to see you." She wrapped herself around his arm. Her gaze glided over his body with unconcealed longing.

"But where is your escort?" Conon searched the marketplace for a noble lord, not in the mood to placate her or indulge her feminine wiles today. "Surely you did not walk down here by yourself."

"Nay. I am here with Sir Rene." She waved a dismissive hand in reference to the respected knight. "He is kind to take me traveling with him, but he is naught compared to you, darling." She squeezed Conon's arm in affectionate reassurance. "I have missed you since your uncle's wedding."

He noticed she did not bother to offer her condolences. She had left Vannes in a huff the night he dismissed her from Elysia's bedchamber. Typical Marguerite. The thought made him appreciate the cool reason of his wife.

They reached a secluded end of the marketplace through no deliberate action of Conon's. With covert nonchalance, Marguerite peered around the fair. As if satisfied with what she saw, she turned eagerly to Conon.

He did not mean to take her in his arms.

Yet she held one arm captive from when he played the gentleman to escort her through the crowd. Now she used it to wrap around her with a lover's familiarity.

"Can you escape your little bride and come to me tonight?" She leaned into him, her words a breathless whisper.

Conon thought about it. Hard. He was still unsatisfied as hell from his unhappy wedding night. Hadn't he just convinced himself what he really needed was an extended roll in the sheets?

Opportunity wriggled enticingly before his eyes.

Well, sort of enticingly.

Damned if Marguerite's breathy voice didn't leave him longing for another, more imperious one. The weighty breast that pressed insistently against his chest didn't go unnoticed, but Conon yearned to caress the more subtle curves of a certain long and lithe female.

Elysia.

"Conon?" Marguerite's urging called him from his sensual daydream of his wife.

"I…um…" Shifting in her arms, he tried to think of a gallant way to disappoint her.

"Conon?" Elysia's unexpected voice almost called him from his skin.

She stood a stone's throw from them, as if Conon's daydreaming had conjured her out of nowhere. The heightened color in her cheeks made him uncomfortably aware of his awkward position.

Not that it mattered overmuch what his treacherous wife thought of him. Still, guilty haste drew his arms from Marguerite as if she were the plague.

"Elysia."

Conon sensed, more than he saw the wicked grin that spread across Marguerite's lips. In fact, he saw that grin reflected in Elysia's surprised gaze. Despite his anger with his wife, he regretted the hurt in her transparent expression.

His wife's lips moved, but nary a sound came out.

Damn. Since when had she been at a loss for words?

"Sorry," Elysia mumbled, then fled the secluded corner of the marketplace to leave Conon in Marguerite's eager clutches.

Marguerite grinned up at him, a giggle bubbling up to her soft, rosy lips.

Conon pressed a finger to her lips, his voice a whispered warning. "Not a word, Marguerite. She is not like you."

As the widow's eyes narrowed with understanding, she stiffened. Her arms fell from his neck. "So it is that way?"

Conon nodded, as surprised as his former lover at his attack of morality. Especially in light of his failed wedding night.

She left in a huff. Typical Marguerite.

Leaving Conon to wonder what the hell it meant that he could find no pleasure with any woman besides his raven-haired independent bride. He did not miss the irony of his going without lovemaking now that he finally possessed the wife and home he always dreamed of.

Damn his morals.

It looked as though he was in for a long dry spell.

Shaking his head in wry humor, Conon couldn't help but be amused that, hungry as he was for a woman's touch, he just let two sought-after females escape him within a few moments' span.

Mayhap he was not so much of a Frenchman after all.

Chapter Fifteen

Daria fluffed her loose tresses under the demure linen head covering she wore for her meeting with the Earl of Arundel. Nervousness urged her fingers to smooth her best silk surcoat and remove any stray wrinkles.

The other cause of her unrest shifted his long legs on the bench beside her, sending skitters of sharp yearning through her veins.

"This is a foolish notion," Leon whispered as he leaned over their shared trencher to pass her a small portion of stuffed pigeon. "Every man here is ogling you."

"It has been a long time since I've been ogled, de Grace, so please don't let your sour mood spoil my fun." She tried to sound as flippant and teasing as usual, but truth be told, a lump of fear settled in her throat at the thought of pleading her case for annulment in front of all these knights.

After two days of petitioning for a formal audience with the earl, Daria received her wish. Unfortunately, it would not be a private meeting. She would be compelled to reveal all the intimate particulars of her forced marriage in front of a tentful of England's warriors.

"I've been ogling you for days, damn it."

Although spoken with gruff rancor, his words caused Daria to flush with pleasure. With all her heart she prayed the earl would help her seek an annulment and throw Oliver Westmoor out of Nevering. Once her marriage to Oliver could be rendered invalid, Elysia would be able to annul her marriage to Conon. Elysia deserved happiness.

And Daria would marry Leon de Grace in a heartbeat.

If the man ever offered for her.

She slanted a cross look in his direction. "I've come to the conclusion that no matter how deeply hungry your expression, sir, you will never give yourself permission to touch."

His silver eyes darkened, so full of naked longing it made Daria's heart pound a desperate rhythm of desire.

"I honor you."

The fierceness of his voice unnerved her. His sentiment was lovely, except that Daria wondered if she indeed wanted to be honored. After five days at Leon's side, hoping in vain for a kiss to match the passion and fury of his others, she could see the merits of a little dishonor at Leon de Grace's hands.

"It is not as if I am wed by my own free will to the man, Leon." Too apprehensive to eat, she pushed her meal around in circles with her eating knife.

"Aye." His hand grazed over her thigh beneath the table. "But I want to be sure I am the last man to ever touch you again, Daria-mine."

She trembled at his endearment, her skin aflame from his caress. Good Lord, she wanted this man.

"I cannot bear the thought of holding you," he whispered, his breath stroking her cheek in a lover's caress, "only to lose you to Oliver Westmoor in the end."

A clanking noise fractured her thoughts.

"Attention!" The earl banged on his cup to gain quiet in the dining tent. "I would hear grievances now, my good men. Pray continue your meals while I lend an ear to Lady Daria Rougemont Westmoor of Nevering Keep."

Finally. Though her knees buckled slightly as she stood, all other traces of nervousness fled as Daria took the floor. Fearless blood pumped through her in long, regular measures as she sailed regally among the makeshift tables to the earl.

Arundel watched her with the wary eyes of a man well used to assessing his opponents. Daria had entertained him many times at Nevering while Simon lived. A good man at heart, the earl was ambitious and driven. He had devoted little time to his own wife when she lived, and even less to his sons as they grew into men. But Daria knew him to be fair.

Let him engage that sense of fairness today.

"Thank you, my lord." Sweeping a deep curtsy, Daria called upon every theatrical instinct to put on a good show.

The performance of a lifetime.

With what she hoped was dignified humility, Daria explained her circumstances. Like a court storyteller, she kept the knights hanging on the edge of their benches as she wove the tale of heartache and suffering she had been forced to endure at Oliver Westmoor's hands.

But most importantly, she reminded her audience, Sir Oliver acted without his liege lord's authority by wedding her. In addition, Oliver stole away one of the earl's other properties to govern on his own.

This last she delivered with just the right touch of haughty indignation.

"Oliver Westmoor has promised he will continue to serve me," Arundel reminded her.

"But he has recently conducted a huge tournament to

gather the most able knights in the country to his side," she countered. "Surely a sign he overreaches his bounds as your vassal."

"As my vassal, his strength does me honor."

Several of Arundel's knights nodded in vehement agreement.

Daria faltered for but a moment. "He seeks to be a direct vassal to King Edward instead, my lord."

The tent went quieter still. Even the dull sound of servers moving among the tables ceased.

All eyes focused on Arundel.

His eyes narrowed in shrewd calculation. "Come here, my dear." He beckoned her to stand directly before him.

Daria went and knelt in dutiful submission to her overlord, her head bowed in deference to his wish. The earl's goodwill would be tantamount to his decision.

"You are an exceedingly beautiful woman, Lady Daria, and I am moved by your impassioned speech." He paused to sip from his cup, his eyes boring a hole into hers all the while. Reaching across the table, Arundel tipped her chin with strong fingers. "But it is not an easy thing to annul a marriage these days, even for very good reasons."

A low rumble went around the room as the knights began to whisper among themselves. Daria imagined they were taking bets on the outcome of the exchange.

Her neck tingled with the sudden certainty that Leon de Grace's brooding silver gaze did not miss any of this. He would not be happy with the turn of this conversation.

"Fortunately you are a very powerful man, my lord." Did her voice sound as desperate as she felt? Daria was out of her depth and she knew it. All her bold bragging to her daughter about how to handle a man.

Ha. She couldn't even convince Leon to take her to his

bed. What made her think she could persuade the Earl of Arundel to do as she wished?

"How much is it worth to you, Lady Daria?" Arundel leaned across the table, his gaze sweeping her form with lazy interest. His finger trailed from her chin, halting just before her bodice.

"I could never repay you, of course, my lord." Her carefully laid plans dissolved along with her forced pleasant expression. "I can only seek justice in the name of what is right and fair, as women are forced to do." She sounded as prickly and indignant as her daughter might if Elysia were standing here in front of this scheming knave.

"Ahh, you are in luck, lady." Arundel smiled, his expression softening. "I would gladly intercede on your behalf if you were to merely grant me a favor in return."

The light of lust in his eyes unmistakable, Daria awaited the inevitable proposition.

A loud crash startled them both. She whipped around to the source of the sound.

"Do you insult the lady, sir?" Leon stood amidst the knights, his wooden bench askew on the floor behind him. Silver fire flashed in his eyes. One hand rested upon his knife in blatant impudence. It seemed to Daria he spoke the words with even more of a French accent than he normally would, as if to make his foreign status apparent.

To Daria's surprise, the earl stood. Sweet Mother in Heaven, things were not proceeding according to plan.

"You have no business here." Arundel gripped his own blade, his stance a clear challenge. "Get out."

"Please my lord, Sir Leon escorts me." Why couldn't Leon allow her to settle this her own way? She flashed Arundel one of her most famous supplicating looks, a combination of eyelash batting and tentative smiling that won over countless men in her courting days.

Unfortunately, Arundel did not bother to glance in her direction. "That explains much. John, see him out."

In a blur of swift movement, Leon jumped over the trestle table and grabbed Daria. John Huntley followed, but not before the knight yanked her between two tables on the opposite side of the tent and out into the summer sunlight.

Commotion exploded inside the dining area as knights bolted after them.

"What the hell did you do that for?" Daria shouted as Leon dragged her along. They ran like the devil was at their heels, her wimple unfurling to flap like a victory flag in the breeze behind her.

"Mount up," Leon urged between clenched teeth, pushing her in the direction of a horse.

She half stumbled over a young squire who polished an already pristine shield beside the animal in question.

"Sorry, lad." For good measure she grinned winningly at the boy before stealing his master's mount. Kicking the horse forward, she flew into the wind, not sparing a glance for Leon's safety until her horse galloped at full speed.

Leaning over the mare's bare back, she clutched the mane with both hands and peered backward. Leon followed close behind on a larger horse, although he, too, rode without benefit of a saddle or reins.

No one pursued them.

They had insulted one of the most powerful earls in England, mocked his authority and stolen two valuable horses. Daria couldn't believe they would be allowed to just walk away. Retribution would come one way or another.

It seemed as if days passed before Leon finally permitted the horses a rest. Guiding the sweaty animals to a narrow stream, he vaulted from the animal's back, then waited to help Daria down. Although angry with him, she was not too proud to allow him to be useful. Sliding into his waiting arms, she then shook off his hands to prance away with indignant strides.

"How long did you plan to kneel before that man, Daria?" Leon mused as he walked with predatory stealth to stand before her. "Until you bartered away your soul to free yourself from Oliver's bed? As if that would have brought you any more happiness. Would you give in to Arundel's lewd demands to escape another man's?"

She sought for the words that would cut him to the core. Words that would shatter him as surely as he shattered her with his self-righteous indignation, but she was fresh out of rejoinders.

"You've ruined everything."

"Ruined what?" Bone weary and supremely disappointed with herself, Daria sank down onto the cool, forgiving comfort of the grassy bank. Idly she plucked long green strands to weave into a slender chain. "By annulling my marriage, I'd hoped to free Elysia from hers."

Leon dropped his head onto his knees. "I can't believe you." His words, spoken to the ground in his dejected position, were muffled.

"It is my fault Oliver married her off in such a crass, uncaring manner." What woman would want to marry whatever man happened to win a tournament? Any worldly woman knew that the strongest, most celebrated men were often the most boorish and unfeeling members of their gender. "The least I can do is help extricate her from the match."

"Conon would have killed me." He rubbed his temples with his fingers now.

Daria almost felt sorry for him. Almost. "Ah, yes, because he would lose my daughter's wealth. My heart aches for him."

Leon lifted his head to meet her gaze. A soulful expression caught at her heart. His hair looked as wind tossed as hers; the long, coal-black strands grazed the collar of his surcoat. "Nay, lady. Conon has his own wealth. He cares for your daughter. I think he may love her." His voice fell to a husky whisper. "Love is a powerful thing, is it not?"

Their gazes locked. Daria had the uncanny feeling he did not speak of Conon and Elysia, but of them. Of Leon and Daria.

Shaking her head to ward off the strange warmth that curled through her womb, she dismissed the notion. "How could he love her? He betrayed his promise to stop her wedding."

"Aye! So he could marry her himself! He cares for her deeply, Daria. He could not abide seeing her wed to anyone else."

She did not actually see him move, yet he was suddenly closer to her. His thigh touched hers. The heat of his body mixed with the musky scent of his skin to tease her senses.

"Just as I cannot abide seeing you wed to anyone else." He breathed his words into her ear, sending a shiver down her neck and spine.

"You have spoiled any chance I might have had to gain an annulment. Oliver will kill me for this." Despite the pleasurable tingle Leon inspired throughout her body, the thought of her marriage to Oliver taunted her, reminding her she could never have a future with Leon now. She might well have no life left at all.

"That is why I am going to abduct you."

Her gaze flew to his face. "What?"

"I am abducting you, Daria Rougemont. Do not even try to escape me." His face was utterly serious. His tone would have been almost frightening if she did not know he would not hurt her for the world.

Daria could not bear to see noble Leon do something that would compromise his honor in the world's eyes. What would people say of such an illicit scheme? She tried another tack. "But I will lose my noble title, my clothes—"

"As if you give a damn about a title and clothes."

By the saints, he saw right through her. "Nay, but you will surely be ostracized, Leon." It was impossible. As enticing as it sounded, she couldn't do it. It would destroy Leon's reputation. "Your king will not take kindly to your harboring a fugitive noblewoman."

Grinning wickedly, he brushed his lips in a slow sensuous trail down her neck. "I am a Frenchman, *chère*. My countrymen cheer such illicit liaisons." His hand crept down her thigh to push her silk skirts high up her leg. "I will not be ostracized. I will be a hero."

"What of Elysia?" Not that she was giving serious consideration to Leon's outrageous offer. She was merely relating the myriad reasons why it wouldn't work.

"Conon will protect her. As I will you." The fierceness in his voice made her shiver. "I will not allow you to go back to a man who would wed you at knifepoint, Daria."

She felt herself weakening.

"I have a small estate in Italy," Leon whispered, cajoling her toward what she wanted more than anything. "We will live quietly as man and wife and no one will be the wiser. The way your husband courts disaster with his overlord, he may not live through the year anyway. Then we could wed in the church." Slowly, his fingers slid to the inside of her thigh. "Although you will already be the wife of my heart."

His mouth covered hers before she could respond. And this kiss was unlike any of the others she had known before. Thought-stealing, bone-melting and soul-deep, his lips crafted pure magic.

"Is that a proposal?" she whispered between kisses.

He played over her womanhood with long fingers, teasing her into breathless sighs. "*Aye.* But as my captive, I warn you—you'd better say yes."

To punctuate his words, he slid his finger deep inside her, drawing a gasp and a cry of delight from her lips.

"Yes. Yes, Leon…." With all her heart, Daria committed herself to the man who would be the husband of her soul. Her rightful mate.

And with more love than his words could ever hope to express, Leon claimed his bride.

Elysia dragged herself from her warm bed in the early morning hours a scant three days after her wedding. Today she would leave Nevering for France once again, this time as Conon St. Simeon's unwanted bride.

Yawning with the exhaustion of another restless night spent dreaming of Conon in Marguerite's arms, Elysia blinked sleepy eyes to clear them of the image. With a half-hearted oath, she cursed Frenchmen in general and Conon most especially.

As Belle stumbled over to help Elysia wash and dress, Elysia could hear Conon arguing with Oliver in the courtyard. Again.

Conon had spent the last three days searching Nevering for the dower fortune he thought she hid from him. He asked every servant and tenant he came in contact with if they had seen the chests delivered to the keep.

He ranted and raved to Oliver that Elysia deserved the

wealth, but Oliver had other things on his mind the last few days.

"What the hell do I care where the wench's gold is?" Oliver shouted back in the courtyard. "You should have thought of that before you laid claim to Elysia. The girl is sly as a courtier and sharp as a serpent's tooth, just like her two-faced lying mother."

Belle muttered prayers beneath her breath and fingered the sign of the cross over herself at the outburst.

"Sir Oliver is even more wound up than my Lord Conon today." Belle pulled Elysia's hair into one long plait to be tucked into a light linen wimple. "I pray your lady mother does not return at this point. His lordship will wreak the vengeance of the devil upon her."

A tremor shook Elysia at the dire prediction. Oliver had discovered Daria's absence yesterday and had been on a rampage ever since. Her mother should never have attempted such a crazy scheme. What would Oliver do to her if she came back? Worse yet, what if she never returned?

Patiently allowing Belle to button the long sleeves on her riding garment, Elysia felt her heart burn with too many regrets. Since crying served no cause, she adjusted the simple girtle at her hips and walked out of her childhood home to face her unfaithful, very angry husband.

"Good morning, my lord." Although it was not in her power to make her voice convey any warmth, Elysia would not have it said that she failed to be courteous.

Turning from his task of testing the horses' saddles and reins, Conon smiled politely. "Good morning, *chère*. We will depart momentarily."

To his credit, he remained civil.

He guided a horse toward her and handed her the bridle. "Unless you've had a change of heart and wish to tell me where your wealth is."

Even knowing Conon to be as unfaithful as the summer day was long, Elysia could not help the longing that slid through her as she looked at him. His eyes undid her every time.

"I have seen no such wealth since we returned to England, my lord." Screwing up her courage, she flashed him her most winning smile. "Although I am sure you must have packed it."

His charm dissolved as suddenly as it had appeared.

"Mayhap you won't make light of the situation when you realize you will suffer the perils of being a pauper right by my side, lady."

By the muscle that tensed in his jaw, Elysia guessed he ground his teeth in a fierce effort to stay marginally polite.

"It is a circumstance that I do not appreciate," she returned, stroking the gentle mare's nose as she spoke. "But one to which I am accustomed. I will see to it that I bring all the necessary goods to begin a small linen trade in France."

Instead of soothing him, her comment seemed to inflame him still further.

"I will not require your assistance to run my keep, lady."

"Then it seems you won't need my assistance for much of anything, my lord. You say you've no need of my linen-making talents, and yesterday's embrace with your mistress proved you have no need of me in your bed." Once she flung her angry accusation, she realized how desperately she wanted Conon to deny it.

"You've shown me the value of independence, lady. I think it would be unwise to rely on you." He stalked away without a backward glance, his dark blue surcoat fanning out behind him in a dramatic sweep.

Heart aching at the rift between them, she watched him furtively as he readied their packhorse and supplies. They traveled lightly because she possessed nothing of value to bring except some linens to embroider, a few flax plants and extra spinning tools.

She tried not to remember the picture of Conon in another woman's arms. Tried not to recall how much he resented his decision to wed her. But as she took up the reins of her horse, she could not help but remember the friendship they had so briefly shared. Perhaps with a little more time they could reclaim some of that mutual understanding.

With the sun scarcely full in the sky, they rode south toward the life of uncertainty awaiting them at Vannes Keep.

Chapter Sixteen

The sea couldn't be more than a league or two distant, Elysia realized as the landscape changed, the air growing more heavy with moisture. Once they arrived at the coast, Vannes lay but a boat's ride away.

They had ridden in silence since leaving Nevering. Tension grew thick between them. She longed to reach out to him, but did not know how. She had never been the kind of person to share her feelings.

Daylight still shone when they reached a lovely glade overlooking the shore. Elysia hoped they might eat a bite before securing a vessel to take them across the sea.

"We will camp here," Conon announced, swinging down from his mount.

"Camp? You mean spend the night?" Sleeping near Conon without walls to separate them might be more than she could take.

"By the time I find a boatman along the coast, it will be too close to dark for my liking. Safest to wait." He stood beneath her, ready to catch her.

Elysia made no move to slide into Conon's arms. She

contemplated finding a boatman herself. She had assumed
they would travel late into the night to reach France and
sleep in their own beds. Here, there was nothing. Just the
two of them.

"You prefer to take your meal on horseback?" Conon
grinned up at her, the wind tossing his hair over his cheek.

One nice thing about him, she had to admit, he could
be courteous and agreeable even when angry. And he was
still angry with her. She could tell by the way he only
spoke to her out of courtesy and necessity. He did not tease
and jest, or pick her flowers.

Or visit her bed.

"I think not," she returned, slipping from the mare's
back and into his arms. His hands lingered strong and sure
around her waist, bringing back a flood of sensual memories from a night when there were not so many garments
between them.

Abruptly, he pushed away from her and busied himself
with gathering wood.

Bereft, Elysia tried not to think what her marriage might
have been like if she had been honest with Conon. He
might have trusted her. He might even have grown to love
her. If only she'd felt she could trust him.

Her deception gave him all the incentive he needed to
take a lover the day after their nuptials. To admit he'd only
wed her out of a sense of duty. Now he expected his rightful bridal portion, but she was powerless to give it to him
as it had never arrived at Nevering. Of course, he did not
believe her. Elysia suspected Sir Huntley or one of Arundel's other greedy vassals had stolen it, but why would
Conon believe her about that?

She had too many other important worries on her mind
now to wade through it anyway. Her mother, for one. Ely-

sia's fear for her mother far outweighed any concerns she might have about her bridal portion.

After a low fire burned brightly at the edge of the glade, Conon left to hunt. Returning in no time, he wordlessly handed her two rabbits, which she cleaned and cooked without comment. Did he think her too proud to prepare her own food? She'd survived lean times before. And cooked her own rabbits.

They ate in silence. Finally, when Elysia thought she would scream at the quiet, Conon cleared his throat.

"Where is your mother, Countess?" He stared at her across the fire, the night sky dimming his eyes to naught but two reflective pools of flame.

"She would not wish me to reveal her whereabouts." That much was true, anyway.

Would Conon be angry if he knew Daria sought an annulment for her marriage, which might, in turn, give him an annulment for his? Or would he be relieved to get rid of her?

Elysia did not know which frightened her more. She already regretted complaining of her marriage to her mother since she'd rather heal the rift between her and Conon than annul their unhappy union.

"She has no doubt taken your bridal portion along with her to prevent me from usurping it."

"Nay! Conon—"

He held up a weary hand to fend off her rebuttal. "The money is not important now. But if she contacts you, Elysia, tell her not to return to Nevering."

"Oliver is furious with my mother, isn't he?" She thought she detected genuine concern in his voice.

Conon nodded. "Enough to harm her. I am certain of it." As if to ward off any sense of intimacy their exchange might have created, he stood and busied himself with storing the leftover wine and bread.

"I will not hear from her," Elysia half whispered. Her heart ached for her mother. What on earth made Daria Rougemont, who had always been content to let Elysia fight the family battles, decide to travel to France for an annulment the Earl of Arundel would surely never help her obtain?

There was a time when Elysia would have laid her fears on Conon's shoulders, but she could no longer do that. Struggling unsuccessfully with tears, Elysia did not hear Conon the first time he called to her.

Or so she assumed when he shouted her name.

Turning, she spied him in the pitch dark of the moonless night only because her eyes had grown slowly accustomed to the lack of light.

He lay on top of a large pallet on the far side of the dying fire. Head propped on his hand, he studied her through narrowed eyes. Surcoat dispensed with, only his tunic covered the wall of muscled chest that Elysia recalled so vividly. What she wouldn't give to make things right between them.

She forgave him for tricking her into marriage almost as soon as her feet touched the top of Nevering's flower-covered southern hill on their wedding night. Conon was too honorable and too caring a man not to forgive.

"Sleep now," he ordered, his voice gruff.

Glancing about for her pallet and finding none, she approached the packhorse to uncover her own linens.

"What do you need?"

"Just getting my linens. I—"

"We have more than enough linens. Come to bed."

Although the invitation definitely lacked the finesse of the first time Conon made a pallet for them to share, Elysia knew it cost him to dispense it.

She stood there, wanting desperately to obey him in this, but—

"What is it now?"

"I've nowhere to change my garments." There were trees around them, but Elysia feared tripping over an exposed root in the pitch dark if she tried to stumble over to one.

"Well I suggest you find *somewhere* to change, lest you want *me* to disrobe you."

Clearly, his words were intended as a threat. A few months ago, Elysia would have accepted them as such. But just now, the voice of her mother popped into her mind, full of devilment.

I will show you how a woman goes about getting what she wants in this world.

Elysia knew what her mother would do. She would fight for a man like Conon.

"Perhaps that would be best." Elysia rushed the words out of her mouth before she could change her mind. As soon as they floated free on the night wind, she wished she could have them back. Conon would rather sleep with worldly women like Marguerite than someone like her.

Silence greeted her foolish statement.

Go to him, Elysia! Daria urged her on.

No bride wished to hear her mother's voice intruding into the marriage bed, but she obeyed the prodding command since she'd failed miserably in that arena on her own.

Closing her eyes as a safeguard against turning and fleeing, she walked to the pallet and lay down beside Conon, her night rail clasped, forgotten, in her hand.

Heart slamming against her chest with alarming force, she made herself take deep, quieting breaths. Then she opened her eyes. Conon stared at her with a mixture of awe and disbelief.

She had reclined much too close to him. If her eyes had been open as she lay down, she would not have positioned herself a hair's breadth away from him. As it was, they were almost touching.

"You—" Conon faltered and began again. "You want me to help you undress?"

The strain in his voice pleased her. Perhaps her mother knew whereof she spoke. "Aye. I do not wish to trip in the dark."

He half sprang off the pallet. "I can light you a torch and—"

She halted him with her hand on his chest. "Nay." With every fiber of her being, she wanted him to touch her. She ached for his strength, his nearness. "Help me."

Proffering her wrist with its extravagantly buttoned sleeve, she waited. His hands trembled when they touched her. Elysia prayed it was from some emotion other than resentment or anger. Had he undressed Marguerite with shaking hands when he took her to his bed? The notion made her belly knot in a wave of fierce jealousy. She would not think of that now while she was fighting to win him back.

"You are an accomplished flirt for a virgin, *chère*." He unfastened the buttons with quick efficiency. "I am surprised."

His words stung, but she refused to let it show. She would sell her soul to sleep in his arms tonight. Even on her wedding night, she was not treated to that sort of intimacy. "Perhaps, as we get to know one another better, we will not continue to surprise each other so much."

Her sleeves undone, Conon's fingers stilled.

Meeting his gaze, Elysia saw a trace of trepidation in his eyes. She couldn't go through with it. Sitting up, she moved to leave the pallet. "I will brave the dark, my lord. You needn't help me."

He gripped her shoulders with both hands to pull her back down. "Don't go."

Gentling his hands, he smoothed the palms over her shoulders. "You expect so much more from me than I can give you, Elysia. One minute you seem such an innocent, so pure and so gentle, and then I recall the cold calculation of your scheme to deceive me. Your independence means so much to you that you would perpetuate a lie and then go so far as to hide your bridal portion from me. It is difficult to trust you, *chère,* when I think you may call upon your hidden wealth one day to leave the husband you never wanted."

His words tore her apart. He thought the worst of her. Perhaps with good reason. And because she had been deceitful to protect that independence in the past, he would not believe her now. Soon, she promised herself, she would uncover the mystery of her missing money to atone for her deception.

For now she needed to make the first overture toward healing their relationship. How would they ever solve the gap of understanding that separated them if neither of them was willing to risk a bit of themselves?

Tonight Elysia would take her risk.

Taking a deep breath, she laid her hands upon his chest as if to borrow his strength. "Then tonight I will expect nothing of you. No trust, no promise of a future. Nothing." It required a supreme effort to suppress her pride enough to say those words. She knew it would be the last time her heart could afford to offer such a gift. "Only, if you feel moved to…passion…I ask that you let me share it with you."

Elysia imagined the groan Conon emitted could be heard for many distant leagues.

"Oh, sweetheart." He rubbed an exasperated hand over his eyes. "I promise you, I am very moved."

Patiently, she waited for him to say something a little more intelligible. Was that a "yes"?

Her nerves stretched thin in the interminable moments as he said nothing. She went to speak—to free him of any guilt he might feel at rejecting her offer—but the shame of her brazenness made the words stick in her throat. Cheeks flaming, she settled for burrowing deeper into the tall summer grasses that filled the makeshift pallet.

Finally his hand drifted to her hip and settled there. Warmth curled through her belly. And hope.

Conon propped himself back up on one elbow and stared down at her, his gaze inscrutable. "It would not be noble of me to accept such a proposal."

His lips hovered above hers with mesmerizing closeness. "Then again, I make no pretense about my lack of nobility, Countess." His fingers stroked over her hip. "I am powerless to refuse such a delectable offer."

He tasted her with infinite care and hunger, pulling her beneath the heated shelter of his body. With deft fingers, he loosened all the ties that held her surcoat together, then tugged the garment over her head, along with the linen tunic she wore under it. Bared to his view, she had never felt so exposed. Conon eyed her so intensely, she swore she could see right through to her soul.

Conon wondered what demon possessed him to accept Elysia's ridiculous bargain. One night with no regrets. No expectations. Ridiculous.

He could never love her. He could never trust her as a husband should trust his wife. All his life, Conon longed for a family that would be more caring than the one he grew up in. Since his youth, he envisioned a wife who would be the completion of his soul.

Instead he got his flawed countess, who cared more about keeping her secret stash of wealth to herself than sharing one bit of her soul with a man. And yet…was he not equally flawed himself?

Thinking of his own imperfect soul he looked down at her, stripped of all garments, utterly bared to his gaze, and saw only purity and innocence. A trick of the moonless night mayhap, but he swore he saw naught but gentleness and beauty.

"Conon?" Her voice, so uncertain, niggled at his conscience.

He should not touch her until he knew how he felt about her. But what man in his right mind could resist her charming offer? Tossing her garments aside, he gathered her slender form in his arms and squeezed her against him. His fingers wound through the silken length of her hair, tugging her head back to afford him better access to her lips. His mouth covered hers, tasting and exploring, rediscovering the passion within Elysia he'd only just begun to enjoy that first night of their marriage.

Tightening his grip, he shifted her beneath him, holding her steady as she sighed, her heart pounding madly against him. This was what he wanted with her—tonight and every night—and damn the consequences once daylight arrived. With the way her hips twitched beneath him, he could not mistake her need for it, too.

Nudging his thigh between her legs, he urged her against him. She was so hot. So sweet. Fierce pleasure coursed through him, demanding completion.

"You are mine."

He sounded like a child with a coveted new plaything, but he had to be sure she knew. In this he would tolerate no misunderstandings.

"I know." She kissed his cheek, the warmth of her lips inciting a heat he couldn't deny.

He had never given her a real wedding night. After discovering her maidenly status, he spent himself within her, never giving another thought to her pleasure. Tonight, he would remedy that. Not so much to please her as to make her his own.

Giving his hand free rein over her body, he delighted in the silky feel of her skin, the satisfaction of her complete surrender. Stroking her hip and thigh, he tasted a trail down to the hollow at the base of her throat, along the feminine curve of her breast.

Selfishly, he remained there a long moment to savor the furious beat of her heart against his cheek, the scent of lavender and leather emanating from her warm skin.

She quivered in his arms, her breath uneven and throaty. Long lashes fluttered and fell on her soft, flushed cheek. Only then did he give in to the temptation of the taut pink crests he teased with his hand. He suckled her, nipped her, taunted her until her leg rode high on his own.

Dispensing with his clothes, he skimmed the inside of her thigh with his fingers, tracing lazy patterns along her flesh until she whimpered with sensual hunger. He'd never heard such sweet music. She gasped his name; her back arched as she clung to him.

Heat fired through him, burning away old anger and hurts until he could only remember this moment, this need. Feasting on her lips, he tasted her mouth with a thoroughness that should have sated him but only left him wanting more. Gently, he covered her feminine mound with his palm, tested her with his finger. The slick heat of her called to him at the most elemental level. She burned with the same fire that consumed him.

He wanted to join with her so badly he ached, but he would not allow himself the satisfaction until he saw those deep brown eyes widen with her own release.

In slow circles he touched her, seeking and finding the rhythm that pleased her. At first she stilled, as if afraid he would stop if she were to move even a breath.

Then her eyes flew open in a vague mix of comprehension and confusion. She wriggled underneath him to break away, but he held her fast with gentle hands.

"No, Conon, I—" Her body arced in a taut bow of rapture before she fell and shuddered with raw pleasure.

For the first time since their wedding night, Conon felt a moment's pleasure at her former innocence. He relished the wonder in her passion-dazed eyes as her long lashes finally fluttered wide.

But he could not give her long to rest or feel wonder. It had taken every bit of his restraint to last this long. He needed her. *Now.*

He laid claim to her then, with as much care and tenderness as he could. Entering her slowly, he stared down at her as her eyes grew heavy-lidded. Closed. Her lips parted, her cheeks flushed as he sheathed himself fully, holding himself there a long moment until the blood pounded through him so fiercely he knew he could not wait.

She moved with him, meeting his every thrust until he reached between her legs to touch the bud of her sex. Her back arched as she cried out, spasms rocking her while she gripped his shoulders with unexpected intensity. Her nails dug lightly into his skin, gently scoring over his back until he could withhold no longer. When he allowed himself his own release, he prayed his seed would be fruitful.

Heart hammering wildly, he slumped alongside her,

gathering her up in his arms to hold her close. He brushed a few stray strands of hair from her forehead as his breath finally slowed, his pulse steadying to normal in the warmth of their shared bed.

Even if Elysia could never love or hold faith in him, Conon was determined to have a child. Children. Then he would salvage a portion of his childhood dream of a family.

Twice more over the course of the long, moonless night, Conon enjoyed Elysia's body, making sure she reached the pinnacle of pleasure each time.

His dream of a family was no longer enough. He couldn't stop craving more—something elusive and unnamed.

Chapter Seventeen

Conon brooded as he folded their bedrolls at dawn the next morning. Struggling to remove the events of the previous night from his mind, he busied himself with any task that would forestall conversation.

What had he been thinking? Of course, he hadn't been thinking once Elysia lay down beside him. And later, lost in a tumult of passion, his heart had swollen with nameless emotions for her. Emotions he would sooner suppress than label.

Now he knew better. He could not take Elysia to his bed without risking his heart. She'd played him false once and would no doubt do it again if it served her purposes.

In silence he charted their passage across the sea and through France to Vannes Keep. Ignoring the long looks his wife cast in his direction, Conon focused on his newly inspired plan to recoup her bridal portion.

He felt certain she had given it to her mother to safeguard for her. Why else would Lady Daria disappear the day of her daughter's wedding? And he did not even care so much that Lady Daria possessed the bridal portion that should now be his by rights. He'd made a respectable sum as a mercenary and could continue to wield his blade in service to a wealthy noble.

What bothered him was the principle of Elysia's fortune. He wanted it as a matter of honor. He would even go so far as to give the cursed money right back to her. But it infuriated him that Elysia continued her independent ways even as a married woman. And Conon would not bear it.

Once they reached Vannes, he would urge her to turn over the bridal portion. Thankfully, he left his keep stripped bare. Perhaps if she thought Vannes had fallen on hard times, she would surrender the disputed treasure.

Failing that, he would besiege Nevering and overthrow Oliver Westmoor. Conon had to battle for everything he had ever gained. Why not this? Even his own wife had to be won like a battle prize.

Elysia watched Conon wage some inner war, his aspect fierce. Her heart ached that their night together changed nothing. When forced to speak with her, he remained civil but distant.

Her spirits lifted when they rode by the small dower property outside the main Vannes lands. She could always take refuge there if her marriage declined any further. Or if Conon's mistress made another appearance.

Willing away the surge of jealousy that roiled at the thought, Elysia spied Vannes Keep ahead. Although she retained frightening memories of Jacques's death there, her heart cherished fond remembrances of time spent with Conon by the sea. Looking back, she realized she began to fall for him that day he tended her wounded foot.

Now Conon's broad back impeded her view. She couldn't seem to wrest her attention from him these days.

"Be prepared." He called over his shoulder as his horse trotted over the smooth courtyard stones. "It has changed somewhat since your last visit."

"How so?" When they stopped, she slid awkwardly from her mare to prevent Conon from having to help.

His expression chilled a bit more as he leaped with smooth grace to the ground. Reaching for her hand, he ushered her forward, playing the gallant. Tension knotted in her belly as her apprehension grew. She had noticed Conon could be at his most charming when angry.

Two older maids hurried from the massive front doors as they approached. The courtyard had grown utterly quiet.

"Welcome, my lord, we did not know when to expect you and things are a mite disorganized."

Their voices faded as Conon brushed past them, intent on steering Elysia indoors. She stumbled into the dark, cavernous emptiness of Vannes. "You've been robbed, my lord." She put her hand to her chest to settle its furious beat, taking in the extent of the damage that had been wrought. "By the saints, they've taken everything."

Swinging around, thinking she should comfort her husband, Elysia was stunned to see the look of smug disgust on his face. He stood, arms crossed in the center of his vacant hall.

"What is it? Do you have an enemy?"

"Nay, lady. I have creditors. Or rather, Uncle Jacques did." Leaning against a rough-hewn trestle table, one of the few furnishings left in place, he studied her through narrowed eyes.

"Jacques's debt amounted to all of this?" Staring at the lonesome walls, Elysia could not believe it. How could one man owe that much money? The tapestries, the exquisite furnishings, the silver... All had vanished.

She stalked across the hall, not waiting for Conon's response. Peering into the growing darkness of the echoing interior, she saw the other chambers lacked their fine appointments, too. Devoid of all decoration, the keep had been stripped nearly bare.

"Apparently Uncle Jacques wed you to keep the creditors off his back," Conon finally replied. "Once he died, his portion of your dowry was not enough to satisfy them. I was forced to sell almost everything."

She paced the great hall, too upset to stand still. Her brain mulled the problem at hand, eager to solve it. More to herself than to him, she murmured, "My bridal portion could have replaced most of this. And a good year of linen would—"

He smirked. "Vannes in its lowly state does not appeal to you?"

Elysia shook her head, tired of defending herself to him. "Did you ever speak with the boatmen who accompanied us from France to Nevering?"

"*Aye*. They assured me the cargo was delivered to Nevering a fortnight after we arrived."

"These men swore they delivered the goods to me personally?"

"They swore everything was delivered to its rightful owner."

"What rightful owner?" For Elysia, the difference sounded significant. "You didn't ask them *who*, precisely?"

"I didn't need to. They knew the wealth came from your marriage contract as well as I did."

And every last one of those men worked for the Earl of Arundel. She now had a good idea where the gold went, but it became apparent Conon would not believe her. Having been caught in a lie already, she might never repair the damage to Conon's trust.

"Very well." She cuffed up her long sleeves with slow deliberation, focusing her effort on what she did best.

Work.

"We can't sleep here with the keep in this condition." She eyed the cold stone walls critically. "If it is acceptable to you, my lord, I would like to take one of the maids upstairs to help me ready the master chamber for you. I can address the needs in the rest of the rooms tomorrow."

"That is fine." For a moment his look of contempt slipped. "Though it may have been easier to just hand over the bridal portion rather than damage your lovely hands."

It amazed her she could love him when he treated her with such disdain. Yet she recalled his kindness before the wedding-night debacle. Only now did she realize the value he placed on trust.

She fixed him with a level stare before she departed the hall. "If you think I am afraid of a little hard work, my lord, you clearly know nothing about me."

Just to do her mother proud, she added a regal tilt to her chin as she sailed out the door.

A fortnight later, Conon watched his wife toil endlessly in the fields as he sat atop his favored riding mount. Much to his consternation, she had worked like a peasant every day since arriving.

The fall harvest season revealed the extent of the land's bounty. Thankfully, there would be plenty of food in the winter stores this year, but that did not satisfy Elysia. No, she would not be appeased until every villager and tenant thrived with good health and full belly.

Today she spent her time helping the women save seeds from each crop they harvested. As they worked, she instructed them how to start small garden plots of their own next spring. The villagers were thrilled at the prospect of personal food stores, independent of their overlord's success or failure.

Yesterday, Conon had witnessed her advising the cook on how to prepare the meals with as little expense as possible. Before that, she had instituted a daily routine for the older boys of the village to go fishing on the shore. The boys enjoyed the liberation from the keep, yet took pride in their contributions. From the number of fish they brought back each day, Conon guessed the village could eat salted seafood for the next two years.

Which led to one of his wife's other grand plans. Elysia taught the girls to dry and salt meat, giving them freedom and responsibility. And, of course, a bit of time to flirt with the boys who brought them the fruits of their fishing expeditions.

So it went, day in and day out. Each morning Conon leaped from his bed, eager for the day she could find no more to do. Until he had to admit his scheme had failed.

Why any woman would rather labor in the hot sun, accumulate calluses, and soil good surcoats with physical toil than live off her wealth confounded him. But one thing was certain. His method of bringing independent Elysia to her senses wasn't working.

So there wasn't a reason in the world to deny himself her bed any longer.

With grateful weariness, Elysia closed and locked the door to her bedchamber late that night, lighting one lone candle out of an effort to be conservative.

Alone at last.

No ladies' maid slept at her side. Because everyone at Vannes labored with basic survival tasks each day, it didn't seem right to add a frivolous duty like helping the lady undress to anyone's list of chores.

And, of course, Conon would not be joining her.

The hard toil of the day made her muscles ache with protest as she lifted her good surcoat over her head. The dinner she prepared did Vannes proud, even though it consisted mostly of inexpensive items like the fish the village boys caught. Fresh food required much less seasoning, so it saved her precious stores of spices.

She dropped a sheer night rail over her head, thinking the knights who attended the meal were a harsh and unpleasant lot. Although she hoped Conon did not seriously consider hiring them, she had no way of knowing the outcome of their visit. They all retired to a private study after the meal, shutting Elysia out.

Brushing the plaits from her hair with a heavy silver comb, she settled herself on the narrow pallet in the corner. When the loud rapping hit the door, she dropped the comb with a start.

"Who's there?" Yanking a clean tunic from the large rock that served as her bedside table, she covered herself.

"Conon." The lilting accent stole through her limbs.

Her heart caught in her throat, as it always seemed to when her husband came near. Elysia prayed he did not visit her to criticize or complain. She did not want any of his unhappy surliness to intrude on her private sanctuary of peace. Still, she unlatched the bolt and opened the door to receive him.

Despite the deep frown on his face, he looked as heavensent as ever. Would he continue to hold her at arm's length if she possessed beauty like Marguerite's?

"Good evening, my lord—"

He stepped inside without waiting to be invited, pushing past her with one broad shoulder. "Bolt it."

Her tiredness dissipated at his words. Renewed vigor leaped in her veins at the harsh command.

Conon was staying.

She fought to suppress a smile as she confronted her scowling husband. He might be here in her bedchamber, but he clearly was not happy about it.

He stood immobile in the room full of makeshift furniture, scrutinizing every detail. He fingered one of numerous linens that hung on the walls in place of tapestries.

Uncomfortable at his careful regard, Elysia sought to distract him. "Wine, my lord?"

Ignoring her, he lifted the linen to inspect the wall beneath, then ran his palms over the embroidered facade. "This will not keep out the draft in the winter, lady."

"The linen serves more for my pleasure than warmth, my lord." One commodity she never lacked was good linens.

"And this?" Conon moved on, touching the huge slab of stone that held her garments.

She shrugged, a bit discomfited he paid such careful attention to the furnishings of her bedchamber. "I like to keep my possessions off the floor."

"Don't you feel like you're living in a cave?"

"Nay." An unwanted flush stole through her. "I feel immensely clever for having turned an empty chamber into a comfortable living space. Is there something you wanted this evening?"

That got his attention.

"As a matter of fact, there is." Turning to face her, his fascination with the furniture vanished. He caught her elbow and pulled her to him.

A tremor shivered through her veins, rendering her still and silent. The last time they shared a bed, Elysia had initiated the intimacy they shared, and he had turned away afterward. Tonight, she would not be so bold. She'd had time to consider her marriage more then, more time to think about how they might one day reach an accord.

Waiting, hoping, she watched him. Fascinated with the candle-infused golden halo around his head, Elysia prayed he would forgive her one day. Because, although she wanted him to share her bed with every leaping impulse in her quivering body, she longed to share his heart even more.

"I come to seek retribution, Countess, for your missing dowry." Had he stepped closer? He suddenly towered above her, sliding his palm under her chin to turn her face up to him.

"Retribution?" A grim thought. Yet the heat of his body told her she was not alone in the delicious longing that slid through her at the notion.

"Aye." His eyes pierced hers as he took possession of her lips. "You must begin repaying me for the huge loss I've incurred by wedding you." The words warmed her mouth in between his kisses.

"I am giving you everything I can by trying to make life better for your people, by—"

Covering her words with a gentle finger, he shook his head. "Nay. Do not go on. I have seen how hard you work, lady, and it aggravates me to think of it."

What man didn't want a hardworking wife?

"I mean to extract payment in your bed, Elysia." With one hand, he stroked down the smooth length of her thigh, returning from the journey with the hem of her night rail in hand. "For as many nights as I wish."

Though his hand ignited arousal in every secret part of her body, she could not ignore the memory of Conon in Marguerite's arms. Pushing him away, she crossed protective arms over her chest. "Perhaps you would prefer the bed of a more practiced woman than I, husband. I must be a grave disappointment compared to your more experienced lover."

"Marguerite has not been my lover since we wed, Elysia."

"You forget I saw you locked in a lover's embrace with her the day after our wedding, my lord."

Shaking his head in vehement denial, Conon clutched her shoulders with insistent fingers. He met her gaze with calm assurance. "Nay. You saw Marguerite attempting to entice me back to her bed."

"And, saint that you are, you denied her." Her words dripped with sarcasm, but her heart cringed at the thought of another woman beneath her husband.

"I tell you, she did not succeed. Can you not trust me?"

"How can I offer you my trust, when you refuse to offer me any of yours?"

She watched a combination of emotions play across his expression: surprise, confusion, perhaps even a glimmer of understanding.

Still, he merely shrugged his shoulders. "I do not know, Elysia."

Since he refused to address the larger issue that loomed between them, she could either continue to deny his touch, or she could take a risk and grant him the trust he could not find in his heart to give her.

"Then I will go first, my lord," she whispered, leaning into him to graze his body with her own. Gathering her courage, she settled trembling fingers upon his chest. "I believe you."

Tension seemed to seep from him. Gentling his grip at her shoulders, he slid soothing hands around her back.

She sank into him, accepting his touch. "If you still

wish to enter my bed for the sake of seeking retribution, I would not deny you."

"I want you, Elysia, not retribution." His voice was naught but a hoarse rasp, thick with desire.

The press of his arousal made her brazen. She brushed the inside of her thigh against his leg with a languid stroke. "Pray, sir, take all you wish."

With a choked oath and a groan, he lifted her in his arms and deposited her on the pallet in the corner. There, he wrought the incredible bliss she remembered from the night spent on the road. He joined their bodies, not with anger or demand, but with tenderness and passion.

And although Conon had arrived seeking to extract payment from her body, Elysia basked in the warming thought as she finally fell asleep that she received as much and more than she gave.

Chapter Eighteen

Conon could not bear to leave Elysia's bed that night, preferring to gaze upon her while she slept. With a critical eye, he memorized her every imperfection, as if their cumulative sum would somehow make her less appealing.

There were the purple shadows under her eyes, testament to the long days of hard labor she forced herself to undertake. Then there was the slight crook to her nose that she once told him was the result of a punch Rubin had bestowed in the difficult days after their father died. Elysia, apparently, felt sorry for her brother's grief and did not retaliate.

Her callused hands upset him the most, but they did not make Conon want her any less.

Indeed all of her little flaws endeared her to him more than the perfect beauty of her liquid brown eyes or silky black hair. Elysia's flaws showed her character.

But another flaw lurked beneath the surface. Her damnable proud independence. Her insistence on taking care of everyone and everything around her.

Conon would never understand what drove her to work so hard, but by God, he had to admire her. Could he forgive her? Forgive her for falsely claiming the independent status of a widow? Overlook the fact that she wanted to spirit away her bridal portion for a rainy day?

Conon was surprised to realize mayhap he could.

Last night, she had believed in him. Even when she had every reason to think he had been trifling with Marguerite, Elysia had trusted him. Her simple gesture heartened him, restored some of his faith in her.

But his tender regard for Elysia was too new, too fragile to risk just yet. As dawn crept through the thin linen she had hung over the casement, Conon left her chamber. He did not want to give Elysia the wrong impression if she woke up and found him still by her side. He needed to think over the events of the night before he foolishly committed his heart to her.

He busied himself with greeting more arriving knights that morning. Slowly but surely, mercenaries made their way to Vannes in response to Conon's recent call to arms.

Settling the latest newcomers in sparse quarters in the garrison behind the keep, Conon was in the process of re-assuring the men that their task would begin at the next dawn, when footsteps approached.

"Have I heard the rumor right?" The familiar voice caught Conon off guard. "The Count of Vannes seeks mercenaries?"

Turning from his task, Conon strode over to shake his friend's hand. "Leon."

"Conon." He grinned, his stance relaxed. Leon's whole manner struck Conon as rather at ease for a man who had deserted his best friend.

Excusing himself to his other guests, Conon shoved his friend out of the garrison and into the noon sun. "Where the hell have you been?"

"That's a fine welcome back." Leon folded his arms

across his chest, resting against the thick width of a towering pine tree.

"You disappeared without a word." Conon rubbed his temples. "And believe me, your timing could not have been any worse. Things have gone downhill in a hurry with Elysia."

"She is as good as my stepdaughter now, Conon, so watch what you say."

Conon paused, allowing the words to penetrate his brain.

"What?" For the first time, he looked Leon over with a hard gaze. The man was changed. Subtly, perhaps, but altered nevertheless. There was a satisfied look about him, as if he had accomplished great deeds and now reaped vast rewards.

"Daria Rougemont is with me and I am claiming her as my bride."

"Daria Rougemont Westmoor, you mean?" Leon couldn't be serious. He could always be counted on to be coolly rational, practical. What sort of stunt was this?

"Nay. Daria Rougemont, soon to be Daria de Grace, but we will speak more of the woman I love at a later time." Leon's expression grew stony as he leaned closer to Conon. "What the hell are you doing collecting a bunch of renegade knights?"

"Oliver would not hand over Elysia's dowry, and neither would my bride tell me where it is secreted, so I am taking Nevering as my due."

"Take Nevering? Have you lost your wits?"

"Nay. I have studied its defenses. I can win it."

"Conon, you have to pay mercenaries, or have you forgotten? Where are you going to get that kind of money?"

"Shh!" Conon pulled Leon even farther from the knights' garrison. "If they think for a moment they won't get paid, they'll walk out on the mission."

"Better that than they slit your throat after you can't pay them back." Although Leon looked furious, Conon noticed his friend lowered his voice.

"You know I earned enough at tournament this summer to give them recompense, should the need arise. Though I admit, it will be easier to meet their demands if I can also secure Elysia's missing dowry." Conon stilled as a disturbing thought occurred to him. "That is, unless Lady Daria already holds the dowry for her daughter?"

"Daria?" Leon's brow furrowed in confusion. "Are you mad?"

"I thought perhaps that is why she disappeared." Conon wondered lately if he was indeed mad. He hardly knew himself since he wed Elysia. "She strikes me as the sort of woman who would risk much for her daughter."

"*Aye*, Conon." Leon clapped him on the back in good humor. "But that is not why she left Nevering, friend. It is a long story."

Conon steered Leon toward the keep, eager to see Elysia's mother with his own eyes and learn what went on between Daria and his friend. He was undecided whether Leon's alliance with Daria factored into his scheme.

"Don't you think besieging Nevering is a little extreme?" Leon asked. "No doubt Oliver holds Elysia's bridal portion. You could merely ensure he gets wind of your plan to attack him and he would probably decide her fortune is not worth it."

Conon shook his head in grim resolution. His mind was made up. "We sail tomorrow, friend."

They reached the keep and entered to find Daria and Elysia engaged in animated conversation. Elysia smiled with joy, a feat Conon had not witnessed since before their marriage. Daria seemed to be acting out some adventure or another, her hands and hair flying in tandem as she mimicked someone in a fury.

"Ladies." All smiles faded as Conon entered the hall, although Daria's reappeared when Leon came into the room close behind him.

"I am sorry we gave you no notice of our arrival—" Daria began.

"Leon has always come and gone as he pleased." Conon noticed the hard look Elysia bestowed upon him. After a moment, he hastened to add, "And as Elysia's mother, I would hope you feel comfortable doing the same. You are welcome anytime."

"Thank you." Daria moved closer to her daughter to drape a protective arm around Elysia's shoulder. Why did the two of them look like coconspirators? Preoccupied with his wife, Conon unwittingly let a long silence fall.

Clearing his throat, Leon stepped amid them all. "We come bearing news."

Conon seated himself on the other side of Elysia. He felt curiously jealous of Daria's hand curled possessively around his wife's shoulder. He plucked up Elysia's hand to hold between his own.

"Daria and I have spoken with Arundel," Leon started, his smooth diplomacy easing over the tension that ran high in the room. "Although he will not support Daria's effort to annul her marriage to Oliver, we think he has seen the extent of Oliver's treachery and believe he will try to oust Westmoor from Nevering."

Why didn't Leon tell him this outside when they spoke of Conon's efforts to take Nevering? It occurred to Conon he had not imparted to his friend the fact that Elysia knew nothing of his plan. He stood again, relinquishing Elysia's hand. "Perhaps the ladies are not interested in this talk—"

"On the contrary, my lord," Daria intervened. "It is because of Elysia you might conceivably add Nevering to your list of holdings."

"Because of Elysia?" This did not bode well at all. A familiar sinking feeling took hold of him.

"Aye." Daria beamed with motherly pride, though Elysia looked distinctly less pleased. "If not for her urging me to seek annulment from Oliver, I would not have had a chance to inform Arundel of his vassal's attempted insurrection. Now Arundel will fight to show his dominion over Nevering. I am certain he would give Nevering into your hands, Conon, with your oath of fealty to him."

Elysia had done all that?

Conon waited to speak, struggling to rein in his temper as he stared at his wife. "You've gone behind my back once again, I see." He ignored her mother's sharp intake of breath.

"At the time, I did not perceive it as going behind your back, any more than you thought twice about tricking me into marriage." Her callused fingers twisted themselves in knots, belying the defiant attitude of her words.

"Lady, you have more than repaid me in kind for that wrong."

"Nay, sir. What I hoped to gain from Daria's visit to Arundel was an annulment for her so I might seek annulment for myself. If Oliver is overthrown as my stepfather, his decision about who I wed would be equally invalid."

A red rage descended over him, and the knowledge that she could do that to him made him even more furious.

"Out." The word barely escaped through gritted teeth.

Daria started, as if ready to defend her daughter. "But—"

His eyes never left Elysia. "Get out."

Without another word, she did as he bid. She did not rush, nor did she complain, but merely plucked up her sewing and departed the hall.

"You miserable bastard." Daria Rougemont soon-to-be de Grace had never claimed to be the dignified woman her daughter turned out to be. She bolted from the hall in a temper, her hair and gown flying in a swirling tempest behind her.

"What in Hades is the matter with you?" Leon threw his hands in the air with exasperated disgust. "You used to be the most even-tempered, smooth-talking knight in all of France. Now you are…" He paused suddenly, as if an idea had occurred to him.

"What?" Conon interrupted. "Miserable that I am married to the most independent woman on earth?"

Smacking a palm to his forehead, Leon slumped onto the trestle behind him. "You are in love with her."

The pronouncement hit Conon in the chest like a blow. "Don't be ridiculous. She is the reason my life is in shambles. Because I wanted to teach her a lesson, I have no furniture. Because she harbors her wealth to herself I can scarcely afford to pay those mercenaries—"

"Because of her clever talent you have some very lovely linens on the walls where tapestries should be." Leon peered around the hall with amused interest.

"I could never love her." A man would have to be a fool to allow himself to care for such a shrewd maid.

"I have made up my mind to the contrary, friend." His companion shrugged. "But I am sure if you keep treating her so abominably, Elysia will believe it soon enough."

Without another word, Leon walked away, leaving Conon to his misery.

* * *

"I can't believe he would talk to you like that in front of your own mother!" Daria fumed as she paced the floor in Elysia's bedchamber.

Unconcerned, Elysia let her speak her piece. While Daria ranted and raved about the injustice of it all, Elysia considered how she would extract the information she needed from her mother without giving away the plan that began to take shape in her mind.

"I can't believe you were able to find Arundel so easily," Elysia interrupted once the ranting had turned into more quiet grumbles.

"Having Leon with me turned out to be quite fortuitous in more ways than one." Daria's face practically glowed when she spoke of the man she hoped to legally wed one day. "It proved easier for him to approach passing knights on the road and ask them if they had word of Arundel's whereabouts. We found him three days into France."

"Where did you discover him, exactly?" Elysia fingered her sewing project, hoping she did not give away too much.

"North of Blois." Daria eyed her daughter suspiciously. "Although I doubt he will remain there for long if he hopes to oust Oliver from Nevering before the winter hits."

Elysia had not thought of that. There might not be much time to get to him.

"What mischief goes on in that serious little head of yours, Elysia?" Daria strode over to Elysia's place on her pallet and sank to her knees.

"What do you mean?"

Daria frowned. "You know perfectly well what I mean. You cannot hide a good scheme from the woman who thrives on them."

Elysia shook her head. She could not get her mother involved in any more dangerous plots. "I am just eager to see

Oliver get what is coming to him. I wonder how many days it would take Arundel to get troops from Blois to Nevering?"

Caught up in imagining all the ways Oliver Westmoor might be humiliated and brought to his knees by his angry overlord, Daria seemed to forget about Elysia's interest in Arundel's whereabouts. Thank goodness.

When Conon had angrily dismissed her from the hall earlier, it dawned on Elysia that only one thing would redeem her in his eyes. Maybe.

After Daria's departure to rejoin Leon, Elysia had ample time to consider her next move. If she could locate her missing bridal portion, Conon might forgive her transgressions. Ever since learning the boat master told Conon the Vannes treasures had been shipped to their "rightful owner," Elysia grew more and more certain where the misplaced wealth lay.

In the greedy earl's lap.

Now she had to get it back. That small fortune represented all that was wrong in their marriage, and all that kept she and Conon apart. She could not change the fact that she had misrepresented her wedding night. But she could change Conon's belief that she hid her bridal portion from him. Finding the wealth might be a way to recoup some of his faith.

No matter the cost, Elysia would uncover the whereabouts of her missing dower. It would be the first step toward winning back her husband's trust.

Chapter Nineteen

Conon lay back on his pallet, idly tossing a small sack of gold in the air and catching it with one hand, just above his nose.

Toss.

Catch.

Toss.

How long had he whiled away the hours, knowing sleep would not come? At first he had been angry when he threw himself on his pallet at bedtime. Elysia's staunch determination to act independently still galled him. She had turned out to be more clever and bold than he had first anticipated. Her scheme was both brilliant and daring, if he could look at it from the standpoint of anyone but the overthrown husband.

In fact, he could almost admire Elysia's incredible industriousness and hard work to get the things that she wanted from life. She actually came from a similar background to his. They both had to struggle to make a pretense of noble living when they had been devoid of funds.

Toss.

Elysia met the challenge with even more success than he had.

Catch.

Snagging the rough woolen sack from the air, Conon jerked himself to a sitting position. Could that be what bothered him most—not her independence per se, but her unflagging ability to succeed in spite of him?

Elysia had created a fortune from a good idea and backbreaking labor. And since they'd arrived in France she had proven she could do it all over again.

Conon thunked the small sack against his head in a gentle but insistent rhythm. Many men would be intimidated by her fierce independence, but such was not the case for him. He had just hoped for a bride who would need and value him. He still nurtured ridiculous dreams of a warm family and loving wife.

But he would never obtain them by banishing Elysia from his hall. In front of her own mother, no less.

He *had* tricked her into marriage, after all, knowing she was the most self-reliant woman in Christendom. Perhaps he could forgive her this once and lose himself in the snug heat of her body.

The idea gained appeal by the instant. Creative ways of awakening his sleeping countess tumbled through his head as he traversed the corridor to her room in naught but his braies. With sunrise still an hour away, he could indulge himself more than once before freeing her to go about her daily business.

Thankfully, Elysia had not locked the door. A ray of hope shone through Conon as it occurred to him perhaps his wife wished for him to join her.

Careful not to disturb her rest prematurely, he navigated

the various rocks in the chamber with caution. Jamming his shin into a huge stone anyway, Conon muttered a curse.

Damn miserable excuse for furniture. Maybe if he bought some new furnishings with the winnings he had from the summer, Elysia would realize she didn't have to work like a peasant. Maybe then she would have time to be the kind of wife he had envisioned for himself.

Kneeling beside her pallet, Conon reached out to stroke her silken hair. Finding only a tangle of bedclothes, he reached farther across the pallet.

More linens.

Leaping onto the makeshift bed, he flung his arms wide in a panicked attempt to find her. Nothing. He lifted the thin linen from the casement to allow the fading moonlight into the chamber. His wife was not there.

"Elysia!" he bellowed the name, unconcerned whose sleep he might disrupt in the hall. "Elysia!" Conon shouted into the corridor.

Running to his chamber for a flame from his dully burning hearth, he brought a full-fledged torch into Elysia's quarters. Light spilled into every corner of her private haven, as neatly arranged as her perpetually perfect person.

"Sweet Jesu, Conon, what's afoot?" Leon stumbled into the chamber alone, though the mate of his heart followed close on his heels. "Go back to bed, Daria," he whispered.

"She's gone, isn't she?" Daria piped up over Leon's shoulder, peeking around her husband with frightened wide eyes. She shoved Leon hard, and pushed her way through.

"*Aye,* Mistress Conspirator." If anyone ought to know the whereabouts of Elysia, Daria would. "Where is she?"

With frantic movements, Daria searched the chamber herself, then turned accusing eyes toward him. "Why don't you tell me, Conon? A newly wed bride should either be awake at night or too exhausted from her husband to roam around by herself."

Caught off guard by the counterattack, Conon found it difficult to reply. "We…did not sleep together last night."

Daria approached him, her bed-tousled hair giving her the semifearsome look of an Amazon warrior in a silk chamber robe. "Let me offer you a little advice, St. Simeon." As she reached him, she planted tight fists on her hips. Conon's own mother had never intimidated him half so much. "Never send your wife off to bed by herself, no matter how miffed you might be. It makes for bad blood in a marriage, and deprives you both of the one thing that might keep you together despite the arguments and misunderstandings."

Fear niggled at Conon's brain. If Daria truly didn't know where to find Elysia, his wife could be in grave danger.

His hand trembled just a little as he extended it toward his mother-in-law. "If you help me find her, I promise you, I shall not fail in that duty again."

Daria squeezed his fingers in gentle forgiveness.

Leon strode to her side, slipping his arm possessively about her waist. "Do you know where she is, Daria-mine?"

Conon shook his head to watch Leon de Grace—his lifelong idol of strength and self-possession—battle an obvious twinge of jealousy.

Daria's brow furrowed in thought. "She must be around the keep somewhere." Seeming to war with a thought, she shook her head violently. "Elysia would never be so foolish to—"

"What?" Conon barked, a sinking feeling in his gut assuring him he would drive the sanest woman to do something stupid.

With frightened eyes, Daria met his gaze. "Elysia wanted to know exactly where we found the earl." Looking helplessly at Leon, she shook his arm in urgent accompaniment to her message.

"Why would she wish to see the earl?" Leon wondered aloud.

The grim knowledge settled over Conon. "To succeed where her mother failed. She goes to gain support for her annulment."

"Nay, Conon, wait—"

He turned to leave, impatient to be underway. Daria chased after him and yanked his arm in a command for attention.

"She no doubt goes to get your precious money back, my lord." Her green eyes flashed fire and condemnation. "My daughter believes returning your gold is the key to righting her mistakes."

Conon paused, considering the words. He didn't care about the money. He cared about her trust.

Could Elysia be that foolish? Perhaps she could be, after the way he had behaved lately.

He shut out Daria's words, stalking from the chamber intent on his purpose—to haul his wife home before the sun set. Saints preserve her if she reached Arundel before Conon found her. From what Leon had confided of the earl, Conon did not trust the man to behave honorably where Elysia was concerned.

He tore through the keep and packed for a short trip, then headed to the stable, struggling to ignore the sick feeling that twisted his gut.

Leon waited for him with a horse already saddled and eager for a ride. "They are north of Blois, a straight shot east. I think you can beat her there if you take the high road. 'Tis more dangerous, but quicker."

Conon nodded his thanks as he mounted and secured his bag.

"And, Conon?" The note of warning in Leon's voice stopped him short. Conon glanced up expectantly, noticing for the first time that Daria lurked in the shadows beside Leon, shivering from the morning air in her thin wrapper. "John Huntley is with the earl."

Fear knifed through Conon's insides, but he nodded acknowledgment before tearing into the streaky pink light of dawn.

Daria worried her lower lip as she watched him go, fear for her daughter making her a bundle of nervous energy.

"He will bring her back safely." Leon's words pierced her fright and she relaxed at the confidence in his voice.

Leon knew Conon and his capabilities well. For that matter, Daria had witnessed her daughter's husband beat back a field of fierce competitors to win her daughter's hand. She must trust in him. "How could she just take off into the night by herself?"

Leon rubbed his hands over her chill skin, chiding her with his glance. "Look who she has for a teacher. You are fortunate she did not turn out more reckless with a role model like you." Planting a kiss on her shoulder, Leon pulled her to him.

"But Elysia has always been so driven by duty and responsibility." She ignored Leon's straying lips down her neck. "You know that girl did not so much as touch a toy after her father's death? What other girl would instantly give up every shred of childhood to fulfill the role as head of the family?"

"Conon will show her how to play again." His words rasped over the swell of her breast.

"As I have shown you?" She giggled at his answering hard squeeze.

"You have not begun to show me any such thing, Daria-mine." Leon's fingers trailed down the length of her silk-clad thigh.

"Liar."

"I demand a lesson."

Daria heaved a long-suffering sigh as Leon swept her off the ground and into his arms. With one hand she cupped his face, reveling in the rough scratch of new growth on his cheek. "You, sir, are a very slow learner."

"With you as my teacher, lady, I will make sure I never complete my studies."

Languishing in his arms with the relaxed anticipation granted to a woman who has a lifetime of love in front of her, Daria thanked God for Leon.

The journey at night didn't scare Elysia half as much as traveling during the day.

Now that daylight shone brightly on the road north of Blois, Elysia feared meeting a stranger. Not even whores or female thieves traveled alone.

To pass the time more pleasantly, she thought of Conon. Although his demeanor had been cold and distant since their wedding night, flashes of Conon's old self seeped through at odd moments. Elysia had spied him checking her flax plants several times since she'd planted them. He even ordered the removal of three trees that blocked the light in her new garden.

Then again, perhaps Conon only took an interest in the flax because he saw the money-making potential of the endeavor. Elysia felt strangely deflated at the notion, reluctant to let go of her fantasy that Conon would one day support her desire to nurture a thriving business of her own.

Far-off shouts drifted to her ear. Afraid to meet a stranger on the road, Elysia steered her horse into the thicket before she realized the shouting emanated, not from fellow travelers, but a huge English encampment.

The earl.

Elated that her journey drew to a close, Elysia urged her horse forward. Too late, she heard the stirring in the underbrush and recalled the camp could be guarded.

A disembodied voice emerged from the forest, though the speaker did not. "My God, if I am not a lucky bastard."

Elysia kicked her mount, but a hand snaked out of the bushes to jerk the reins near her horse's head.

John Huntley unfolded his long length from his covert position in the woods. "Not so fast, Countess."

Elysia's heart plummeted. She shouldn't have come here alone. Her fierce pride and sense of independence had overruled her good sense, and now she would face the consequences.

Even as she gulped back her fear she prepared for battle. She reached for her knife, shielding her movements within the folds of her gown. Slowly she unsheathed the weapon.

"Release the mare, Huntley. I have a meeting with your lord," she said, surprised at the tone of cool detachment she managed.

He wavered only a moment, then shortened his grip on the reins. "The earl would never ask you to come to Blois, Elysia."

"I would not interfere with his plans if I were you." Her nervous fingers worked the handle of the knife round and round in her palm.

"What business would he have with you? Unless..." He shook his head. "Your husband could not be so foolish as to send *you* to retrieve the Nevering fortune." Huntley looked about the trees, as if half expecting someone to attack him from behind. "Does he use you as the lure?"

In spite of her fear, Elysia's heart raced to think her guess had been correct. The earl possessed the missing money.

"Nay, sir. Do not come any closer until you speak to the earl." Forcing her shaking hand to be still, she clutched the knife and poised herself for any false move.

She thought herself prepared for anything, but instead of reaching to pull her from her horse, Huntley yanked her leg with one swift jerk. He tossed her to the ground before she knew what happened.

By the time she pushed herself upright, Huntley had already run off her mare. "This has been a long time coming, Lady Elysia." He knelt on the ground in front of her before she could scramble to her feet.

Memories of the last time he touched her assaulted Elysia. His filthy hands on her flesh… Fear and anger steeled her.

Miraculously, the knife remained in the death grip of her fingers, still hidden at her side. Breathing deeply to calm herself, Elysia waited for an opportune moment to strike.

That moment arrived when the first thing the greedy animal did was double forward to put a hand up her gown— exposing his neck and upper back.

Big mistake, Huntley.

She gripped the knife and thrust the blade into his back, unmoved by his howl as she kicked up dirt in her attempt to escape him.

But in his pain, he fell on top of her. The ponderous weight of his body pinned her to the ground. Not weakened yet by blood loss, he seemed to have the strength of ten men when he backhanded her temple.

With her last coherent thought, she prayed Conon would forgive her.

Chapter Twenty

After riding hard all morning and changing horses twice, Conon thought he should be nearing the English encampment. Whenever his fears for Elysia threatened to overwhelm him, he did his best to recall his fury with her. How could his intelligent, practical wife risk her neck to annul their marriage? Did she resent him that much?

Pausing in a clearing to establish direction, Conon heard a man bellow. Uncertain what he would find, but unable to ignore the shout, he turned south in the direction of the sound. As a series of shouted oaths and epithets assured Conon he moved in the right direction, a warning pricked along the back of his neck. The angry voice sounded forebodingly familiar.

Suddenly the vicious cursing stopped. The forest road grew ominous in its silence.

Conon looked in all directions for some sign of movement, but the thicket grew so dense it betrayed nothing. Concentrating on the stillness, Conon waited for the slightest sound.

A muffled woman's cry sent him charging through the

heavy underbrush, heedless of thorns and branches lashing at his face and arms. Though the feminine voice remained indistinguishable, Conon knew with icy certainty who had made that soft whimper.

He prayed his instincts were wrong. That the pitiful sob he'd heard belonged to anyone but Elysia. If Elysia were hurt or worse— Conon didn't know what he would do.

Squeezing through a thicket of trees, he found his wife. The tableau before him froze the blood in his veins. Elysia lay on the ground beneath a senseless man, her bare legs exposed to the earth and sky. Eyes closed, body unnaturally still, she was pinned to the ground while a knife protruded from the man's back.

Conon leaped from his horse and ran to Elysia. He didn't need to look at the big knight's face to know the man's identity. John Huntley had vowed to avenge himself on Conon. The bastard had obviously kept his word.

Conon pulled the dead man off of his wife and scooped Elysia into his arms. He swept her tunic down over her legs with one hand while he placed a gentle kiss on her throat.

Her heartbeat thudded dull and warm beneath his lips. Relief flooded him. For her sake, he prayed Elysia had not been molested. For his own sake, he merely thanked God for her life.

Sifting through her silky black hair in search of a bump, Conon found nothing amiss. Only when he wiped some of the blood from her face did he discover the series of deep bruises in the distinct imprint of a man's hand and a small cut by her eye. The majority of blood darkening one of her sleeves seemed to be Huntley's, however, for Elysia was otherwise unmarked.

Conon lifted her awkwardly into the saddle, then settled in behind her. He cradled her with one arm, gauging the safest path away from the English camp before anyone discovered Huntley.

Only when they were several leagues from Blois did Conon stop. Gently pulling Elysia to the ground in a protected glade, he needed to hold her, check her. The residual fear from finding her with Huntley and covered with blood left him shaking.

Still.

He should have been riding with all haste to the coast this morning, but he could not think of anything but Elysia just now.

His mercenaries waited for him to lead them in battle to take Nevering in his name, but that cause did not strike him as important today. Unfurling a crumpled wool blanket from his travel bag, he draped the pine-needle-blanketed ground with its warmth and laid his wife upon it.

Elysia slept as if dead. Although the blue vein at her throat still pulsed strongly, Conon grew more fearful. He'd heard of people never waking from a head wound.

What if he never looked into those deep brown eyes again? Never loved her again? In a moment, he assured himself, he would go. For now, he could not rid himself of the feeling that if he watched over her carefully, she would awaken. More than once he peered into her expressionless face, wondering if there was any chance in the world she had foolishly sought Arundel to reclaim her bridal portion as opposed to seeking his support for an annulment.

Preposterous though the hope might be, Conon wanted to believe Elysia did not hide her wealth from him. What if his wife had been motivated by the noble, though reckless, cause Daria suggested?

She goes to get your precious money back.

Oddly, Conon found it mattered less to him what her

reasons were for leaving. He had found her. His countess lived and breathed here in his arms.

At a slight movement of Elysia's head, all other thought evaporated. Conon stroked her cheek and shook her gently, calling her from the heavy sleep. "Awake, *mon amour.* Look at me."

Elysia heard Conon's voice from far away, wanting nothing so much as to believe he could be right there beside her. Concentrating on the effort, Elysia pulled her eyes open to see him. Her heart smiled to look upon him.

Yet he looked so worried. "Conon?"

"I'm here." His hand shook as he stroked her cheek.

Elysia could not remember the last time he had touched her with such tenderness. Her eyes drifted closed again as she relaxed in the comfort of the knowledge that he watched over her.

"Did he hurt you?"

The question brought back a swarm of frightening images. Opening her eyes again to chase away the memories, she shook her head. "I don't know. He hit me and then I…"

"What about before that. Did he…"

The memory chilled her inside. She recalled that all too well. "I stabbed him."

A light touched Conon's deep blue eyes, rendering them the color of the summer sea. His voice sounded surprisingly soothing. "I know."

It had been so awful. At least Conon did not seem angry. Then another idea shook her, frightening her to her very soul. Struggling to sit up, she clutched Conon's surcoat. "Is he dead?"

His arms lifted her just a little, and he propped her against his chest so she might lie back against him. "*Aye, chère,* but not by your hand. We fought when I found you and he fell from a ledge into the sea."

She suspected Conon merely sought to protect her with this version of Huntley's demise, and for that, she was grateful. Still, she couldn't truly regret Huntley's death. He had violated his knightly code of honor and abused her person most vilely. Still, her rash action of traveling alone had hastened him to his end and for what? She had come no closer to securing her bridal portion from the earl.

"I will obtain the gold when I feel better." She wished she could reassure Conon on that point.

"You truly believe he has it?" He sighed the words into her hair as he kissed the top of her head.

Gooseflesh pricked the skin on the back of her neck as it occurred to her she rested between his long, powerful thighs to recline against him.

"Huntley confirmed it," Elysia confided lazily, the money seeming less important when she was in Conon's arms. "Arundel keeps it in his possession."

Conon went still. Every muscle in his body seemed to flex and turn to steel. "Arundel would steal the wealth of his own ward?"

"Mayhap he thought to protect it." She skimmed a hand along his arm, a vain attempt to soothe him. "He did not plan to see me wed for some time, after all. He may have told Huntley to bring it to him rather than leave it at Nevering."

Conon curled a hand around her chin. "Your mother informed him of our marriage. He knew full well your wealth should have been returned."

Elysia felt his anger palpitate between them, though for once, it was not directed toward her. If anything, his annoyance calmed her, wrapping her in his watchful protection. He would take care of her.

"All this time, I thought you were hiding it from me."

"You had every reason to mistrust me, my lord. I do not blame you."

He trailed gentle fingers over her hair and down the curve of her neck. "I will make war on your overlord, lady. He will pay the price for cheating my wife."

"You do not have to—" Elysia stopped midstream, suddenly realizing her words would not be what Conon wanted to hear. She had tried so hard to win his approval by being self-sufficient and turning Vannes into a prosperous keep once again. But perhaps that was not what Conon needed. Mayhap he wanted to help her as much as she wanted to help him. "Then I select you as my champion."

"I have already assembled men, Elysia." Conon lifted a wary brow at her response. "My mercenaries will take Nevering."

He would be challenging far more than Oliver Westmoor's power. By waging war on Nevering, he would be taking on one of the most powerful earls in England. Still, she bit her tongue. Conon was the military strategist. Certainly he knew what he was about. But she could not resist offering her aid.

"I will help you if you want me to."

"Nay." He pulled her closer, squeezing her fiercely. "I require no assistance." His voice turned low and husky as he fingered the neck of her bodice.

Warming at the intimacy of his touch, Elysia wondered at her own wantonness since meeting him. That he could arouse her so soon after her bout with Huntley surprised her. But his touch bore no resemblance to Huntley's cold brutality. And Elysia needed Conon's touch, his tenderness.

Would he still want her after Huntley's vile assault?

She snuggled more closely into the strength of his chest.

If he pushed her away now, she did not think she could withstand it. Allowing herself the luxury of reveling in the play of his hands upon her, Elysia relaxed in his arms. Like a bee drawn to a favored summer bloom, Conon's fingers traced a sure path to the peaks of her breasts.

Unbidden, a moan escaped her lips. He tilted her chin with his fingers and met her gaze. Glacial blue eyes probed the depths of her soul, looking as uncertain and wary as she felt.

"I need you, Elysia." Tunneling his hand through her hair, he brought a handful to his cheek to brush silkily over his face. "But only if you are willing…. If it is not too soon." Allowing the hair to fall, he reeled her in next to him like a prize catch.

His solicitous concern curled through her heart and squeezed. Yet Elysia had not thought of stopping. She craved his touch, his attentive care for her body after John's assault.

"Nay. I need you, too."

Desire rocked her when his hips grazed hers. Conon had not spoken to her with such tender affection since their wedding night. And she had missed him sorely since then. Her body craved the silver-tongued Frenchman who could talk her into a swoon with his sinful promises and wanton suggestiveness.

Dappled sunlight warmed her still further, patterning their bodies in leafy shadows. Garments melted away from her fevered skin at Conon's touch. "This time will be different, *chère*. I promise you," he whispered, the hard length of his body held tantalizingly close over top of hers.

His hand palmed her belly, robbing her of speech. "I will give you my babe this time, and you will nurture it with even more devotion than your flax plants, *aye?*"

Her empty womb convulsed with answering longing at

the thought. Tears bathed her eyes at the gentleness in his voice. Unable to bear his absence a moment longer, she wrapped her arms around his neck to pull him toward her. "I swear it."

Slowly and sweetly he drank from her lips, mating their mouths in a primal rhythm. Conon descended to kiss her breasts and belly, inciting her flesh wherever his lips touched. Elysia moaned in hungry anticipation of a deeper touch.

"All in good time, *demoiselle*."

The whispered words were like an invocation to her flesh, breathed out over her belly. Conon lifted himself up on muscular arms, while the sun imbued him with a golden glow, burnishing him with angelic light.

"You know as well as I, Elysia, the best plants grow in the most fertile soil."

A mischievous glint in those blue eyes promised something beyond her comprehension. Watching her every movement, as if taking delight in her confusion, Conon slid those strong arms under her thighs.

Her heart fluttered a nervous dance. "Conon, I don't thin—"

Then his head descended and Elysia's every objection was lost in a torrent of heady sensation. The dull ache that hungered for him transformed into a sharp torment of need. "Conon, please…"

Her words were swept away in a shattering instant as Conon pushed her over the inevitable brink of pleasure. The world behind her closed eyelids grew dark for a moment before it exploded into a dazzling display of white light. Spasms of fulfillment rocked her, leaving her clinging to her husband.

Conon loomed above her like a pagan god in all his glory, his blue eyes still as determined and driven as ever.

Saints alive, there was more.

In the overwhelming moment of her own pleasure, she had nearly forgotten the point of it all. But now, gazing up at her husband, Elysia remembered the best was yet to come.

He stared down at her as he entered her, as if willing her to look back at him. Elysia found she could not look away if she tried. His gaze held her as surely as his body did, and she wanted to weep with the joy of it.

A profound difference marked their lovemaking this time, an ineffable sense of understanding that had been markedly absent when he came to her on those two occasions since their wedding.

This time, he lacked the bitter resentment and condemnation. His touch spoke of forgiveness, of a new trust. Whether he would admit it to himself or not, Elysia could feel that Conon had grown to care for her just a little bit.

The notion softened her heart and made her squeeze him tighter still. Even knowing he might not ever return the sentiment, Elysia could not help the feeling that bubbled up spontaneously inside her.

"I love you, Conon."

Eyes widening, Conon descended to her and took her mouth in a soul-stealing kiss. In that moment, he found his own release, and although he did not return her promise of love, he bathed her womb with the promise of the future.

Elysia hoped it would be enough to carry her through the battle that still lay ahead.

A sennight later, Elysia puttered in a dim crofter's kitchen, a scant league from Nevering Keep. She cut beans and stirred soup alongside her hostess, Anna Weaver, despite the woman's insistence she did not need help.

Elysia hated idle hands.

"So my lord Conon thinks we can aid him in winning Nevering?" Anna asked softly, more to prevent any passersby from hearing their conversation than for the sake of the soundly sleeping newborn in the cradle beside her.

I will give you my babe this time.... The sight of the precious infant recalled Conon's words to her that night in France. The image of Conon's baby in her womb clutched at Elysia's heart.

"Aye." Elysia dropped the soup spoon and gazed into the cradle with thoughtful eyes before turning her attention to Anna. "If we can smuggle in Conon and a few of his knights tonight, we could avert a big standoff with Sir Oliver and take the keep with little bloodshed."

She had been surprised at Conon's scheme because it did not require an excessive display of force. In her experience, men often preferred to flaunt their prowess rather than follow the most practical route. Certainly her brother had never wanted to take the more sensible paths in his life. But beneath Conon's chivalrous exterior beat the heart of a warrior, a knight who could overcome whatever odds Fate offered him, even when they looked insurmountable. She loved that about him.

He had agreed to let Elysia go into the village outside Nevering to convert some crofters to their cause.

"It is a good plan, my lady." Anna paused in the midst of pounding down a small amount of wheat for the next day's bread. "But we won't need to sneak my lord Conon in tonight."

"We won't?" Elysia panicked, wondering if she had been wrong about Anna's allegiance.

The woman smiled and winked. "Nay, because my own Joseph serves as master of the watch tonight. He will open the gate wide to Conon St. Simeon."

Elysia could not believe their good fortune. "Would he really?"

"Aye. He hates serving Oliver. Most of the men do." When the baby stretched and frowned as if to cry, Anna rocked the cradle with her foot. "And the Count of Vannes made quite an impression here, don't forget. He won over many of your former men-at-arms by practicing with them."

Conon seemed to win people over quite easily, Elysia thought, as she watched the infant settle to sleep. She smiled to think of her own babe. Hers and Conon's. "Then I better make haste to tell him the news." She gathered a traveling cloak around her. "Does the guard still change at sunset?"

"Aye." Anna mopped her head with a clean linen. In the close quarters of her hut, the cooking flame overheated the small space. "Joseph will look for you at nightfall."

Impetuously, Elysia squeezed the kind woman's shoulders.

"I hate to mention it, Lady Elysia," Anna whispered as she pulled out of her embrace. "But is there any word of your mother?"

The thought of Daria's latest adventure lightened Elysia's mood. "Conon and I convinced her to go to Italy, where she will remain unless the Pope grants her an annulment." She made no reference to Leon de Grace. She did not care to have her mother's honor questioned in any way. "We did not want her near Oliver during the battle."

"Thank heaven. He is livid about her departure." Anna tucked a blanket more snugly around her babe's neck. "We have all feared for her safety if she returns."

"While Oliver Westmoor lives, she will not." She said a small prayer of thanksgiving that Leon de Grace insisted on it. Bidding Anna goodbye, Elysia hurried out of the hut and to the forest's edge where Conon waited. She pushed a peddler's cart in case anyone from the keep happened to notice a figure leaving the village.

Feeling daring and nervous as she drew near the camp, Elysia peeled back her hood to assure the men who hid in the woods of her identity.

"Elysia." Conon appeared to her first, leaping down to the earth from a low branch of a pine tree. Soon other men followed, until the forest rained with mercenary knights. "What news?"

Casting a wary glance about, Conon escorted her to a private spot in the forest and waited to speak until she took a seat on a dead log. Her husband played the courtier even in a crisis.

Quickly Elysia explained Anna's idea.

"Perfect." He grinned that devastating smile of his, leaving Elysia giddy with pride at her meager accomplishment.

"You'll do it, then?" Elysia kept waiting for him to point out the flaws in the plan and readjust it. She had finally realized Conon did not appreciate her never-ending attempts to be independent. She wasn't sure how much help or advice he would accept from her.

"I'd be a fool not to, Elysia." He bowed formally before her, as if they met in a great hall and not a clearing in the pines. "Thank you."

She watched him stride over to his men, commanding their attention with his lifted arm. As the mercenaries scrambled to sharpen blades and oil armor for any possible battle, the quiet of the forest was replaced by the dull clanking of weaponry and shields.

Watching Conon give last-minute orders and making preparations, she wondered how he felt about her. Since the lovemaking they shared after the incident with Huntley,

Conon had been more solicitous of her health and her opinions, but there remained a distance between them.

Although he obviously had come to care for her to a certain extent, he did not share the depth of feeling Elysia expressed that day. Just before nightfall, he sought her out privately, drawing her far from his men to speak to her.

"I go now, lady, to win your birthright as your dowry. Do I have your blessing?" His words, formal and stiff, tore at her heart.

How could he not know? She removed the silk that covered her hair and wordlessly tied it to his sword, repeating her actions from the day he won her hand on the tournament field. "Go with God, my lord. And my favor."

He nodded, as remote and distant from her as ever. Elysia could not bear the coolness between them.

"Conon." Stamping her foot after her mother's fashion, she tugged the sleeve of his tunic. "Wait."

He watched her with scant interest, yet she pressed forward, worried she might not have another opportunity to convince him of her love. What if he never came back?

Drawing close to him, she trailed her hand up his chain-mailed chest to his cheek. In the deepening shadows of the coming night, his blond hair dulled to burnished brown. Under cover of the dark, he looked less an angel and more a man.

"You deserve this." Her words rang with conviction. "Since I failed to restore the bridal portion to you, I can only hope you will obtain Nevering as a recompense for what I've lost."

His expression grew more grim. "I do not do this for recompense, Elysia. Not anymore." His voice knifed through the still clearing, low and fierce. "I do this for *you.* For your honor and for your vengeance."

"But Arundel has cheated you of your money—"

"It's not about the damn money." He sheathed his sword and gripped her by the shoulders. "I have money, Elysia. Enough to manage Vannes. And if that is not enough, I will sell my sword arm to the highest bidder."

"But there is not even any furniture at your keep, my lord." How could he think he had money when he couldn't afford to furnish his own holding?

He swiped an exasperated hand through his hair. "Jacques's creditors cleaned me out, but I have since recouped enough wealth to replace nearly everything." He cast his gaze heavenward toward the rising moon and thunked his forehead with the heel of his hand. Twilight fell as they spoke. "I hoped to make you surrender your fortune if your circumstances were more meager."

"So you chose to work me to the bone in the hopes I'd submit under the strain?" Of all the low-down, sneaky things to do. Her mouth fell open as she gaped up at him.

"I didn't know you'd take it upon yourself to right the ills of the entire village. *Sweet Jesu,* Elysia, I've never seen anyone work so hard." He cradled her face in the palm of his hand, tipping her chin to meet his eyes. "And the more you slaved away, the madder I got. It's like you had to prove to me you didn't need me for anything—you could take on the world by yourself."

A bit of her anger died at his words. "I never wanted to prove I didn't need you. I hoped to show you I could help you."

His grin was slow and sheepish, and took Elysia's breath away. "*Aye, demoiselle.* But it is a difficult thing to realize your wife does not need you."

Just when she thought they were getting close to understanding each other, she realized they were as far apart as they had ever been. "I cannot be someone I am not just to soothe your pride, my lord."

"I know." His blue eyes grew dark and unfathomable as he plucked up his fallen shield. "But perhaps we will grow to trust each other in the future."

Their moment of closeness had passed, leaving Elysia cold and shivering in the night air. He looked ready to depart, as if eager to be away from the woman who would never be the wife he had hoped for.

Now he prepared for battle—a battle he sought to win for her sake—and she could not bear the thought of him embarking on his mission without understanding the depths of her feelings. "I still hope we can have more than just trust between us, Conon."

"*Aye*. But first I must take care of you as you have taken care of the people of Vannes." Perhaps he could see her confusion because he forged ahead. "I will win Nevering to avenge you. Even if it is not important to you, it is significant to me."

Elysia couldn't understand. He would stake his love—their future—on the outcome of a battle?

"I will not be like your brother. I will not make excuses to you, nor will I rely upon you to take care of everything."

A light snow began to fall, the first of the season. Soft dots of white swirled around them, too beautiful for a night that would result in deaths and destruction. She wished they could simply enjoy it, the way they had gazed at stars and strolled the French seaside together.

But Conon St. Simeon was not the carefree knight she had once imagined. Beneath his playful exterior lay a complex and vastly wonderful man.

His mercenaries began to clamor for him from the other side of the trees. Now that it was fully dark, they needed to wage their attack. Her time with him had come to an end.

"Win your battle then, my lord, and return to my side." Elysia reached up on her toes to kiss his cheek. He took a step back, but she held his hand. "And know this, Conon. I may not need you to shelter me or feed me or clothe me. But I need you to be happy. I need you to be complete." Whispering the words through a veil of snowflakes, she released him to his fate.

Watching their cloaked figures disappear into the night, she prayed fervently that he would emerge victorious. And for once, she would have to content herself with merely praying. Like it or not, battle was his trade and her hands would have to remain idle for a few hours.

Gathering her dark cloak over her head, she stepped into the clearing and prepared to wait.

Chapter Twenty-One

Elysia's words echoed in Conon's mind as he led five of his men through the village toward the keep. It challenged him to be furtive when he felt as tall as a tree and utterly invincible.

Elysia's chaste kiss shattered his last defense against her. She might not be the kind of wife he had once dreamed of, but she was all he dreamed of now. All he wanted.

How could he not love a woman like that?

The whispery brush of lips that equaled her idea of a kiss inflamed him far more than any skilled seduction at the hands of one of his worldly widows.

Because it came from Elysia.

His independent wife.

A tremendous sense of well-being filled him until he thought he would burst with his pride and joy. As much as Conon wanted to take Nevering in order to avenge Elysia, a victory tonight could not compare with the feeling of winning his *demoiselle*'s love. It was a prize with more value than he could measure.

Nothing could stop him this night. Nothing.

Stealthily, Conon and his men entered Nevering. With incredible ease, they imprisoned any guard on the watch who did not embrace their cause, then admitted the rest of the mercenary knights.

By midnight, with barely a shield raised or a sword thrust, Conon controlled Elysia's former keep. All that remained was awaking Oliver Westmoor and informing him of the news.

A chore Conon relished.

Recalling the man who had forced Daria Rougemont to wed and bed him at knifepoint, Conon thought it best to rouse Oliver with the feel of cold steel at his traitorous throat. The deposed lord opened his eyes in immediate realization.

"Do not move, Westmoor, lest you feel the misery of a French blade." Conon stared down at him with grim satisfaction.

"I do not know where your infernal bridal portion is, St. Simeon," Oliver hissed between clenched teeth, though his eyes betrayed his fear. "Pray do not kill me for that which I've never laid eyes upon."

"Nay, sir, I will kill you for falsely promising me that which you've never laid eyes on." Conon increased the pressure of his knife against his captive's neck, though he had no intention of doing Oliver real harm. "A man of your stature should take more pride in his word."

Sneering, Oliver lifted a brow. "You must admit, St. Simeon, I gave you quite a treasure anyway. Elysia Rougemont can spin gold from straw, it seems." He snorted in disgust. "Would that her mother had been half as talented."

"I did gain a treasure, Westmoor, though by no help of yours." Raising his hand, Conon punched the former ruler of Nevering in the temple, rendering the man temporarily senseless.

The muffled yelp at the door distracted him.

Elysia stood framed in the portal, her hood pushed back so that her midnight locks spilled in all directions over her cloak. Eyes wide, she worried her lower lip between her teeth. "Did you kill him?"

He ignored her question. "What the hell are you doing here?" She should have been safely tucked away at Anna Weaver's house. Fear for what might have happened to her and relief that it hadn't mingled in his heart. Hadn't she frightened him enough for one lifetime the past sennight?

The harshness of his question seemed to snap her out of her fear. Waving aside his concern with harried impatience, she closed the distance between them. "I promised myself I would not interfere, Conon. But one of the laborers in the flax field spied the earl and his men pausing enroute to Nevering to speak with a traveler near the river. They will be close to the gates by now."

"Sweet Mary." Conon had not expected Arundel to arrive for at least another few days. It would be a miracle if he could get all of his men to their posts in time.

In his gratitude, he forgave her somewhat for not obeying him. "Thank you for coming, *demoiselle,* you know I could not have done this without you."

Dropping his unconscious burden back on the bed, Conon raced to the door, surprised to realize how invaluable his wife had become to him. Not only had he come to trust her, but he had discovered an independent wife could be of immeasurable help.

Elysia watched him, marveling at his speed and grace. Curious to see what he would do next, she followed him out the door.

Vaulting up onto the gallery banister, Conon gave her a rakish grin. "Tie him up then, *chère,* so I might meet our guests."

Yanking a corner of an elaborate tapestry from its moorings on the wall, he leaped from the balcony with a warrior cry, using the wall hanging to break his fall. Landing neatly on a trestle table in the hall below, he grinned up at her before sprinting out the main entrance.

Elysia observed his antics in mute surprise, amazed he could find levity in a situation such as this. And sort of pleased.

As horrible as this day might turn out to be, she couldn't deny the hope that beat anew in her breast. Conon seemed to have forgiven her. Even better, now that he would battle Arundel and avenge Elysia, he seemed to have forgiven himself. She had not seen him so lighthearted and full of wit since their wedding night.

Despite repeated reminders to herself that they were all in dire trouble if the earl entered the gates, Elysia could not help smiling as she searched for strong rope.

Elysia watched over her captive nervously. Although he remained trussed up like a Michaelmas roast, she would not fail in the responsibility Conon entrusted her with.

She had tied a lead rope from her sleeping prisoner to herself. That way she would know if Oliver tried to escape during the night. Despite the unforgiving hard surface of the oak chair she curled up in, Elysia closed her eyes to rest.

Conon's voice bellowed through the keep at dawn. "Elysia!"

"I'm here!" she shouted, instantly awake, struggling to free herself from her self-imposed captivity. "I am stuck and—"

Flinging the door open, Conon appeared. Spying the rope around her waist, he hastened near, a thunderous look on his face. "What on earth?"

The proximity of those broad shoulders and well-muscled arms distracted her. How could she have transformed into such a wanton in the few times her husband had touched her?

He tugged on the knotted rope. "What happened?" Turning accusing eyes toward the bed, Conon looked ready to do battle with Oliver.

Westmoor still slept soundly, however.

Shaking the seductive thoughts of Conon from her mind, she sighed. "I feared your prisoner would escape."

Working the knot with deft fingers, he freed her. "*Sweet Jesu*, Elysia, you didn't have to stay here with him."

"You left too soon for me to get complete instructions."

He grinned. "So I did. And it was a near thing, *chère*. I got there just in time."

"Arundel is locked out?" Elysia could hardly believe it.

"*Aye.*" He rocked back and forth on his toes, a gleam of pride lightening his eyes to the hue of a summer sky.

"You did it!" Throwing her arms around him, she squeezed him with all her might.

Although he pried her gently off him, he still smiled. "*We* did it."

"Nay, Conon, 'twas your—"

"No." His smile faded. "I am proud of what I have done here thus far, Elysia, but I would have you acknowledge your part in the scheme, as well." He held her at arm's length, his voice stern and authoritative. "You got us here, Countess. This is your victory as much as mine."

Taken aback by the powerful presence that seemed to emanate from her husband, Elysia nodded her silent agreement. "We make an admirable team, my lord."

Tugging her by the hand, he led her toward the door. "Come."

"Where are we going?" Tripping after him, Elysia glanced back to her prisoner, still sleeping soundly with his limbs tied in every direction.

Conon moved quickly, as familiar with Nevering's awkward twisting corridors as she was. The fortnight he'd spent in residence that spring had been time well spent.

"The north tower, above the earl's camp."

"But—"

"You will see."

Effectively silenced, Elysia followed him up a narrow staircase.

The north tower housed munitions and food stores. When they reached the top floor of the small square tower building, Conon pushed her down low to crawl with him across the floor.

"They'll never see us, Conon," she admonished, knowing he made her creep along to protect her from potential flying arrows.

"It doesn't hurt to be cautious."

Cautious?

Was this the carefree man she had fallen in love with? The Conon St. Simeon who arrived late to his own wedding? The man who walked barefoot in the surf, covered her bed in flower petals and made love to her under the stars?

There was something different about Conon now. An ineffable confidence evident in every line of his body.

Motioning for her to remain just inside the chamber, he moved with stealthy grace out onto the low balcony. Elysia watched him peer between the battlements before he returned to her side and slumped next to her on the floor.

"I want a united front when we talk to Arundel or else I wouldn't ask you to go out there with me." Taking her hand, he moved to stand.

Rooted to the spot, Elysia held him back. "What will you say?"

"It is a surprise." He arched an eyebrow in teasing invitation.

Knowing he would keep her safe, she followed him out onto the balcony behind the crenellated rampart. Conon situated her close to one of the battlements, presumably so he could push her behind the thick stone if an arrow came flying.

For his part, the Count of Vannes leaped up onto the wall, impervious to the fact that a fall from that height would kill him.

So much for caution.

"Arundel!" Conon shouted, his voice echoing out over the expanse of green lawns.

Elysia watched the muddle of knights below until a man came to the forefront of the crowd, his rich red garb with the fur collar proclaiming his status and position even at this distance.

"I am here, trespasser," the earl shouted back, his voice easily carrying the short distance to the low tower wall. "Open my gates at once."

Arundel's retinue looked well-trained and battle-ready on their fresh horses. The earl probably stopped to refresh himself at Westmoor Keep on the way to Nevering. Elysia guessed Sir Oliver would be in grave trouble with the earl for allowing Arundel's lands to descend into such turmoil.

"Impossible, sir," Conon returned, the wind whipping his hair and tunic as he stood on the precipice's edge.

Elysia grinned at his daring.

Conon smiled down at her for a moment, as if sensing her approval, then turned back to the earl. "I have claimed

Nevering as my hostage until you return that which is my wife's due."

"I have naught that belongs to your wife, knave."

"Ah, but you do, my lord earl." Conon's manner could not have been more gracious if he were seated in the king's private chamber having this discussion. "You have my wife's bridal inheritance, which served as her dower when she wed me. I demand payment at once, or you will never set foot in Nevering again."

So that's what he was up to. Elysia hoped Conon did not overplay his hand. The earl would hate feeling bested.

Even from her distance, Elysia could see the cocky tilt of Arundel's head at Conon's bold remark.

"Are you so sure of that? My intelligence tells me you cannot have but ten men in there with you."

Conon grinned wide. "Is that the same intelligence that told you there was a chance you could walk right in and take Nevering last night while Oliver Westmoor slept?"

Elysia smothered a laugh. Conon postured with such smug arrogance.

The earl would never know how close he had come to doing just that. If Conon had not sped out to the gates the previous night with all haste, Arundel's troop of some fifty knights would hold Nevering now.

"The king will not stand for this, St. Simeon."

"When he finishes his war in France I'm sure he'll stop by and lend you his aid, Arundel."

Everyone present knew there was no end in sight to the king's war with France. Silence met Conon's remark.

Conon shouted, "It is a simple trade. You will immediately return all of the wealth that rightfully belongs to Elysia, or I will set up a profitable residence here with the presiding queen of the European linen trade and she will reap enough gold to assuage her losses."

Elysia bristled at the clear implication she was his chattel. As if sensing her annoyance, however, Conon turned to flash her a lopsided grin of apology. His face hidden from Arundel, Conon raised his eyebrows at her, as if to say he had no idea what to expect from this negotiation, either.

In that moment, she felt a deep and abiding connection with her husband. She understood him perfectly, and the knowledge filled her with warmth.

"Tell him you want his decision by nightfall," Elysia prodded, swept up in the spirit of the demands.

Without hesitation, Conon turned to his audience, the public mask of self-assurance falling immediately into place. "We would have your decision by nightfall, Arundel, or the deal is off. My wife quite likes her home here, you know."

Bounding off the wall, Conon pulled her back into the shelter of the tower chamber behind the balcony. The crisp autumn air blew into the room unchecked by any tapestries.

The sun's warmth lit the room. The smooth stone floor glittered with sparkled flecks in the bright light of the slanted morning rays.

"Conon." She held his hands when he would have moved toward the door.

"Yes?" Though he looked as innocent as a schoolboy, Elysia suspected he knew exactly what she had on her mind.

"You gave the earl an ultimatum."

"That I did." Apparently Conon was not going to be very forthcoming.

"I'm a little surprised at how you worded it."

Conon nodded. "I had to be stern. Did you think your husband has no backbone?" He looked gravely offended.

She shook her head, growing serious. "You referred to the money as something that rightfully belongs to me."

He curled his hands around hers, cradling them between their bodies as he drew nearer. "It is yours, *chère*. That is why they call it a 'bridal portion.'"

Warmth spiraled through her, heating her far more on the inside than the sun's paltry rays could on the outside. She had the feeling Conon was trying his best to take care of her again. And she loved it.

"But it belongs to the husband until he dies. You are within your rights to call it your own."

He grinned. The sun caught strands of gold in his hair, illuminating him from behind with an angelic glow. "But I will not. You will keep your own blasted money for all the hardships I put you through. Get a ladies' maid or some ribbons for your hair or—"

She laughed. Sweet heaven, could he make her laugh. "It's a bit much for ribbons, my lord!"

"Buy ribbons for the crofters' wives. Their daughters, too." He shook his head. "I don't care, Elysia. Spend it on your new linen venture. But I will have none of it."

Sensing the futility of arguing the point with him, Elysia's mind turned to more grave matters. "What if Arundel chooses to battle with you? What if you're harmed? Or—"

He held up his hand to halt her list of fears. "First of all, I am Conon—the tournament champion of Nevering and all-around capable knight. I will win if it comes down to a fight."

Men! How could he be so—

A gentle hand beneath her chin interrupted her thoughts. He tipped her gaze to meet his. Blue eyes held her spellbound. "But Arundel will not cheat you, Elysia. Your honor is worth more to me than my life."

Did her heart stop beating? Or maybe it had just melted under the sweet caress of his words. She forced herself to speak, needing to form the question that had haunted her ever since their wedding night.

"You have forgiven me, then?"

Encircling her with his arms, he pulled her close. "*Aye.* The question is, do you forgive me?"

Her heart warmed that he would ask her. "Aye." Still, she yearned to hear words he had not uttered.

"Thank you, Elysia." He ran his fingers through her hair, smoothing it off her face and down her back. He brushed her cheek with his own. "I love you, wife. More than I ever thought I could love a woman."

She did not respond so much in words as in a sigh of complete and utter fulfillment.

Conon laughed, skimming his hands down the length of her body to pull her hips to him. "*Mon amour,* it is my goal to hear that little cry time and time again today."

Her eyes widened in surprise as he left her to bar the door behind them. "Here?"

Conon pulled her cloak from her shoulders and threw it ceremoniously on the floor behind her. Then he stalked toward her with clear intent. "Here."

Letting out a little squeal when he caught her, Elysia giggled as he tumbled her to the floor, ensuring she fell into the protection of his arms.

"What have we to do besides wait, anyway?" Conon asked in muffled tones as he bent to kiss her neck. "There is one thing I would like you to agree to first, however."

Surprised at the sudden serious note in his voice, she met his gaze, waiting. Though he seemed pleased, she couldn't staunch a tremor of nerves. Judging by his expression, whatever he wanted was of great importance.

"I want to bring Eadred home with us, to foster at Vannes."

"Yes. Of course, yes!" Laughter bubbled in her throat, as irrepressible as the joy that grew in her heart. "His mother will be so happy, Conon. We will care for him as if he were our own."

Any last trace of tension between them dissolved. Conon wrapped her in a bear hug to squeeze her breathless. "Although we will have many of our own, as well."

"St. Simeon!" A shout interrupted them. Conon's hand stilled on its path down her bodice.

"Arundel." They said the name in unison.

Elysia caught his idle fingers and pulled him to his feet. They walked out on the balcony to face the news together.

Conon squeezed her hand, and she knew he felt as nervous as she did. Not bothering to leap onto the wall, Conon remained by her side, holding her hand as he called down, "I am here."

"My Elysia has been fully entitled to her bridal portion all along. I am more than happy to deliver it to her new home in France."

Elysia and Conon exchanged skeptical glances.

"I want an emissary to go with you to see that the deed is done, and then I will gladly welcome you through your gates."

"Done. Send a man down, and I will see him to the coast this afternoon."

Conon raised his brow in plain surprise.

"Next year will be Nevering's most profitable yet," Elysia confided, guessing why Arundel would give in gracefully. "A whole new flax field has yielded a full harvest for weaving this winter."

"Do you want me to keep Nevering?" Conon asked.

"And give up generations of your family's inherited wealth?"

294 My Lady's Favor

He shrugged. "Only say the word, *chère.*"

Elysia laughed. "Send a man down!"

"I am sending a man down, Arundel," he shouted. "Consider our bargain struck." Conon turned to look expectantly at Elysia. "Your most profitable year ever?"

"Aye, my lord." She laughed at the naked greed in his eyes. "But I will soon make Vannes as profitable. With your blessing, that is."

Conon spanned her belly with his hand. "As long as our union is fruitful, I care not for the profits."

"I think a couple needs to sleep in the same bedchamber to accomplish those goals, my lord," she whispered, wrapping herself around him.

"I think we need to start addressing this issue right now." His hands dipped low to catch the hem of her gown and travel the length of her thigh.

"What of the man you would send to Arundel?" Breathless from the shivery response his touch ignited, Elysia whispered the words.

"He has made you wait long enough for what is yours." Conon laid her back on the cloak on the floor. "He can wait until I show my wife how much I love her."

"I hope it takes a very long time, my lord."

"I swear to you, *mon amour,* it will."

Epilogue

"Papa! Look what *Grandmère* showed me!"

Conon squinted against the bright sun to watch eight-year-old Rochelle thrust and parry with the light sword her grandparents bought for her on their trip to Italy. Tall and lithe, Rochelle's graceful figure grew more like her mother's everyday.

Eadred, already a hulking lad at sixteen summers, fended off her eager blows with a wooden staff. To Rochelle's credit, she put the boy through his paces.

"Beautiful, Rochelle!" Conon shouted, well pleased with her new talent. "Perhaps you'd better don protective gear, Eadred. Your new opponent shows fine form."

Eadred scoffed, only slightly more tolerant of females than he'd been eight summers ago. "I can manage one small girl."

Rochelle's tutor, *Grandpère* Leon, looked on. "She is as quick with the sword as her Uncle Phillipe, I'll warrant."

"Phillipe is not my uncle!" Rochelle protested hotly, increasing the rain of blows on poor Eadred in her annoyance. She refused to call Leon and Daria's son, who was a mere month older than she, "uncle." "He is my cousin, and not half so good with his sword."

"Rochelle." Conon forced a note of warning in his voice, though it did no good, as Leon laughed at her antics.

Bestowing a halfhearted glare in his friend's direction, Conon grew distracted by a little hand tugging at his surcoat.

"Papa, the baby is done eating now," five-year-old Lisette explained. Ribbons askew in her golden-blond hair, she turned pleading eyes upon her defenseless father. "Mama wants us to come take her."

He scooped her up in one arm. "Then of course we will go get her, little Lisette."

"Me, too, Papa! Me, too!" the imperious voice of three-year-old Cherie demanded. Her green eyes flashed the same emerald fire as her grandmother's. "I want to play with Baby Nanette."

"She will want to frolic with you too, *mon amour,*" Conon assured her, plucking up Cherie with his free arm.

Rounding the flower gardens filled with lavender and sweet marjoram, Conon inhaled the fragrant beauty of his wife's private outdoor bower. Surrounded by young fruit trees and filled with exotic flowers, Elysia had planted the hidden haven after her linen trade's first successful year in France.

"Oh, good, Conon, you are just in time!" Seated in a luxuriously padded chair, she cradled a newborn against her breast. "Nanette would play for a while before her nap."

Dropping his squirming charges to the ground, Conon winked at his wife. "I've brought her the best entertainment she could hope for."

Conon saw Elysia lay their infant daughter on a thick

pad of blankets. He smiled as she reminded Lisette and Cherie about the gentle touch to use with a baby.

"I *know,* Mama," Cherie returned, looking mortally offended. "Nanette is our baby, too."

Pride filled him, as it did every day Conon watched his daughters grow strong. And independent.

Elysia grinned up at him, her lovely face the original inspiration for his four beautiful daughters. "The babe is in good hands then, it seems."

She walked into his arms, more precious and valuable than the wealth of Vannes or the riches of her lucrative linen trade. He knew no man whose prosperity rivaled his own.

"Where is Rochelle?" Elysia asked, absently kissing his shoulder as she monitored the girls at play.

"With your mother and Leon. She is learning to use the sword they brought her."

"*Mon Dieu.* I did not think they truly meant to teach her."

"Daria says it is important for a woman to learn how to do more than sew."

"She has adopted scandalous notions since she married your friend." She shook her head in amused resignation.

"Ha! You mean my friend has adopted some scandalous notions since he wed your mother. 'Twas Daria who returned from Italy with a taste for sword fighting."

"An odd thing to learn on your wedding trip," Elysia admitted, laughing. "I think Mother just wants to ensure the girls can fend for themselves."

"My girls have me to protect them." No harm would ever come to his angels. Not while he drew breath.

"Thank Heaven they have you." Turning in his arms, she rose on tiptoe to kiss him.

His reaction was fierce and immediate. Because he practiced chivalrous restraint while she convalesced from childbirth, he hadn't visited her bed since the babe arrived. He took long, deep breaths to maintain composure.

Sliding back down to her feet, she winked as she moved toward the children. "I only wish I did."

That could only mean one thing. *Convalescing time was over.* Conon reached for her, but his wife danced away, her teasing laughter designed to torture him.

"Papa, look!" Rochelle's voice interrupted his lascivious thoughts. His daughter entered the bower with a huge hamper in hand. "Cook made a picnic!"

Daria and Leon followed close behind, a large jug of wine between them.

His heart ached with want of Elysia. Had it only been a few weeks since he last took her to his bed?

"Tonight," she promised. "You will be well rewarded."

The girls exclaimed over each new confection they withdrew from the picnic hamper, but Conon barely took note. Bedtime would come early tonight, for certain.

"As will you, Countess."

Elysia joined the girls on a blanket among the wealth of blooming flowers. "I already am, Conon St. Simeon," she whispered, rubbing her cheek against Lisette's golden head with a mother's contented smile. "I already am."

* * * * *

if you enjoyed My Lady's Favor, be sure to look for Joanne Rock's next release,
THE LAIRD'S LADY
*coming in September 2005
only from Harlequin Historicals*